OUR MAGIC HOUR

Jennifer Down was born in 1990. *Our Magic Hour* was shortlisted for the 2014 Victorian Premier's Literary Award for an unpublished manuscript. Her work has appeared in the *Age, Sydney Morning Herald, Saturday Paper, Australian Book Review*, ABC's *The Drum* and *Blue Mesa Review*. She writes a monthly column on words and language for *Overland*.

jenniferdown.com

OUR MAGIC HOUR
JENNIFER DOWN

TEXT PUBLISHING MELBOURNE AUSTRALIA

textpublishing.com.au

The Text Publishing Company
Swann House
22 William Street
Melbourne Victoria 3000
Australia

Cover and book design by Imogen Stubbs
Typesetting by J&M Typesetting

Printed in the United Kingdom by CPI Antony Rowe

National Library of Australia Cataloguing-in-Publication entry
Creator: Down, Jennifer, author.
Title: Our magic hour / by Jennifer Down.
ISBN: 9781925240832 (paperback)
ISBN: 9781922253477 (ebook)
Subjects: Australian fiction.
Love stories.
Melbourne (Vic.)—Fiction.
Dewey Number: A823.4

For my parents, and for Sophie and Lilly.

All The World Was Alive

For months afterwards Audrey tried to make sense of things. She wanted to remember what had happened.

She knew one morning she'd put on *Horses* and paraded around in front of Nick. Jerky shoulders, wishbone legs. She was wearing his shirt. It fell to her knees; the sleeves swallowed her hands. He sat at the kitchen table and pretended to ignore her until he couldn't, then he said *You look like you're about to perform an autopsy*, and she flapped the cuffs at him and said *I can't! I've got no hands!* and he said *Come here, you idiot*. They made love in the backyard while the tea and toast went cold. The threadbare towels hung stiff on the clothesline. That was a morning hazy with heat.

Katy had called one night.

'My shift finishes in an hour. Do you want to get tea? Just us?'

Audrey drove to her side of the city. They took fish and chips to Stony Creek Backwash, sat under the bridge in the cooling hour. It was just them and the gulls. The factories were quiet.

'This is my favourite view of the city,' Katy said.

'Mine's Ruckers Hill. Reminds me of living with your parents. Trams to school.'

'That was fun, having you sleep over all the time. Adam got so jealous. He was a real bitch about it.'

Katy's family ate dinner together every night. Her parents umpired at weekend netball matches, took orange quarters for the girls in their pleated skirts. Audrey's parents destroyed each other.

'I only ever come here with you,' Audrey said. 'You're the only person I know on this side of town. Is that the new uniform?'

'Your taxpayer dollars at work.' Katy arched her back in mimicry of a preening model. 'You ought to see the dress. It's awful, makes my tits look enormous. A *shelf* of bosom.'

'And you get to wear those sexy non-slip shoes.'

'I know. One of the girls said I looked like a TV nurse. You know, the matronly one who's firm but fair, never has sex,' Katy said.

'We could do something with your hair—something Nurse Ratched.'

'Get fucked.'

Audrey slung an arm around Katy. 'There's no face I'd rather see if I were in a hospital bed,' she said.

Katy grabbed a couple of soggy chips and mashed them against Audrey's lips.

The gulls wheeled and cawed for the scraps. Audrey looked across the creek to the city. Katy brushed her hands together, wiped them on her skirt. She lit a cigarette. She had to try again and again, one hand cupped. The lighter was almost dead, or it was windy. Audrey was never sure afterwards. She could only see Katy sitting there on the boardwalk: navy skirt, ankles crossed primly, face a rictus of effort as she tried to light her cigarette.

• • •

There'd been a housewarming one night. Audrey knew because there were photos. Patrick fussing with the camera. *Hang on, hang on.* She and Nick standing by a window with a heavy curtain, arms around each other. Audrey's cheeks ached. Nick slid his hand down the back of her jeans.

'You're smiling like a nice Liberal couple,' Paddy said.

Audrey laughed, and that was when he took the photo. 'A pair of young homeowners who do it missionary style,' he said. Audrey stretched up on her toes to bite Nick's earlobe and the camera flashed again. Paddy moved on. Nick said *That won't look like us at all.* They hid behind the curtain to kiss like a couple of kids.

By the time the pills hit at last they'd already started home. They looked at each other in the back of the cab. Everything was funny. In the shower Audrey said *Make it hot.*

'Pill chills,' said Nick.

The air conditioning broke at work around that time. There were no windows in the conference room. Audrey dragged in one of the ancient portable units, the kind that only shift hot air around a room. On the way back to the office she'd stopped to buy the kid an icy pole.

Audrey emptied the pencil case onto the table.

'How old are you, Hayley?

'Five.' The skin around her mouth was stained red like a birthmark.

Audrey traced her own hand on a piece of paper, then the child's.

'Audrey?'

'Yeah?'

'Can we go on the floor? I like lying on my tummy when I'm drawing.'

'Of course we can. Grab the textas.'

'Brady has connecter pens but I'm not allowed to use them.'

3

'You can use as many of these as you want.'

Audrey sat beside her on the carpet. Someone had scratched BETH PIG CUNT into the side of the table. She spread the paper in front of them. Two sheets, two red outlines of hands. *How many fingers are there, Hayley?* The child's hair was in a ponytail and damp strands stuck to the back of her neck. *Can you tell me about five people you can talk to when you feel sad? Or five people you can tell a secret to?* It was slow work.

The air conditioning was broken for three days, but a cool change came through before then, and it stopped feeling so urgent. That might have been the week when the newborn baby died in a parked car, or it might have been the week the inquest was announced. After a while it was hard to be sure.

Audrey went to see her mother one afternoon. Must have been the Saturday. Visits to Sylvie began with the long drive out to the peninsula. Audrey kept watch for the familiar markers: the silos under the Nylex clock as she slipped on to the freeway; the overpasses; the flat ugly road lined with native trees; the hill in Frankston where you could look back and see lights dotting the bay line. The guilt and forgiveness happened in the car, like a Catholic ritual. Audrey's knowledge of Christianity was patchy, censored by her father, but she'd read about indulgences. Exceptional forgiveness; less time in purgatory.

The drive was longer than the visit. Sylvie was in the shower when she arrived. Audrey sat on the end of her mother's bed and listened to the monologue drifting from the bathroom. Sylvie spoke mostly about getting older. She was afraid of ageing, she didn't like living alone, she wished Bernard hadn't moved out so young, she missed their father.

'What if I paint your nails?' Audrey said.

'No, I don't want it.'

'Come on. You'll feel better.'

Audrey chose the colour: ballet pink. They sat at the kitchen table, Audrey holding her mother's bony fingers. She still wore her wedding band. She regarded Audrey impassively, giving the occasional murmur to point out where the varnish was too light or had smudged onto her cuticles. Audrey worked with her face bent close.

'There. All done,' she said. 'See—they're nice.'

Sylvie looked at her with such open, childish gratitude that Audrey was disarmed.

After her nails dried Sylvie smoked a cigarette by the sink, her features puckered. Audrey waited at the kitchen table. She felt twelve again.

'Je vais faire du thé. T'en veux?'

'*Non*, Maman. Sit down and relax for a moment.'

'How's your brother?' Sylvie asked.

'I don't know. I haven't seen him in a while.'

'Why not?'

'I've been busy,' said Audrey. 'I called Bernard on Thursday. He said he'd been to school.'

Sylvie stubbed out her cigarette and flicked the butt into a potted maidenhair fern. She looked at the white wall, where a shadow of the jacaranda outside was stencilled. She began to twist her knuckles.

'Your sister calls me every second night,' she said. 'She has news.'

'Irène's always been the one with the emails and photos.'

'You don't like talking to me.' Sylvie was winding up.

Audrey looked at photographs lined up on the sideboard. 'Have you been taking your medicines?' she asked.

'Of course I take the medicines. *Sois pas condescendante avec moi.*'

'I just wanted to make sure.'

'You just wanted to make sure. Why don't you make sure your brother is okay? Why don't you call me more?'

Audrey picked up her handbag. 'I don't need to sit here and listen to this.'

'*C'est bien le problème.* You never want to listen to me.'

'I'm going to leave now,' Audrey said.

Her mother's cheek smelled of talcum powder and tobacco. As Audrey closed the door she knew that Sylvie would still be watching the murky projections of the branches on the wall.

Audrey and Nick lay on the couch with the pedestal fans spinning.

'How was your mum?' he asked.

'Twitchy.' She turned to him and touched the neck of his T-shirt. 'I'm scared I'm going to be like her.'

He kissed her. 'You won't be,' he said.

Another morning—Sunday, Audrey knew, because Adam had told her—Katy and Adam ate breakfast at the Espy. They went back to his place past the market stalls and the flats. Audrey could picture it: Adam chattering, jubilant; Katy pulling her hair into a braid as they walked. Him in a crumpled jacket, her in a sundress. They would have sat on the lawn, played at lazy fantasies.

'What about him?' Katy tilting her head.

'In the cowboy shirt? Nah,' Adam said. 'Couldn't compete with a good wank.'

They cackled on their backs, legs in the air like beetles.

It was hard to keep track of days. Eventually there came a time when Audrey thought she'd been at that Sunday breakfast, too. The markets swarming below, the ferry getting smaller as it heaved away from the mainland. All three of them hungover, collapsing on the grass together.

What Audrey knew for certain was: on Sunday evening, she and Nick made dinner for their friends. Emy brought flowers and a cake.

Katy stood at the bench with a knife and carved radishes into tiny flowers. 'You put a knob of butter on it'—she held one up—'and then you dip it in sea salt. Mum used to do them for dinner parties. They're the best. Here—open your mouth.'

Audrey couldn't remember what time Adam arrived, or which of Nick's friends were there. Probably Patrick, maybe Mark and Yusra.

Everyone crowded into the kitchen until Nick had the fire pit going. They ate in the backyard, plates balanced on knees, while their faces got shadowy.

'When I was a kid, I used to speak with this really Strine accent,' Emy said, 'but once I was a teenager, it was more about how I dressed—like, when I started uni I had this horror of being mistaken for an international student. Isn't that awful. I wore Doc Martens every single day.'

'Because you were really alternative,' Adam grinned. She kicked his shin.

'Look at you in that sweater, you willy,' Katy said. 'I don't think you're in any position to judge.'

They sat close together. It was a long dusk.

Nick and Emy washed the dishes while Audrey, Adam and Katy sat in the yard. They'd known one another the longest. They'd been thirteen, plankton in the enormous high school. They still fitted together in the same way ten years later.

Adam was sprawled on the banana lounge, arms tucked behind his head. Audrey and Katy were on the plastic lawn chairs.

'Oi, what's going on with you and Jarrod?' Adam asked, turning to Katy.

'I don't know. I think it's just become friendly.'

'How so?'

'It doesn't matter.'

'Yeah, but it's shitty when things like that don't work out.'

'We weren't together,' Katy said. 'It's not as though it's the end of a relationship.'

'But it's the death of an *idea*.' Only Adam could get away with that kind of sentence. Katy looked towards the house. Nick's voice floated from the back door—*You can clean that shit up. That'll teach you to bring an uncooperative cake. Did you even do Home Ec? Nah, it's all right, we'll just have the ugly pieces, look*—

'But what makes you think—' Adam started.

Stop pushing, Audrey wanted to say.

Katy was folding into herself like a telescope. 'I don't know, I was trying to do nice things, and—you know, sound him out, but I think maybe I was expecting too much,' she said. Her hair, pinned in victory rolls at the start of the night, had come loose; her lipstick had worn off.

They were silent. Nick and Emy were still carrying on in the kitchen. Emy was bellowing *I will not be lectured on misogyny by this man*. Nick roared with laughter.

Katy drove Adam home and stayed over at his house. Audrey could imagine it. Adam, drunk and exuberant, leaning over the console. *Kiss me, Kate!* he would have said, and she would have pecked his cheek. Audrey knew how they slept: Adam with his throat to the gods, Katy curled beside him. She might have got up and poked around his things, drunk a beer from the fridge, flicked on the television.

Adam said that Katy left early Monday, before he was awake. She'd made a plunger of coffee, lukewarm by the time he found it, and written a note. Adam was hungover, late for his nine o'clock class.

Audrey could picture Katy in her old Volvo, in the same clothes she'd worn the night before, shaking a cigarette from its pack at the lights on Barkly Street. It was a sunny morning. She drove to the

Dandenongs, to the reservoir at Silvan. No traffic going away from the city. Through the window was all hairpin bends and great friendly trees whose leaves were turning. Katy parked in the picnic area. It was still early. When she opened the door she heard magpies.

Audrey was watching television with Nick on Monday night. She remembered everything.

She went to get more wine from the kitchen, saw Katy's coat draped over the back of a chair.

'Katy never came to get her coat,' she said.

In less than an hour Katy's father would call to deliver the message, and Audrey would be crouched on the floor, lungs dragging, and Nick would be beside her, and the coat would remain on the back of the chair in their kitchen, an exoskeleton left behind.

When it was quiet, when Nick had fallen asleep with his hand on her back, Audrey imagined what happened that morning—

The yellow rag tucked around the hose, neat as a swaddled baby. Yellow is the colour of luck: newly hatched chickens, sunlight and stars in children's pictures. It has nothing to do with the damp smell of death.

Katy's hands clasped in her lap, as though she were waiting for a bus. The witness who wept as he gave his statement. He'd been driving a seniors group to the reservoir. Walking back to his bus he saw the hose stretched from the exhaust to the cabin, saw the girl's limp head from behind. He ran, wrenched at the doors and beat on the windows, yelled through the glass.

He'd phoned an ambulance and sunk down by the car door, clumsily making the sign of the cross, kneeling on the gravel.

Suppose the car had been newer, with a catalytic converter. Suppose someone had got there sooner, or she'd been called into work.

Audrey was sick with it.

. . .

The Wednesday morning after, Adam sat at Audrey and Nick's kitchen table. When he didn't have a cigarette between his knuckles, he kept his palms flat on his thighs. His shoulders were square; his knees shuddered.

'We all saw her on Sunday night,' he said. 'She stayed over at mine, for fuck's sake. I didn't realise.'

'None of us did, mate,' said Nick.

'Yeah, but you'd fucken think somebody—she changed, somebody should have noticed. There were all these signs. We just ignored them.'

Audrey realised she'd been holding her breath. She thought she was going to say something reassuring, but she just gasped: 'Her poor parents.'

Adam covered his eyes, let out an animal noise.

Audrey touched his arm, but he drew back. 'What's wrong with you both? Why aren't you crying? This is *sad!*' he yelled. 'She's—so—selfish!'

He would not be held. He crouched on the floor and sobbed.

After the funeral they all hobbled back to the Shields' house, the backdrop to Katy's first milk teeth and last day of secondary school.

Audrey shut herself in the bathroom and sat on the edge of the tub. Here was the bud of every drunken misadventure they ever had. See *her* bending into the mirror, smudging black dust beneath her eyes, see her with her knickers around her ankles as she schemes from the toilet, see Adam leaning out the window with a sneaky cigarette. Audrey lying in the empty bath, laughing at them, always the first to get drunk.

Audrey put her face to one of the big towels, tried to breathe through the thickness.

Nick was talking to friends when she returned. *C'est un vrai gentilhomme*, her mother always said. Audrey knew he was overcome. She'd seen him standing with his hands in his pockets outside the church. He'd held her while the pictures of Katy played on the screen. He said it was okay when she didn't want to look.

Audrey watched everyone in their black clothes. Every day from now on was just further away from Katy. It was a carsick feeling; it was weak arms and enervation. She'd eulogised her friend, bastardising Montesquieu: *Here rests a girl who never rested before.* Her father would've been proud. His was the only other funeral she'd been to.

'You all right?' Nick asked when they were alone.

'Are you?'

'Yeah.'

He watched her watching the mourners, leaned close. 'All these people loved her,' he said in her ear.

All the years, all the love: all wasted.

They limped outside. The city was spread below them, a neat grid of lights. Its golden veins stretched out to the suburbs. *This is my favourite view of the city*, she'd said at the Backwash, and Audrey had said *Mine's Ruckers Hill.* This one.

Nick turned the car keys over in his hand. Neither of them moved from the verandah. The trees rustled, the leaves stirred. All the world was alive.

They stood still in the dusk, faces jaundiced by the streetlight.

At home Audrey stood in the kitchen. Nick switched on the kettle, loosened his tie, went to get the mail. He took a knife from the drawer and slit open an envelope. Audrey studied his face, the awning of his brow, his throat. He had the purposeful Adam's apple of a thin man. His hair always needed cutting.

He stacked the rest of the mail on the table and glanced at Audrey. 'You did good today.'

'What did we do after Dad's funeral?' she asked.

'What?'

'I don't know what to do,' she said. She was fixed to the spot. 'I can't believe I have work tomorrow.'

He looked at her carefully. 'How about if I run you a shower.'

'It's okay, Nick. I'm fine.'

He followed her into the bedroom.

'There was a Lou Reed doco on SBS,' he said. 'After your dad's. We came home and we were both spent, and we watched that. You were worried Sylvie would—you know—so you kept calling her.'

'That's right,' Audrey said.

'You were wearing that dress.'

Audrey reached behind for the zip and tugged at it.

'Could you—' She turned her back to Nick. His body appeared behind hers in the mirror. She was still wearing her heels. Even with the false height, he was a head taller. He brushed her hair to the side and caught her eye in the reflection as he fiddled with the dress.

He smiled. 'You always want to try yourself before you let me help you.'

She felt a release. Nick drew the zip all the way down, kissed the back of her neck, her spine. The dress was slipping off her shoulders and Nick's mouth was there and she was surprised, then, at how close she wanted him. But in the shower, when they fucked slowly, wet skin on skin, Audrey thought it made sense, after all, since there was nothing left to say.

Months afterwards, that was how she recalled it. But things might have been different.

Strange Triangles

Audrey could hear voices inside before she rang the doorbell. She banged on the glass pane. Giddy laughter: her brother's, and a girl's. The rain fell while she waited on the front stoop. St Kilda was straggly in the wet.

Bernie escaped when he could, like Audrey, like Irène. For a while he'd shared a flat with some other lost boys, but he lived alone now. He was happier in his new house, a squat weatherboard with a rotting verandah and a lone fig tree in the front yard. Audrey brought him frozen meals and paid what remained of his rent after the government allowance he got for living out of home as a student. He attended school occasionally. Their mother thought he was responsibly passing his VCE. She lived alone now, too, in the old house in Tyabb that was too big for one person. Since their father had gone, relief leaked from the whole edifice.

'Bernie?' Audrey set her umbrella down by the door and let herself in. 'Hello?' There was music coming from the bedroom, summery guitars and a man's voice. The music of her childhood, a song her father had listened to.

'Come on,' the girl was laughing. 'Fair's fair.'

'Fair, I'll give you fair in a minute.' There was a squeal.

Audrey went to the kitchen and made an instant coffee. 'Hey. Bernie,' she called again. Someone turned down the music, and her brother appeared in the doorway, all swagger and grin. He was wearing a pair of socks, underwear and a dress shirt.

'Good morning,' he said brightly.

Audrey nodded at the doorway.

'Company?'

'My *girlfriend*,' he hissed, 'is in *that* room.' He ripped open a teabag with his teeth.

'Girlfriend.'

They stood, contemplating the cheerful, tuneless singing in the next room.

'I don't have any money for the train. You owe me,' the girl's voice called. She was happy; Audrey could tell without seeing her face. *'Bernard, you owe me / some money.'*

Audrey raised her eyebrows at Bernie over the top of her mug.

'Can I ask you a favour?' he said in a low voice. 'Can you lend me some, quick?'

'What?'

'I just need forty bucks.' He saw her face. 'Please.' Audrey fumbled for her purse. 'Thanks,' he said. He kissed her cheek. 'I'll pay you back.'

'Bern, Bern, Bernie-e-e / I know you think it comes for free / But you owe me some motherfucking money / For that motherfucking E...'

'For what?' Audrey said. Too slow: the girl drifted into the kitchen and Bernie slapped the notes into her palm.

'See?' he said. 'I told you I'd come through, so you can stop singing and catch your train.'

'Hullo,' the girl said, looking at Audrey. 'I'm Hazel.'

'Audrey. I'm Bern's sister.' They smiled at each other. Hazel put the money into her pocket. She was a schoolgirl and a beauty, long-limbed and unhurried. She leaned against the fridge and held out a hand for Bernie's tea. The three of them made a strange triangle.

Audrey turned to the sink and rinsed her mug.

'I'd better go. I'll see ya,' Hazel said.

'*C'est ça? Tu t'en vas?*' Bernie asked.

'I don't understand,' Hazel laughed. 'I'll see you tomorrow night.'

'See you, Hazel. Nice to meet you,' Audrey said.

'Yeah, you too,' the girl said, and left, her light hair hanging down her back.

Bernie and Audrey listened for the door to open and close.

'God, you're a shit,' Audrey said, following him into his bedroom. His mattress was an island in the middle of the floor, sheets and blankets puckered. Beside it, an overflowing ceramic ashtray from the Big Pineapple. Damp teabags sat sourly in mugs. Books were piled in towers around the room. Junot Díaz, Alice Munro, a book of Diane Arbus pictures, school textbooks with weak, fat spines. The window was stripped of curtains. An enormous Egon Schiele print was peeling off the wall.

'You're a shit,' Audrey repeated, picking up a crumpled piece of paper and pitching it at his head. *'I'm a little fucked-up French boy. Come around to my flat and we can listen to New Order together while we get high.'*

'Don't be a cunt,' Bernie said, dropping to the mattress. 'The girls like it.'

'Yeah, *you* like it,' Audrey said, nudging him with her toe. 'Don't ever trick me into lending you money again.'

'It was just one pill.'

'That's all it takes, idiot.'

'*T'es pas ma mère.*'

'No, I'm not, so stop acting like a child.' She picked up the ashtray. 'Go to school or something.'

'Go to school!' Bernie sat up. He laughed and hung his head. 'I'm sorry, Audie. I'm really stoned. Hang on, isn't it Saturday?'

'Just testing.' She touched his soft dark hair. 'I made you some more meals. They're in the freezer. You look skinny. And answer your phone. Maman was flipping out.' She picked up a small yellow book from the floor: Zola's *L'Assommoir*.

'Was this Dad's?'

'Yeah.'

'Can I borrow it? I haven't read it in ages.'

'Yeah.'

She put the book in her bag, carried the ashtray to the kitchen and dumped the cigarette butts into the bin.

'Thanks,' Bernie called from his room.

The music came back on, louder than before.

Audrey drove to Adam's. She parked beneath a spindly eucalypt and climbed the concrete stairs with one hand on the banister. She heard music pouring out from the apartment. The security screen trembled with the noise. Adam opened the door wearing nothing but a pair of briefs.

'You told me you gave up wearing those last year,' Audrey shouted over the music.

'I like my tighty-whities,' Adam said, 'and if I want to wear them—'

Audrey shut the door behind her. She turned down the speakers. 'Been practising your killer moves?'

Adam shrugged. 'This morning I got up and went for a run, boiled an egg, had a shower, put on some Pulp. I just feel really good.'

'Dancing in your undies.'

'Yeah. I thought I'd go out tonight, too. She wouldn't want me sitting around. That's what everyone says. You know, keep busy.'

He was running a hand through his hair over and over as he spoke. Audrey's eyes flickered to his pupils. 'I read on the internet about carbon-monoxide poisoning,' he went on. 'It's a peaceful way to go. I think that's important. It's just like going to sleep. You don't feel your central nervous system start to collapse. You don't know, but your blood's toxic.'

'God, Adam,' Audrey said, 'you don't need to read that.'

He crumpled to the floor. She crouched beside him.

'Who found her?' he said. 'She wouldn't have even looked the same.'

Audrey pictured Katy's face, discoloured and horrific. She sat down hard. Adam was sobbing. 'This is the worst feeling. I can't fucking stand this.'

Audrey clambered to turn off the music. 'I'll make you a coffee.' She couldn't look at him, so pitiful in his boyish underwear. He got up and stood before her, shrivelled and tentative, waiting for direction. 'Put some clothes on, for God's sake,' she said at last.

They sat at the kitchen table.

'She hated your tighty-whities,' Audrey said.

Adam laughed thickly. 'She made me give them up. My New Year's ressie last year. I kept a couple pairs.' He wiped his nose. 'She didn't hate many things, though, did she?'

'Just yappy dogs.'

'Milky tea.'

'Voyeuristic television programs.' Audrey looked down at her mug. Toxic blood.

'Did you say you were at Bernie's before?'

'Yeah. He had a girl over.'

'Tell me,' Adam said.

'I don't know what to tell. He's a deadshit. Everything's such a *battle* with him.' Adam was holding his glasses in front of his face. There was a fingerprint smudge on one of the lenses.

'Come on,' Audrey said. 'Let's go out.'

Adam shook his head. 'I can't.'

They stood in the doorway of the apartment.

'It'll get better, Adam.'

'Yep.'

She touched his arm. 'Call. If there's anything.'

Outside it was warm and raining. The bitumen was steaming. Could it still be the same fuggy Saturday? Audrey slid the key into the ignition. She wondered if Adam was watching her from the window, and waved in case.

He'd made her look at photos. He took out a Kodak packet from the chest of drawers, and suddenly Katy was there. Ashy blond hair that caught the sunlight, heavy-lidded eyes, strong shoulders. She pulled a face at the beach, next to Adam; she stood seriously on the sand alone, looking down the camera lens with her unfashionable sunglasses; she was vicious playing Scrabble with Audrey, Emy and Nick in her lounge room; she paused to smile mid-conversation, holding a plastic takeaway container in one hand, a fork in the other.

Adam was looking for a clue. There was nothing there. *I want to talk to that guy she was seeing,* he'd said. *Jarrod. Where can we find him? I bet her parents don't even know.* Katy was spread all over the table in little six-by-four squares. No crime scenes; there was no detective work to be done. Audrey longed to open the kitchen window and press her face to the fresh air.

She wanted to tell Nick about it as they walked to Smith Street for dinner, but she couldn't explain it. Looking at pictures with Adam didn't sound so unreasonable.

The restaurant light was dim. Audrey traced her fingertip over the laminex tabletop where her wineglass had left a ring of condensation. She thought to say *I went to visit Bern and Adam today, and Bern was high and Adam was something else, and neither of them was wearing pants, and I had to shout at them both just to get in the door.* Nick would see the funny side. He always said it was Audrey who'd shown him how to laugh at bleak things, but she was sure she'd learned it from him.

The food arrived. Nick waited until the waitress left before he spoke. 'I don't know why I said my day was all right,' he said. 'It was shit.'

'How come?'

'A woman in Fairfield tried to hang herself from a light fitting and it fell out of the ceiling.' He nudged his beer bottle. 'And an OD. We got there too late. The father found a note.'

'Are you all right? Does Tim know what happened?'

'No.'

'Do you think you should tell him?'

'And say what? *Sorry, mate, you'll have to take care of this one on your own. I'm just going to find myself a nice embolism. It's a bit close to home, a friend gassed herself the other week.*' He set down his fork. 'Sorry,' he said. 'That was awful and it's not your fault.'

'It's okay.'

'It's just work. You know.'

'I know.'

'I have to be able to do it.'

She looked at him across the table. 'It's okay. I know,' she said again. Nick nodded.

They'd shared friends from the beginning. They met three times without meaning to. First at the Gasometer, in the draughty space by the bandroom, for Yusra's birthday. Audrey was a sleepy drunk sloping out of her chair and under Nick's arm. The second time they escaped a party and ran out into the night. They shared a joint lying on the dry grass of Royal Park. He told her what he knew about the stars, about ancient gods and wars; chaos, the nothingness from which all else sprang. He said, shyly, *My mum made me do classics in high school.* The third time was at a gig, and they were together after that. He taught her to drive, called her Spencer because Adam did. She waited a year to introduce him to her family. That first dinner he sat like a clenched fist, and nothing happened. Driving home she said *You don't believe me, do you.* He was stunned. *Of course I do.*

Remember the pneumonia was Nick's way of trying to convince her he was right about something. When they'd first moved into the Charles Street house together, Audrey caught a cold that got steadily worse. For weeks she shook her head blithely at Nick, a newly qualified paramedic, and coughed into her tissues. She finished her student placement at QEC. When he came home one night and found her feverish and bloody at the throat, with her jumper on inside-out, Nick bundled her into the car. She argued with him all the way to Emergency. By the time she was in a four-bed ward with a nasal cannula she'd already began to laugh at it. They laughed about most things, eventually.

The phone sounded in the middle of the night. Audrey lurched sideways.

'Hello?'

'What do we do?' A throbbing, awful voice.

'What? It's late, Adam. Are you all right?' Audrey sat on the floor.

'What do we do now?'

'What do you mean?'

'I don't know.' He was crying again. 'How do you know what to do? I can't *stand* this. How are you doing it?'

Audrey scraped her fingers through her hair. Nick was awake. He switched on the bedside lamp and rolled over to watch her.

'You just have to keep moving,' Audrey said. 'And try to sleep at night. It'll get better. You have the bad days first, and then some

20

good ones. And then one day you'll realise you've had all these good days in a row, maybe a hundred.'

'How do you know?'

'Everything's always worse in the middle of the night. Go to sleep, and then when you wake up everything will look better.' She rubbed her eyes. 'Are you safe? Do you want me to come over?'

'It's all right. Sorry I called.'

'Don't be sorry. Just get some sleep.'

'Okay, Spence. Okay. 'Night.'

''Night.'

She climbed back into bed.

'You said the right things,' Nick said.

Audrey reached for the light. She was cold. 'How would anybody know what to say.' She touched his face, the plane of his cheekbone, with the flat of her hand; traced his lips with her fingers. He looked wide awake.

It had been a fortnight. Audrey was homesick for everything that had come before.

When they got together she was twenty. It was endless silly mornings in the kitchen; bike rides around the creek; kissing in the back of taxis, in cinemas, on street corners. Nick made her laugh in a new way. While at university he worked as a kitchen hand in a café in Rathdowne Village—*The Toorak of the north*, he said—and Audrey would meet him when he finished in the afternoons. They'd walk to the park, or back to his apartment on Blyth Street that he shared with Mark, or sit out on the pavement with expensive European beers, him in his daggy checked chef pants, not caring. If he was pissed off about something, it became funny in the retelling. So many afternoons lying on his bed waiting for him to shower, to stop smelling of mint and garlic and mushroom, or sitting on the cold tiles, talking to him while he squirted shampoo onto his head. He had a pleasant voice when he sang, or maybe she was just used to it. One Labour Day he invited her up to the Murray with his family. When he found out she couldn't swim he spent hours at the Northcote pool, teaching her to turn her head to the side and suck in air every four strokes, to cup the water and draw it towards her, to think of her feet like flippers. A half-roll of film, left over from a disposable camera he'd taken to a music festival, he used up on her, on the ordinary. Audrey tying back her hair, Audrey in the kitchen with a book and a beer. The two of them kissing, the tops of their heads obscured by the camera's flash in the mirror above the bathroom sink. When Audrey laughed and said *Why don't you go out and take pictures of your friends*, he said *I don't want pictures of them*. In the mornings when she had to get up and go to work or class, he watched her dress.

'What are you doing? Come and lie in bed with me.'

'I already slept there,' Audrey said. He looked up at her through boy lashes. 'I'm going to be late. I've already gone. What's the past tense of bye?' But she lay down beside him, looked at the rooftops out the window, the flats, the trees with their timid branches. It was the first time someone had said *Please stay*.

It was getting so the warmth dropped out of the days quicker, and the sun was thin. Audrey supervised an access visit between a mother and her fifteen-month-old boy in a playground. The baby walked around unsteadily. Every few minutes he'd find something on the ground, or start to run away, and Audrey would get up to chase after him.

Audrey sat him down across from his mother again. He watched her intently for a moment, but she could not capture him: he lost interest and turned back to Audrey. He smiled with a slack mouth and reached a hand for her hair, making the gurgling noises of a six-month-old baby.

The woman leaned forwards, trying to get his attention.

'Brooklyn,' she said, touching his blond crown. His eyes were swimming-pool blue. Audrey looked to the mother's face to see if they were the same, but her pupils were stretched wide.

Audrey turned her head. It was all the privacy she could give them.

When the grief came, it was primitive and crippling. Audrey was kneecapped at the coin laundry; in her fluorescent-lit cubicle at work; sitting on the rooftop at the Labour in Vain, surrounded by friends. Minutes before, she'd been laughing so hard she thought she would vomit. Walking through the university after a conference, her head full of early intervention programs until suddenly it wasn't. Glimpsing a thickness of hair that did not belong to Katy, hearing her dry cackle in someone else's throat: impossible logic puzzles, a kick in the guts. She was struck crawling down Punt Road on the way home from seeing Adam, cars slowing in a stream of lights. Rolling to a stop just past Domain Road, where the hill fell away again and bared the Yarra and the silos and the football ground and the commission flats and the suburbs and trees whose leaves spilled brown and veiny. Tim Buckley on the radio and Audrey was unravelling.

When she got home Nick had left for work. *Saving lives*, his mother told friends. Audrey wrote another card to Katy's parents to say she was thinking of them. She lay on Nick's side of the bed and began to re-read *L'Assommoir*. She woke with a wet face, Nick's arms around her. The room was strange and bright. The thought crawled into her mind, unbidden: *We won't survive this, any of us.*

'You okay?'

'I was dreaming.' She'd stopped crying. She couldn't even remember what the dream had been about. 'What time did you get home?'

23

'Just now.' He touched her hair. His T-shirt said CODE RED! VALUE OUR AMBOS.

'Adam called again tonight,' she said. 'I don't know what to do for him.'

'We've all just got to get through it. There's no map.'

There was a bad smell in their kitchen. At first Nick didn't notice it. *Something's died under the house*, Audrey kept saying. *Must be a possum or a rabbit.*

'You'd know about it if there was a dead possum under there,' Nick said. But after a few days he could smell it, too. 'Reckon it's the sink,' he said. He took the strainer out and poked around with a wooden spoon. It wasn't a terrible odour. It didn't really smell like a dead animal. Only a dampness, something pungent and mildewy.

She drove out to her mother's house for dinner. She was the first to arrive. She wasn't sure if she could face Sylvie alone.

Adam answered on the fourth ring.

'It's only me,' she said.

'Hi, Spence.'

'How are you?'

'I'm okay.' His voice so soft she could hardly hear it.

'Just okay?'

'Yeah.'

Her sister's family had arrived. Audrey watched Irène and David approach the front door; she watched them take it in turns to greet Sylvie. Five-year-old Zoe was in her school uniform. Sylvie feigned shock at the sight of her.

'When are you thinking of going back to school?' Audrey asked.

'I don't know. I think I've fucked it. I've missed too much and I didn't email anyone.'

'All right.' It was an hour from here to Adam's flat, an hour back.

'I'm going to Maman's for dinner tonight. Do you want to come? Nick's working. I could use the company.'

'Nah, it's okay. Tell her I said hi.' He must have sensed her panic down the line. He said, 'I'm okay. Really. Just need to get it together.'

'Okay,' Audrey said. She let her head drop for a moment.

Sylvie opened the door with a cigarette between her fingers and held out her arms for an embrace. She said *P'tit lapin* the way she always had. She examined Audrey as they separated. 'Are you taking care of yourself? Where is Bernard?'

'He couldn't come. He has a SAC tomorrow.'

'C'est quoi, ce SAC?'

'It's—' Audrey followed her mother down the hall to the kitchen. She waved at David and Zoe as they passed through the lounge room. 'It's like a test. It counts towards your exams.' She'd invented the SAC. Bernie was probably sitting on his bed, high and happy.

'And Nick? He is working?'

'Yeah, he's on night shift.' She poured herself a glass of wine and leaned against the bench. 'Is there anything I can do to help with dinner?'

'I will tell you.'

Everyone mumbled through grace at Sylvie's request. Audrey was tired, glad for the simple conversation. David's going to Singapore in April. His first overseas work trip. If they'd had more notice, they could have all gone together. It would have been nice for Zoe to see another country. Sylvie is volunteering at the old people's home. She's made some lovely friends. The elderly people are so sweet. Sylvie is kind too—she takes them biscuits and flowers and puzzles. Irène is planning to pick up more copywriting work now that Zoe's at school. She just wants to make sure Zoe is all settled. She'll start looking in a few weeks.

'And how are Mr and Mrs Shields?' Sylvie asked.

Audrey froze. *They're devastated*, she wanted to say. *They will come to dust.*

'Helen called last night,' she said instead. 'She didn't say much. I'd sent a couple of cards and she thanked me for those. Wanted to know how I was doing.' She cleared her throat. 'She and Steve seem very strong.'

'I can't even imagine it,' Irène said. The five of them were quiet. Zoe was swinging her legs, oblivious.

The grandfather clock struck eight.

'Adam's the biggest worry,' Audrey said. 'He's not doing too well.' She finished her glass of wine and excused herself. From the next room she heard the conversation turn.

The sisters stood at the sink to wash and dry the dishes.

'It was a nice service the other day,' Irène said.

'Thanks for coming. You didn't have to.'

'God, Audrey, she was family.' She was polishing the cutlery with the efficiency of a waitress. 'You spoke well.'

Audrey felt something, a filament of steel wool, stuck beneath her fingernail. She held her hand to the light, but she couldn't see anything.

'I like your dress,' Audrey said. 'You look like Maman.' She caught them both unawares, but it was true. Irène had their mother's wild hair and regal nose, but she was taller, broader across the shoulders. Audrey had their mother's frame. *Little-boy legs*, Sylvie had said once, standing in front of the mirror naked and hollow-thighed when Audrey was a child.

'It's funny.' Irène hung the tea towel on the dishrack. 'I was thinking the same thing about you when you and Maman were standing in here before. I think I don't notice it as much because she's always flapping around,' she said, 'and you're so still.'

Audrey could feel the tiny steel fibre lodged under her nail.

26

It was a mild, monotonous pain.

The strange smell was still in the kitchen. Audrey scrubbed at the bottom of the fridge. She knelt in front of the pantry and looked at the onions.

'How long have we had these potatoes?' she asked Nick.

He shrugged. 'Since the weekend, maybe. Not that long.'

He took apart the sink, lying on his back like a mechanic looking under a car, sheepish about his lack of expertise.

'There's nothing there,' he said at last, exasperated. 'It's clear.'

Sometimes Audrey thought she was imagining the odour, when cooking smells covered it or when the afternoons were warm enough to leave the back door open. But when she got up in the morning it was there, clammy and foul.

As long as she was still moving, still thinking about the next thing, there was no need to think of Katy. She caught the tram down to the Children's Court. She visited the Richmond flats, Odyssey House. She drove to Mill Park for a home visit, asked for a police officer to accompany her.

'Only thing, love,' he said. 'Have to take a guvvy car. We haven't got one spare.' Audrey drove. He was a grey-faced man about the age her father would have been. Audrey could tell he resented having to come with her. She jollied him along at first, then gave up when the traffic got heavier.

The client refused to use pads or tampons. When she stood up to put the baby in his highchair, blood trailed to her ankles and made neat crime-scene spots on the linoleum. The visit passed without incident. The car was waiting on the nature strip where they'd left it.

'Sorry to drag you out here,' Audrey said. 'I thought the boy-friend might have been home.'

The officer wedged himself into the passenger seat. 'She's living like a fucken animal,' he said from inside the car.

Audrey looked back at the house. Plastic venetian blinds clacking against the open window, overgrown bougainvillea by the front door. She thought of her father. *Fucken animal.* Which was the Zola novel where the lovers had fucked and killed like beasts? Her mother might know.

Back at the office she called her brother.

'Are you at school?' she asked.

'Y-y-y—nah, I bailed on Psych. I might go back later.'

'Promise?'

'I'm not gunna promise.'

'Six months, Bern, that's all you've got left. Can't you just do it?'

He said *Yes* petulantly, to get her off the phone.

In the tearoom Sean watched her spoon Nescafé into a mug that said *München Weihnachtsmarkt.* He was standing by the sink, forking pasta out of a plastic container. Audrey wondered if he'd heated it.

'You didn't want to give Johannison another shot?' he asked.

'Sorry?'

'Bradley Johannison. He's done his dash, has he?'

'I don't think access is a great idea,' Audrey said slowly. She watched the bolognaise sauce spatter his shirt collar. 'He breached an intervention order and left Mum with a head injury.'

'Nah, good on you,' Sean said. 'That's ballsy. I just mean—I mean, he was never after the kids, he was pissed with Mum. And he came through that new program.'

'There is no rehabilitation for someone like Bradley Johannison,' Audrey said. 'He's not going to learn to get better.'

Sean shrugged. 'Good on you,' he said again.

'Would you have given him another shot?'

'Look, he's not my client. I guess I think you're a bit more interventionist than I am. That's all.'

Audrey reached past him for the milk. Her coffee turned the colour of mud, of the driveway at her mother's house after rain.

She phoned Nick. He was ramped out at Sunshine.

'Spence,' he said, 'what are you wearing?'

'The blood of my enemies.' She sat in the empty conference room to tell him about Sean.

'*Interventionist,*' he said. Audrey imagined his eyebrows wiggling.

'The way he said it—like I was Thatcher.'

'Maybe he was coming on to you,' Nick said. 'Maybe he's got a thing for—what did he call you?—ballsy women. Fuck him. Don't doubt yourself. Everyone else in that office wants to adopt you. Have you told Vanessa?'

She went for drinks with the other workers. Audrey liked being friends with older women, liked the stories about their children and husbands. Audrey could not relate: her only point of reference was Zoe, and she saw her only occasionally. These women's kids dressed up as hotdogs for school plays and put gumnuts up their noses and masturbated in the cubby house. Audrey sat with her wine and her disbelief, never saying a word. When she left it was after midnight. She wondered if Nick was still awake.

'Hey! Audrey!' She turned around. Emy was sprinting down Sydney Road in heels. Audrey held out her arms and Emy fell against her, breathless. 'Are you going home? I'm fucked. I've got to be up at five-thirty again tomorrow. Do you want to get a cab together?' she asked.

In the taxi Emy leaned her head on Audrey's shoulder. 'I haven't seen you since the funeral,' she said. 'How's Adam doing?'

'He's missing Katy. He won't leave his apartment.'

'I called the other night and he bit my head off. I wish there was something I could do.'

29

'They'd been friends for a long time.'

'And you, too,' Emy said. She sat up. Her glasses sat crookedly across her nose. Audrey wanted to kiss her.

Emy yawned. 'I'll call him tomorrow. See if he wants to come out and get breakfast on the weekend. I'll tell him I want him to give an assessment of Ben. You and Nick should come, too.'

'How's it going with Ben?'

'So good,' said Emy. She lolled across the back seat, rested an elbow against the window. 'Really *easy*?'

They looked at each other in the grey shadows. Nicholson Street flashed by outside the window, weeknight-sleepy.

After work Audrey took the tram through the city to St Kilda. She stood opposite three private-school boys in blazers. They could have only been twelve or thirteen. They were eating Wizz-Fizz, scooping the sherbet out with their index fingers, and watching the floor show: a junkie couple screaming at each other at the far end of the carriage.

'You waited till you got home with those fucken sores on your cock, and then *you* called her.'

'You're a fucken headcase, that's right, I don't know your number and I don't wanna know you.'

Audrey tried not to listen but her jaw was clenched. It was dusk. The sun flashed in orange points between the buildings.

In supervision that afternoon her manager Vanessa had asked about Katy. Audrey was not prepared. She was sitting with manila folders in her hands. Vanessa was saying *It's not the ideal caseload*, and Audrey was saying *It's okay, it's manageable*, and then Vanessa said *How are you going, anyway? How's your pain?*

Audrey asked Vanessa about training in infant mental health. It was a clumsy change of subject.

Nick described pain on a one-to-ten scale. It was how he was trained to ask patients. Audrey had questioned it. *It's not discrete*, she'd said, *And anyway, pain is relative*—and he'd kissed her and laughed and said it was only an assessment tool.

The schoolboys were gone. Where they'd sat, a man in a suit was brushing the knots from his daughter's hair. Her fingers worked a hair elastic.

Audrey looked away.

Adam's car was gone. Audrey climbed the two flights of concrete stairs and sat on the step outside his door. A middle-aged man came out of the next apartment and surveyed her as he locked the screen door. He said *Good day* and moved past her towards the stairs.

Audrey walked to the end of the landing. She looked down at the street, held out her hands to the air. She sat in front of his apartment again. She waited for twenty minutes before Adam appeared, carrying a couple of plastic shopping bags.

'Oh, shit! Sorry, Spencer, have you been waiting long?'

'It's okay, I just got here.'

Audrey realised she'd been expecting something terrible, but Adam was clean-shaven, clear-eyed. He pulled a bottle of Omni out of the fridge. 'It's happy hour,' he announced, and poured them each a glass.

They sat on the couch.

'You look better,' Audrey said carefully.

'I feel a bit better,' Adam said. 'I just keep having these dreams.'

'What sort?'

'I don't know. Weird dreams. Like I dreamed I was the one who found her in the car. I keep having that one. And I dreamed *you* died, and I had to tell your mother, and—you can imagine—she lost her shit. We were in a schoolyard.' Audrey said nothing. Adam took out his cigarette papers. 'I had a dream I married her.'

'That's a funny thing to dream of,' Audrey said.

31

Adam shook his head. 'You're my best friend, but I would have married her.'

'What do you mean?'

'What I said. I fucken love you, Spence, but she is…the kind of girl you'd marry. She's so warm. You're hard.'

'Hard.' Audrey hated the catch in her voice.

Adam didn't look up from his tobacco pouch. 'We have to squeeze things out of you. But she used to tell us everything, you know? That's why I don't get it. What she did. I just feel so abandoned.'

Before she had time to realise, he'd pressed his mouth to hers. His hands bracing her cheekbones, leaning in and over her; soft lips, strong mouth.

Audrey pulled away. Adam put his face to her neck and let out a cavernous groan. She stroked his hair, felt the firmness of his skull.

'Come on, Adam, you don't want to do this with me.'

He gave a heaving sigh and put a hand over his eyes. 'Oh, fuck it. Fuck this. I'm sorry.'

'It's okay.'

'No, it's not. Everything's turned to shit.'

His skin was hot beneath her hands.

Nick was waiting for her with some flaccid pizza. He was engrossed in *Law & Order*, but Audrey couldn't pick up the storyline. She pushed the pizza around. The grease stains on the bottom of the box reminded her of inkblots. She got up and tipped the crusts into the bin. Katy's jacket was still on the back of the chair in the kitchen. Audrey fingered its collar. She shrugged into it and rolled up the cuffs. It came almost to her knees. She went back into the lounge room wearing it.

Nick hadn't moved. He glanced up at her.

'Oh, Spence,' he said. Audrey could see he was trying to gauge the spirit in which she'd done it. 'It looks so different on you,' he said at last. 'It was a jacket on her, but it turns *you* into a detective, or something. You look like a small bloke.'

Audrey sat down beside him.

'Adam kissed me today,' she said.

'Yeah? How was it?'

'Like kissing my brother. Oh, come on,' she said, and corked his arm. 'It's not funny.'

'He's pretty messed up, isn't he. Oh, listen,' he said, 'I worked out where that smell was coming from.'

'Where?'

She followed him back into the kitchen. On the mantel above the fireplace was a vase of rotting flowers. The water was rancid.

'Are they the ones Emy brought that night?' Audrey said. Up close the smell was putrid. 'I can't believe we didn't see them.'

She carried it out the back door, Nick trailing her, picking up the dry petals that fell away. Audrey tipped the yellow water down the gully trap. She set the vase on the bricks, wiped her nose with her wrist. The smell was in the back of her throat.

'How come you didn't chuck them out when you found them?'

'I wanted you to see it,' Nick said.

Before bed Audrey stood in front of the bathroom mirror and filled the sink with water. Nick was stretched out on the mattress like a great praying mantis. She could see his legs and feet reflected in the mirror. They spoke to each other through the doorway.

'Do you reckon she meant to do it?' he asked.

Audrey turned off the tap and leaned over the sink. *Stop speaking like that*, she wanted to say. It was just like Nick to hope it had been an accident.

'She drove where no one would find her and locked all the doors,' Audrey said. 'Of course she meant it.'

'No, but—what do you think happened?'

Audrey rubbed the washcloth over her eyes. Her mascara left two uncertain smudges like moth wings on the fabric. She wrung it out again.

'I was scared of her when we first met,' Nick said.

'Scared.'

'Well, intimidated, I guess. She was so protective of you. I don't think she ever actually *said* she'd cut off my balls, but the threat was always there.'

'Stop it. I'm going to cry,' Audrey said, but she was holding the washcloth over her mouth.

Nick went on. 'It was almost an aggressive kind of loyalty? She loved you all so much.'

'Just not herself.'

Audrey remembered sitting on Katy's couch when she'd first started seeing Nick. *I'm trying to work out how much I like him,* she'd said. *Just think,* Katy said. *Next time you're in bed cuddling or whatever, just think, 'If he died in my bed right now, how upset would I be on a scale of one to ten?'* Audrey had spilled beer on the carpet laughing.

She pulled the bathroom window to. The nights were getting cold.

They didn't know how to talk about it. Nick had sounded as though he were talking about a person still alive: his voice was no more strangled, no deeper than usual.

'Audrey.'

'Hm?'

'Come and lie down next to me.'

She turned and stood in the doorway, holding the dripping washcloth. Nick was on top of the covers. His hands, balled into fists, covered his eyes.

The Cooling Hour

Nick got up before it was light to take his grandad to the Anzac Day service. Audrey watched him dress. He stuffed his old woollen beanie into his pocket, grabbed his wallet from the dresser. He turned off the lamp and told her to go back to sleep.

The muddy light was struggling through the window when she woke again. Nick was climbing onto the bed. Water droplets hung from his nose and eyelashes.

'You're soaking wet,' Audrey said. She sat up and put a hand to his cold neck. He was still wearing his hat.

'Not much gets past you.' He pulled off his saturated T-shirt. Audrey rolled on top of him and pinned his chest between her thighs.

'Is it next weekend that you get your three days starting Friday?' she asked.

'Weekend after,' Nick said. 'Why?'

'I want to get out of the city. I'm going to book something.'

'That's very wild and spontaneous for you.'

She leaned forwards and kissed him. He pretended to struggle, but she held him down.

It rained silvery and thick. They went to Nick's parents' for lunch. Audrey sat with his mother in the kitchen while the television bellowed football in the next room.

In a simple way, Audrey liked Nick's family better than her own. She envied his modest, happy childhood. She envied him his younger brother, who captained sports teams and did his homework and got clumsy-lucky with girls; his father, who had a Monty Python quote for every occasion.

Audrey's father had been an academic. He taught French history, the Revolution. He liked stories of grandeur and triumph, the process as the result. Their house was full of books. *The Protestant Reformation. Signs and Symbols in Brecht. The New Orpheus. The Growth of Philosophic Radicalism.* He read less after he lost his job, but even in the commission flats his books had made little columns on the bathroom tiles, propped up lamps in the living room, overflowed from milk crates by the front door. There was an illustrated children's bible, given to them by Sylvie's parents, of which Neil did not quite approve. Audrey had read it lying on top of the ducted heating vents. She rarely got further than the first few pages—Adam and Eve, Cain and Abel, the Tower of Babel, all technicolour savagery. Neil was always sure to remind her it was a myth. He liked to say, in his embarrassing French accent, *Je suis un homme raisonnable.*

How it began was, Neil went to France to study. He could not speak the language. He met Sylvie. He was in love—with her, but also with the idea of marrying an exquisite dark-haired woman who propped her chin in her hands and adored him. He didn't finish the PhD and she came back to Australia with him: *Fuck knows why,* they'd both say later and laugh, and it became their private joke. Things were simpler back then. Neil loved reading and learning.

Sylvie loved listening to him. She had not finished high school. She thought he was the sun. They went to the beach, to the pub, to the promontory for the weekend. He studied; she worked odd jobs. They got married and had children: one, two; they could no longer afford to be adolescent and adventurous. Things started to disintegrate. Neil got a proper job. Sylvie stopped working and started fucking somebody she met at the library. *At the library,* said Neil incredulously. He cried in front of her, on his knees, and she pressed his head to her belly and stroked it lovelessly. She was ashamed. She stopped seeing the man from the library. They had a third child, and somehow they struggled on. It was hard for Neil to find work. It was hard for him to be at home with the children. It was hard for him to stop drinking.

Sylvie sometimes said *He was a very calm man when we married,* as though Irène and Audrey were somehow to blame. She'd always been flustered trying to explain things to the doctors in Emergency, as though it were a shock each time.

Whenever Audrey visited the bathroom in Nick's childhood home, she paused in the hall to study the photos of him and his brother as kids, grinning and impossibly skinny. Nick, the big brother, with his arm around Will at a surf beach somewhere. Nick asleep on his bed in his jocks, aged maybe seven. School photos, bashful teenage smiles, angry skin. A seaside holiday, a tent in a wet forest. There was an early photo of Nick and Audrey at a costume party, dressed as Richie and Margot Tenenbaum. An odd picture for hanging; Audrey barely recognised herself.

In the kitchen Paula was slicing a teacake into fat wedges.

'How's your mum, love?' she asked.

Audrey reached for the plates. 'She's okay at the moment. My niece Zoe started prep this year, and Maman's obsessed. She calls her every night so she can listen to Zoe do her reader.'

A sudden volley of cheers from the television. Nick's grandad:

37

'Other bloke's built like a brick shithouse. Didn't think Dempsey had a chance.'

Audrey rode her bicycle to the Shields' house. She hadn't seen Katy's parents since the funeral, but they checked on each other every so often. She took the long way through the Edinburgh Gardens. The light fell through the trees. It was too pretty a day for a belly full of dread. Audrey's legs were heavy. She was still in the trousers she'd worn to work, and she wished she'd changed.

There was no right thing to think about. Either it was Adam, moving around his apartment, or it was Katy, who got sad so suddenly, so secretly, that none of them had even noticed.

Fifteen, in the schoolyard, the athletics carnival. Katy with one hand over her eyes, watching the boys jump hurdles. Audrey had a cracked rib. When Mr Spivelli had asked why she wasn't participating, Katy said, 'Have you ever had to run the 1400 metres with *cripplingly bad* period pain, sir?'

'Why didn't you just say she's got a busted rib?' Adam asked.

'Because then people ask questions, dickhead,' Katy said. Audrey was so grateful she forgot to say thank you. She put her hands to the grass, watched the tufts sprout between her fingers. She was used to the two of them speaking for her, or over her.

Sixteen, late at night after the party. Katy crawling into bed beside Audrey, legs thrashing, hissing *Do you know how ugly penises are?* She'd seen Dylan Ford's cock in the back of a car. She wasn't sure how to hold it but Dylan didn't seem to mind. *He didn't want to do anything else after*, Katy said. *Do you think it was me?*

Seventeen, on the back porch at Adam's parents' house, watching an electrical storm roll in. Katy imitating their dance moves. *And Audrey dances like this*—bobbing and twisting, thighs pulsing, limbs flying. Textbooks strewn uselessly on the porch. Biscuits for your afternoon tea, a braid for your hair, washing on the line, wind in the lemon tree.

Eighteen, stretched out on the oval at school. Katy grinning, saying *Anyway, no men are ever good enough for your friends*, grass stuck to her woollen jumper.

Audrey power-pedalled up High Street against the tepid wind. She stopped at the lights by the tram stop at Ruckers Hill. Did not look back at the city.

Steve was out in the front garden tying stakes to the roses.

'Hullo, love,' he said. 'Hellie said you'd call round. Good to see you.' He didn't move to touch her. 'She'll be inside.' Audrey gave him a smile that she hoped was not apologetic.

Katy's mother was a woman who showed her teeth when she laughed. She asked you what you meant when you were lazy in conversation. She looked much the same as she always had, only tired, and Audrey didn't know why she was surprised. What does the mother of a dead girl look like, anyway? When Audrey left home at seventeen she'd stayed with the Shields for a few weeks, sleeping in Katy's double bed. Banana pancakes for breakfast, television late at night, Katy sneaking cigarettes between the front door and the tram stop on the way to school.

Helen set out biscuits and switched off the radio. Audrey asked after Katy's sister. They talked about Nick, about Audrey's work, her mother. Helen talked about the holiday that Steve wanted to take.

'One day I'm keen on it, the next I can think of sixty reasons why we shouldn't go. I suppose it's all part of the process.'

'Of course it is. You'll get through it.'

Helen gave a heaving laugh. 'This isn't fair on you,' she said. 'I'm sorry.'

'Don't be sorry. It's not your job to make it fair.'

Helen's chin trembled, but she recovered. She looked from the table to Audrey, cleared her throat. 'What about Adam?' she asked. 'I've been worried about him. I wasn't sure if he'd come with you today.'

They told each other to take care at the front door.

Steve was on his knees in the garden bed. He straightened up as Audrey wheeled her bike to the front gate.

'Thanks for coming by,' he said. Clumps of earth and weeds were strewn across the brick path. The garden smelled of things uprooted, earth turned over.

'I wish there was something I could do. I've always loved it here.'

'None of us can go back,' said Steve.

The sky was a deep lavender when she rode home. It was all downhill, all green lights, sweeping into the Hoddle Street bus lane, flying past the train station. When she pulled into Charles Street she saw Adam's little Datsun parked outside the flat, and her guts lurched.

She went through to the backyard. Nick and Adam sat opposite each other in the dark. She flicked on the floodlight and chose a seat next to Adam. Nick offered her a beer.

'How was your day?' Adam asked.

'It was okay.' Audrey fiddled with her earring. 'How about you?'

'I can't sleep. I think I'm going nuts.'

'Do you think maybe you should see someone?'

'That's great fucking advice, isn't it.'

'Hey,' said Nick. 'She's trying to help you, mate.'

Adam's hands fluttered helplessly. 'I just want her back,' he said. 'I just really want her back here, with me.'

'I know,' said Audrey.

'We slept together once.'

It was so absurd that Audrey felt she'd missed something: he couldn't be talking about Katy. When she realised he was serious, she felt left out. It stung that they'd never told her.

'What are you talking about?' she said.

'It was the summer after we finished school, and we were bored, and she just really didn't want to be a virgin any more. She came around one day and we fucked in my parents' house. You reckon I should see someone.' He was hoarse. 'Sorry, Spence. I'm sorry.'

'I can put you in touch with somebody, if that's what you want. It might be for the best.'

'For the best,' Adam echoed. He stood. 'Fuck off.'

Audrey heard him bang through the house. She didn't have the energy to get up and make sure he was all right. Underneath the tugging panic there was guilt.

'You couldn't have done any more,' Nick said.

Audrey watched the back fence. 'How long was he here for?' she asked.

Nick squinted at his watch. 'Hour and a half.'

'Are *you* all right?'

'I'm rooted,' he admitted. 'It's hard.'

'I don't know what to do for him.'

'You said the right things. You couldn't have done any more.'

'I just want him to feel better.'

'It's okay. It's tough,' Nick said.

Audrey moved across the table and kissed him. She ran her fingers up under his shirt.

'What do you want to do for your birthday?' she asked suddenly.

Nick shifted. 'I haven't thought about it,' he said. '*Should* I do something?'

'Why wouldn't you?'

'I don't know if anyone feels much like celebrating.'

'It can't be like this forever.' Audrey wished she hadn't turned on the floodlight. It was making sharp, ugly shadows. 'I'm sorry,' she said. 'Do what you like.'

Nick shrugged. 'Maybe just get a few people down to the Stando.'

'Today her dad said *None of us can go back.*'

Nick looked surprised. His arms went around Audrey again.

'I'd forgotten you were going to see them this afternoon,' he said into her hair.

The phone began to ring inside. Audrey moved to get up.

'Just let it go,' said Nick. 'They'll leave a message if it matters.'

Yusra's birthday, their loose anniversary that they never celebrated. When she sent around a message saying *Come to the Great Northern!* Nick sent one back that said *Yus, you didn't have to do that for us.*

It was long dark by the time they left the house. They walked down Gipps Street swinging their hands.

'Yesterday we picked up this guy playing footy,' Nick said, 'and he had a depressed cheekbone. The pain was so bad he was spewing.' Audrey said nothing. She could tell he was being careful. 'How old were you when your dad—'

'Twelve,' she said. Nick winced. A quick shake of the head, a squeeze of the hand, as though that could undo everything. 'We waited till the next morning, then Maman drove me to Emergency. She told them I'd been playing soccer. I was terrified the doctor would ask what position I played.'

She remembered crying when her sister touched her face with a tissue. Her jaw felt wrong when she opened her mouth. *Everything's double,* she'd said. Her sister said *It's probably just the pain,* but in the morning Audrey's face was lopsided and her eye was sunken. She was still seeing double. At the hospital they said it was from the fracture. The doctor drew a diagram of the muscles around the eye, explained what had happened. When she thought about it now her eyes watered.

'Weren't they onto you?' Nick asked. 'Didn't they call for a social worker that time?'

'We got the story straight in the car on the way there. We didn't look like—you know, like *clients*. Dad would have been polite. Asked all the sensible questions.'

'He was a prick.'

'I don't really remember it,' Audrey said. 'It's okay, you know.'

'Do you miss him?' he asked.

'I never did.' They leaned into the gritty wind. Audrey tried to explain it. 'It's not static,' she said. 'It doesn't make sense. Sometimes I'm so filled with rage, it's like—if I could go back and see him doing that stuff to us, I'd kill him on the spot. Sometimes I'm still scared. And then sometimes I have this weird sad feeling, because you can call him a prick, but I still disappointed him.'

'How?'

'When I was little I read so much. I was so determined about everything.' She dug a knuckle into her other palm, the fleshy part between her thumb and forefinger. 'He wanted me to be more.'

'More,' Nick said.

'He used to teach us about history. The Spanish Revolution. Steve Biko. The end of the Ottoman Empire. I thought he knew everything. He'd talk about the fall of the Berlin Wall and I thought he'd watched it happen. Irène used to get bored, but I loved it.'

'You were probably just happy he was doing normal dad stuff.'

'I know that now.' Audrey went on kneading her hand. It was releasing a strange, sicky pain. 'But I used to remember the names and dates for him. I read everything he told me to. I got put in those gifted programs at school. And then by the time I was sixteen, when we moved out to Tyabb, I'd dropped my bundle. I think at some point I realised girls like me didn't grow up to be foreign correspondents or barristers or whatever he was hoping.'

'You did the best you could,' Nick said. 'It was survival, not the-world-is-my-oyster. You were commuting hours to school on the other side of the city.'

43

'That was all I had.' The pain in her hand was exquisite.

'I know,' he said gently, 'I just can't understand why you cared so much about what he thought.'

He glanced down at her fingers, still working away furiously.

'What are you doing, you goose?' he asked. He took her hand in his again. The ache stopped.

They were ill-prepared for a weekend away. The weather forecast was erratic; Audrey threw beach towels and coats in the back of the car. Nick had come home from work in the middle of the night, gone to a union meeting in the morning and slept the rest of the day, only waking when Audrey got back from her work. He stood in the kitchen and watched her pack yoghurt and beer into a bag.

'Can we stop at Mum and Dad's?' he said. 'It's on the way.'

'We could drop in coming home on Sunday.'

'Nah, I want my wetsuit for the weekend.'

She looked up. Her heart turned over at his sleepy expression. 'We're not in a hurry, are we,' she said.

It was raining so hard it looked like dusk. Nick fell asleep while they were gridlocked on the bridge, rolling out west. On Radio National they were talking about cities at risk of earthquake.

Audrey stopped for petrol before Geelong. Nick woke. They stood on either side of the car and shouted over the wind.

'Do you want me to drive the rest?' he said.

'You take the corners too fast around the cliffs.'

'I'll be careful.' He was unshaven, smiling. His was a good-hearted face.

'You tired?' she asked.

'Not any more.'

He went into the servo as if to prove his use, came out with coffee and a bag of lolly snakes. Later his kisses tasted of artificial raspberries.

The bad weather blew over them, the sky a fleshy colour. When they hit the coast, Nick pulled into the first carpark and they stood looking at the ocean, a couple of surfers bobbing gamely below.

As they approached the lighthouse Audrey turned off the radio and looked sideways at Nick.

'I know what you're going to do, you bloody nerd,' he said, and she was already singing the *Round the Twist* theme song as loud as she could, shouting it through the window.

'Maybe we should watch that when we finish *The West Wing*,' Nick said.

'I think it's one of those things that wouldn't date well. It was really good when we were ten.'

'I reckon it'd be great if you were Bernie.'

'It'd be terrifying to watch when you were high.'

They dropped their things at the cabin and went to the pub. They wore coats and sat outside to eat dinner. The light faded. Car headlights inched their way around the shoreline. Nick said *They're like a string of pearls* and then looked shy about it. Audrey would have given him anything at that moment.

In the morning he was up early, moving around the room. He made Audrey a coffee and set it on the bedside table. He joked about the tiny motel cups.

'You're so awake,' she mumbled. 'Come back to bed. It's dark.'

'I'm going to the beach. You wanna come?'

'I want to sleep. Come and be a bed slug with me.'

'I'll be a bed slug tomorrow.' He pushed some hair from her forehead. 'Sure you don't want to come? I brought Will's wetsuit. I'll teach you.'

'I'll meet you down there later. I'll bring proper coffee.'

Audrey could not sleep after he left. There was a sliver of light on the wall, falling through from the edge of the thick curtain, and she watched it turn from grey to gold. Eventually she got up. The shower faced an enormous mirror. Something about Katy's hatred of her body had dulled any feelings Audrey had about her own. On a bad day she might be ashamed at its flat lines, childlike proportions. Mostly she didn't think about it. Still, she was glad when the glass fogged over and she couldn't see herself any more.

She walked to the beach at Fairhaven. There were five or six surfers out. She couldn't tell which was Nick. His old car was parked by the foreshore, and she sat in the driver's seat to wait for him. After a while he came loping up from the beach, elated, dripping from his hair and earlobes.

'Oi, Spence, are you aroused by my neoprene?'

'You look like a tadpole. Or a sperm.'

'I don't know what your mother told you,' Nick said, peeling off his wetsuit, 'but I covered the reproductive system a bunch of times at uni, and sperms do not look like this.'

'I know. I read *Where Do We Come From?* They've got top hats.'

Nick spread his towel on the car seat. Audrey could smell the sea on him. 'How'd you go?' she asked.

'I'm pretty rubbish at it,' he said. 'It just feels really good. You forget how good. Me and Will learned at Breamlea, but this is still my favourite beach. I wish I got to do it more.' Audrey thought of the photos in the hall, the boys on the sand, joyful faces, that insane physical energy. She'd heard Nick and his family talk about those holidays so many times that the memories had almost become hers.

'Want to drive round to Apollo Bay?' he asked.

They stopped at every lookout along the way. It was a thick steel sky; a mean ocean.

'I reckon you did well to get out there this morning,' Audrey said, 'before the change hit.'

On the beach their figures were reflected in the wet sand. They stood over the rockpools with their shoes in their hands. The wind had picked up. Audrey kept pushing her hair from her face. Her jeans were wet at the ankles.

'You all right, Spence?' Nick said. 'You've gone quiet.'

She felt suddenly deflated. 'I don't want to go home.' She looked up to the foreshore. The soft sand was flying in a grey haze. She thought of deserts.

The flowers were delivered to Audrey at work, an overflowing bouquet of orchids, lilies, sunset-coloured roses.

'Nick in trouble?' Penny asked.

'Not last time I checked,' Audrey said. The other workers leaned over her cubicle to admire the extravagance, jiggling tea bags in their mugs.

'Remember being a sweet young thing and getting flowers?'

'Pete only buys me flowers when he's really in the shit—once, he got me a vacuum cleaner for my birthday—'

Audrey fumbled with the card.

'*Hey baby, happy Tuesday, you'd better do my favourite thing tonight, love Nick?*' Josie said.

Audrey shook her head. 'They're just from a friend.'

'Thought it was too good to be true.'

There was a larger envelope tucked inside the arrangement. Audrey tore it open when she was alone. Half a foolscap page fell out, lined with Adam's ragged capitals.

Dear Spence, I don't know how I turned into such a mean bastard but I'm sorry. I've been wanting to apologise about the other night but I was <u>so ashamed</u>. You and Nick and Mum and Dad have been telling me I should see someone for weeks. I'm sorry for being so stubborn. I think I'm scared I'm the weak one, when everyone else is getting by. I'm scared that if Katy got sucked under, the rest of us are on thin ice. I know what you'd say to that, but I can't help it. Anyway I made an appointment. Just wanted to tell you I'd done it, and I'm sorry. I know you miss her too. Thanks for being patient with me when I'm no good. I love you. Adam.

Nick was at work. Audrey left the flowers on the sideboard and went to contemplate the fridge. There was a thumping at the door: Adam.

'I was thinking of moving back over the north side, seeing how much I'm round here,' he said, 'but now I have a grief counsellor in Prahran so I might just stay where I am.' The clouds moved fast behind his head. The sky was bruised.

'Adam.'

'I'm sorry. I feel like I've been an arsehole. Or hard work, or something.'

'Don't say that. I wasn't trying to palm you off. I just think you might need someone more than me. For this.'

'I know.'

Audrey stood aside and he moved past her into the house.

He was talking—theatrically, extravagantly—like he used to. 'I had my first appointment last night,' he said. 'I had this idea it would be lying on a daybed surrounded by pot plants or something. But she's nice. Pretty conversational. Her name's Olivia. She's funny, which is good. I just feel better already, having talked about it with someone who didn't—someone *outside* of what happened. Mum and Dad have been trying, but I just couldn't,' he said. 'I went round for dinner last weekend, when you and Nick were away, and Mum was asking me about placement this semester. I said I hadn't been to uni since week two, and she started crying. And then everything was just horrible. And I'm not fair to them. I forget they loved Katy, too.'

'I'm going to get changed,' Audrey said when he drew breath at last. He followed her into the bedroom and sat on the unmade bed.

It was exactly what Katy would have done. Audrey felt a hot new ache bloom in her chest. 'I realised,' Adam said, 'I am very afraid of forgetting her, or how it actually was. I've been sort of fixated on commemorating her.'

Audrey thought of the photos spread on Adam's table, his ceaseless interrogation of the past. He'd call her at work to tell stories, or confirm some obscure detail.

'Have you eaten?' she asked. 'I was going to make risotto.'

He sat on the bench while she made the preparations. The flowers quivered on the sideboard.

Audrey did the right things: cut the tips off the stems; changed the water. On the third day she wrapped them up again. The coloured paper was still near the top of the recycling bin, just beneath the weekend newspapers. After Nick left for work she drove to the hills. Up in Beaconsfield the side roads were unmade. She counted three white crosses picketing the dusty shoulder. Everything was dry and grey and green. She found the reservoir. The dam seemed enormous. There was a pebbly embankment leading down to the water. Audrey parked under a gum. She walked down to the lower carpark, hands in her pockets. It was warm enough if you stayed in the sun. She could hear kids playing in the park below.

She walked back to the car, took the flowers from the back seat where they sat on top of the street directory. In the last parking space there was a velvety feather, full and black. She left the flowers there.

At home Nick asked *How was work*, and Audrey said *Fine*, and they did the quiz in the newspaper.

The pub was humming with gentle weekday noise when Audrey arrived. Emy was not there. She sat down at a table to wait. She watched the street outside darken through the tall window.

Emy swept in: bought a drink, dropped her bag and squeezed Audrey's hand in a single motion. 'I just found out before I came here,' she said, 'I've been offered a job in Tokyo.'

'Congratulations! What an opportunity!'

'Do you think?'

'What do you mean? Of course it is. How long for?'

'The contract's for a year, with the firm. I haven't even thought about it properly. I don't know what to do.'

'Why wouldn't you?'

'You know, with Ben.'

Audrey nudged her. 'I didn't know it was so serious! Is it *lerve*?'

'Sort of. I don't know. Yeah, it is, a bit. God, listen to me. I ought to be euthanised.' She kicked her legs under the table and finished her drink. 'I can't sit here, I'm too wound up. Can we go for a walk?'

They walked up Brunswick Street all the way to the Edinburgh Gardens, Audrey wheeling her bike, only stopping to buy a bottle of champagne, which they uncorked sitting on the grass. A group of boys were running football drills on the oval. Their loud calls cut through the traffic noise. Emy couldn't sit still: she sprang to her feet, she paced, she rolled on the lawn in her expensive-looking jacket.

'Mum and Dad'll love it. All those years of Saturday Japanese school.'

'Tell me about Ben,' Audrey said.

'You know there's a word for it? For someone who's a foreign-born descendant of a Japanese immigrant? It's not as though I'm going *home*. I haven't been there since I was twelve. I'll look like I fit, but I won't.'

'Just do it. It's only a year.'

'Is it?' Emy said, and thumped the empty bottle against the earth. 'Is that all?'

Audrey rode her bicycle home and slept easily.

'Beat this for a day at the office,' Nick said, climbing in beside her at 2 a.m. 'An eighty-two-year-old guy with dementia wanders into a closet and gets lost. Four days later staff find him, and Tim and I get the job of pumping him full of saline while he sobs for his wife. Who died ten years ago.'

Audrey opened one eye and rolled over to face him. 'Ten-month-old baby who's been sexually abused.'

'How do you know?'

'She has an STD.'

'Fuck.' He flicked off the light and drew her to him. 'You win.'

They made it through the front door blindly, laughing and clutching at each other.

'But why Good Friday? Why is that the day when everything's shut?'

'It's because we're meant to be sad,' Audrey said.

'It's because Jesus died on the Friday. Maybe we're supposed to play at being dead by not being able to buy milk.'

Nick had her arms pinned above her head, but she felt the vibration of her phone in her pocket. 'Hang on a second.'

It had stopped buzzing. They looked at the screen. 'It was only your sister,' Nick said.

'I know, but I had about six missed calls from Maman. Hang on.'

Nick leaned against the door. Audrey set the phone on the sideboard, dialled voicemail on speaker. Irène's voice filled the hall.

'Audrey, it's me. Have you spoken to Bernie? Maman and I can't reach him. He's not answering the phone. I'd go around tonight but I've got to pick up Zoe's friend. She's having a sleepover. Anyway, let me know.' Audrey reached out and batted at the phone. Nick was kissing her neck.

'How's the expectation,' he said, 'that you'll just drop everything and go round to Bern.'

'Maybe I should.'

'Come on. How many times has this happened? He's always fine.'

'Yeah.' She shed her jacket. 'I'll go tomorrow.'

All night Audrey woke again and again, and every so often Nick would be awake, too, and their bodies would shift into new shapes, and once Nick reached for her as if in a panic, and once Audrey thumped to the kitchen half-awake and stuck her head under the tap to drink, and once she turned over to face Nick, who was open-eyed, and they began to kiss in a dream, bodies just coming to, and she saw the dull shadows from the streetlights passing over his face as he came, and he covered her body with his and she felt his breath in her hair, and they held each other, and the whole time they never said a thing.

Bernie was alone when Audrey went round the next day. 'Your bell's not working,' she said. 'I brought you some frozens.'

'Thanks.'

She followed him into the kitchen. 'Have you been going to school?'

'Yeah,' he said earnestly. She believed him. He was honest most of the time.

'How's your art?'

'Good,' he said. 'Do you want to see my folio?'

Bernie painted in oils and sometimes took pictures. His sketch-book was three-quarters full with digital photos he'd pasted in.

'I've been using Dad's old camera, too. Film's so expensive.'

There was a series of prints from a party. Two boys passing a joint between them, sitting on a tiled verandah. Light streaming through a bathroom window. A girl talking. She was speaking with her hands, holding them up near her face: the fat fingers slightly curved, as though she were holding a pair of binoculars.

'These are really good,' Audrey said.

He looked embarrassed.

'Bern, do you remember living in the Wellington Street flats?'

'A bit. I would've been about seven,' he said. 'I remember what it was like inside—the lift and stuff. I don't really remember the school, but I know we used to walk. Sometimes Maman took us.' He closed the folio. 'Why?'

'Nothing. I had a dream about it a while ago,' she said. 'Do you want a coffee?'

Driving home she phoned her mother, then her sister. Later Nick laughed listening to her re-enacting it all.

'Maman said *Be patient, he's just being a teenager.* When I moved out I had to phone her twice a day, sometimes more.' Nick handed her a mug. 'Thanks. So then I call Irène. *Thanks, Audrey, I know I never visit our brother and I have six hours of spare time each day when my only child is at school, but somehow I just can't find the fifteen minutes to drive to Bernie's house. You're a lifesaver.*'

'It's weird when you get nasty. I think I'm getting turned on.'

'Hang on, I haven't told you the best bit. At the end, Irène goes *You've never seen Bernie high, have you?*'

'Wow.'

'I didn't tell her I accidentally paid for his pills the other day.'

'What about when he was stoned at your dad's funeral?'

No one else but Nick would have found it funny.

Audrey's phone rang. He looked at her, daring her not to answer it.

'Hello?'

'It's me.'

'Hey, Adam, how did the session go yesterday?'

'Good, really good. Listen, can I drop around now?'

'This is all so *intrusive!*' Nick hollered when she hung up. He made a joke of it, but Audrey knew he was frustrated.

'I'm sorry,' she said. But he was already kissing her forehead, heading for the shower.

He came out dressed in his uniform, hair wet.

'We might get to see each other one day,' he said, fastening his watch.

'Everything's stranger than normal.'

'It'll swing around again.'

Audrey touched the back of her hand to his. They linked fingers.

Sylvie phoned four times while Audrey was with her client. Audrey knew better than to worry, but she left work and drove out to Tyabb all the same. The sun was low in the sky, the houses huddled together. The wind flattened the long grass by the foreshore.

Sylvie had a head cold. She was flushed and unhappy. She sat at the table in a dramatic slump. She fiddled with the cord at the waist of her dressing-gown. Audrey boiled the kettle and kept her hands busy slicing lemon.

'I had coffee with Helen,' she said.

'Oh, *que t'es sympa*, going to see her before you came to see your own Maman. I've been so lonely here, I feel like nothing is worth it.'

Audrey found the honey and spooned some into her mother's cup. 'We organised it a while ago. I just wanted to know how she was doing.' She knew she sounded defensive. 'It's hard to get out here during the week.'

'You don't have to visit me like I'm some *vieille bique* in a home. Just call me.'

'I do.' Audrey set the cup of tea in front of her mother and sat down. 'I called you on Tuesday. I told you about Emy, remember?'

'Yes.' Sylvie poked at her hair. 'Why don't you do something like that?'

'What, work in Japan?'

'Something exciting, at least. Take a risk.'

'There's not a lot of scope for overseas travel with child protection.'

'Why don't you try something else? Do something you like.'

54

'I like my job.'

Sylvie lit a cigarette. Audrey reached for the ceramic ashtray.

Nick phoned while she was stopped for petrol coming home.

'I got caught up with Maman,' Audrey said. 'I'm still on my way.'

'It's okay, I haven't left work yet. That's why I'm calling.'

'What's happened?'

'It's not a big deal.' A pause. 'Some fruitcake held Tim at knife-point today. They made us go to debriefing.'

'What?' On the bowser there was a sticker prohibiting mobile phones. She fumbled with the petrol nozzle. The foul-smelling liquid trickled over her hands. 'Were you there?'

'Yeah, I had to intervene. Nobody was hurt or anything. The debrief's taking longer than I thought. I just thought I should call.'

They arrived home at almost the same time. The house was cold. Audrey kept her coat on as she flipped through the mail. Nick went to the fridge.

'I don't want to go to the gig tonight,' he said, reaching for a beer. 'I want to drink this quickly, so I can't get called back to work later. Then I'm thinking burritos. Then maybe some *Sopranos* or sloppy sex. Either way.' He gulped a mouthful, offered the bottle to Audrey, and wiped his sleeve across his mouth. 'It's like we don't stop any more. I just want to stop for a second—'

'All right,' Audrey said.

They walked to Gertrude Street to pick up the food, and stood waiting outside the restaurant. Audrey watched Nick's face. He saw her looking.

'Are you all right?' she asked.

'Yeah. It was a long day.'

'Was the guy with the knife charged?'

Nick nodded slowly. 'He had Tim's collar, and he kept saying *I'm gunna fucken kill yerrr*, and Tim was just waiting for something to happen—for the guy to stab him, or for me to do something.'

'He was lucky you were there.'

'I was scared.'

The waitress waved at them from inside.

Walking home, Audrey imagined it without wanting to: blood springing from his neck, the blade cold and mean. She sunk her face into the collar of her coat.

'How was your day, anyway?' Nick asked.

'I got my flu shot,' Audrey said. 'I had a scary dad on the phone. When I was leaving I asked for a security escort to get to the car and they sent a woman my size. What else. Vanessa said we can expect our caseloads to double by December.'

'What about the inquest?'

'I sort of don't want to talk about it,' she said. 'Is that all right? It's just work.'

Nick held out his hand for the bag of food. 'It's all right,' he said. 'When does Emy leave?'

Nick's birthday at the Retreat. It was the first time in months Adam had come along. He and Emy smoked and gossiped out the front. Audrey didn't know what to do with all her relief.

It seemed like everyone in the pub was there for Nick. Audrey saw him in flashes: his narrow back at the bar, his face under the pool table lights, his hand reaching for hers as she slipped past him on her way to the bathrooms at the back of the pub.

Yusra was queuing for the toilets, applying a deep red lipstick.

'It's you!' she said delightedly, opening her arms, and Audrey said *Yus, you're the warmest person I know.* They talked all the way back to the bar, heads bent together while they waited for their beer. They sat in one of the booths. The wallpaper was puckered as if from water damage, patterned with sailing ships.

Yusra said *How have you been holding up.* Intelligent eyes, cloud of dark hair, lipstick on her glass. Audrey didn't have a thing to say.

'It's okay,' Yusra said. 'We don't have to talk about it. I'm sorry.'

They were weepy-eyed laughing minutes later.

'I think changing hands should be a signal. Wrap it up. We're done here,' Audrey said.

'Same if you have to stop for a drink break while you're giving head.'

Emy, then Ben, slid in beside her on the seat. Adam's face appeared across the table.

'I am drinking Collingwood,' he announced.

'Is it okay?' asked Yusra.

'Well—I don't *know*.'

Loud, happy voices. Warm bodies, safety in numbers. It was almost normal.

Nick and Audrey stayed in bed all morning, laughing feebly at themselves.

'I don't remember getting home,' Nick said. 'It's been a long time since that happened.'

'Do you remember vomiting in the shower?'

'Filthy.' He shook his head. 'Sorry, Spence.'

Audrey's mouth tasted of stale party. 'Do you want to go for a drive?' she asked.

'I feel pretty seedy.'

'Fresh air,' she said. 'Let's go over to Williamstown.' His hand found hers under the blankets.

Everything was funny in an indulgent, sleepy way. Nick winced as he leaned forwards to pull on his boots. Audrey waited for him to wash his face. When he saw her lying on the bed in her coat, he said, 'Well, come on, are we going or not?'

'Don't know if I can be bothered,' she said, and they laughed again.

'What a bloody effort.'

At the gate Nick gestured for the car keys.

'Do you want me to drive?' Audrey asked.

'It's okay. I'd rather have something to concentrate on.'

They rolled over the bridge. Audrey wound down the window, leaned her arms on the ledge. The river and the factories whipped by outside. Her hair licked her face. She glanced at Nick. He loved driving with the windows down even when it was cold.

'You know that sort of guilt you have when you're a kid?' Audrey said.

'How do you mean?'

'Like—not wanting to go somewhere with one parent, or having to choose whose car to ride in. Being disappointed by a gift. Not being satisfied by an explanation,' she said. Not protecting one parent from the other.

Nick looked at her quickly. 'What made you think of that?' he asked.

'I don't know,' she said.

She felt shy. He smiled at her, but his brows were drawn together. Maybe he was trying to understand. She wished she hadn't said anything.

They fell asleep on the grass by the water, then it was late in the day, and colder. Driving home Audrey kept an eye out for the Backwash. Nick fiddled with the radio, settling on Johnny Cash. Audrey glanced at him incredulously, and he began to sing along, word-for-word, and she said *You're a dag*, and he pulled the car over in the carpark by the refinery. Audrey slipped out of her seatbelt to lean over him. She kissed him, clutched at his jacket.

'Someone will see us,' Nick said. His mouth found her neck. Johnny Cash ended. There was a thick silence before the announcer started talking, dead air. Audrey was kissing Nick's eyelids, tugging at his jeans.

'It's like it was before,' he said, all in a breath.

Audrey sat back. Her hands fell from his chest. 'What do you mean, *before*?' she said.

'Come on, Spence.'

Audrey suddenly felt foolish, straddling him in the car like a teenager. She slumped onto the passenger seat. She looked out at the power station rising in the sky.

'I feel bad when I forget about her for an hour,' she said.

'I know, and I don't want to forget,' Nick said. 'I just feel like it's everywhere. We talk about it *all the time*.' He was wild in the eyes.

Audrey nodded. 'Do you want to get out for a bit?'

They walked out on the boardwalk past the mangroves. She hiked a leg over the rail; so did he. The city seemed a good thing to look at: its lights were just coming on, the air was pretty in the cooling hour. Audrey did not like having the West Gate Bridge looming behind her. She couldn't say why it seemed so sinister. The last time she'd been here was with Katy, but she couldn't say that, either.

Her fingers were cold. She had to flex her hands to make them real again.

'Happy birthday,' she said.

'Been a good one. Thanks for last night.'

Nick's legs dangled over the water. He laid his head on her shoulder. Audrey stared at the oil terminal. The big tanks sat squat.

They walked all the way out to the rocks and sat there. The sun fell buttery from the pylons, beamed gold off the river. Audrey looked towards the chainlink fence with its warning sign, Border Control, and saw three rabbits run out to the Mobil drums, but they were gone before she could say anything. Nick was watching the punt chugging towards Fishermans Bend. Audrey got up and walked to the fence. She wondered if she'd imagined the rabbits.

'I don't know if I locked the car,' Nick called suddenly. They looked at each other again. Nick shivered. He said, 'We'd better go back.'

The Real Wild

Before Emy's going-away party Audrey and Nick got drunk at home, then they were running late and Nick still hadn't written a message in the card, and while he was bent over the table trying to think of what to write, 'Mesopotamia' came on the radio and Audrey did a silly dance with flailing arms. Nick put his head down on the table. He was coming off a fourteen-hour shift.

'Wake up,' said Audrey, breathless. 'This is very serious. We're going to a party.' She stopped jumping around. 'You don't have to come if you're too wrecked,' she said.

He lifted his head. 'Nah, I'm scared you might dance like that in public.'

They arrived just as the speeches were starting, and hung back in the doorway. Audrey looked around the room. She waved at Adam. Everyone was standing close, flush-faced, ready to raise their bottles and glasses. On the wall over the couch, colourful cut-out letters read SAYONARA EMY!

Patrick had his arm around Emy in the centre of the room.

'Listen,' he said, 'what's the first thing you see at the start of *Lost in Translation?*'

'Scarlett Johansson's exquisite arse in those see-through undies!' Emy shouted.

'A thing of beauty.' Patrick cleared his throat. 'We thought it'd be nice if you had something to remind you of us. So we had a little photo shoot—a couple, actually...' He produced a bound album and opened it: pasted inside, pictures of their friends pouting and clowning in flesh-toned underwear.

'This is disgusting,' Emy said, 'it's great.' She shrieked when she got to the photo of Nick, thin and hairy and mock-wistful, gazing out a window in his apricot-coloured jocks. A few wolf-whistles went up, faces turned to Audrey and Nick. Someone called *You're a lucky woman, Audrey.*

In the bathroom later, Emy collapsed onto the toilet and Audrey sat on the tiles with her back against the door.

'I'm fucked,' Emy announced cheerfully. She kicked off her knickers. 'I'm just the safe side of a really lavish vomit.'

'Where's Ben? Is he here?'

'He went to the servo to get some more ice. He's in a bit of a shit about this whole thing. We're not really sure what we're going to do.'

'What do you mean?' Audrey said.

'I said a long-distance relationship might be hard work. Now he's sulking.' Emy stood up and examined her reflection. She turned to Audrey. 'It'll sort itself out,' she said. Audrey wanted to hold her tightly. Someone had put a daisy in an empty VB bottle on top of the cistern.

Drinking, dancing, talking in the bathroom, out in the yard: Audrey lost Nick for a while, and found him in the hallway under the bald light bulb.

'Hey,' she said in his ear. 'What are you doing?'

'Can we talk?' His voice was shivery.

'What?'

'I said, can we talk? I'm freaking out.'

'Are you okay?' Audrey asked. She looked at his pupils. 'Have you taken something?'

'Jordy gave me something to keep me going.'

'What the fuck?'

'I feel heaps better. Can we just talk for a second?' he said again.

Audrey followed him down the back of the house to the laundry.

'I've been feeling really bad about Katy,' said Nick. 'I just keep thinking there must've been something we could have done. We must've missed something.'

Audrey leaned against the washing machine. The room was quiet and cold. She felt the blood run faster through her body. 'I can't talk to you about this tonight, Nick.'

'What if we just don't listen to one another? Maybe she tried to give us hints. I keep thinking about the night before, when everyone was round at our place. We must have missed something. I feel horrible.'

'It's the speed.'

'It's fucking not.' Mad eyes. Audrey was scared to touch him. 'I can't stop thinking about it, all the time. Things keep happening so quickly, and we never stop to process any of it. Your mum's always threatening suicide. We just ignore her.'

'You don't know her like I do. She's been threatening it since I was nine.'

'We don't listen to one another,' Nick said again, voice rising. 'You're not listening now.' He was hysterical, arms flung out.

Audrey gave a short laugh. 'Are we having an argument?' she asked.

Nick drew back, and then his fist was in the wall. White shreds and dust fell to the ground like salt as pulled out his hand. He stared at it; cradled it with his other. There was a rough hole in the plaster.

Audrey looked at the wall. That old familiar feeling was in her arms. Enervation, adrenaline: too much of one of them. When she and Irène were children they'd called it the floppy arms before they stopped talking about it.

She stood very still.

Patrick appeared at the door. 'Everything okay?' He saw the jagged hole. 'Fuck, mate,' he said. He looked from the plaster to Nick to Audrey, pressed right into the corner of the room.

Nick stared goggle-eyed at the wall. *You fucking idiot*, Audrey wanted to say, but even her mouth was weak. She left him standing there with Patrick.

She went to the kitchen and got another drink. Adam came looking for her.

'Ben just told me what happened,' he said. 'You okay?'

'Yes.'

'Did he—'

'He did a line of speed and put his fist through a wall.' She saw something flicker across Adam's face. She remembered that expression, the one she hadn't seen for years, the one Katy made when she saw Audrey's bruises at the swimming pool when they were fourteen. Now Adam was ready to make pitying noises in his throat. 'I'm fine,' she said. 'I'm just going to go outside for a bit.'

'Do you want me to come?'

'Would you mind if I just—if I were just by myself?'

She finished her wine in the backyard. She was watery in the legs. She watched a possum run along the fence and disappear into the lantana below. Nick came and stood beside her. She couldn't look at him. She watched the black shapes of the garden moving in the night.

'I don't know why I did that,' he said.

Audrey dropped her head. 'No.'

'I was just so tired, and it's making me loopy. But that's not an excuse.'

Audrey folded her arms and turned to him. 'My dad did that once, when he missed Maman's face. There is no excuse.'

'I'm so sorry,' Nick said. He was ashen, a cartoon of a man pleading. He knew her well enough to feel the weight of his mistake. 'I've never done that before,' he said. 'It's not me. I don't know what happened. I'm sorry.'

Audrey didn't want to go back inside to the party or stand out here with him, but there were no other choices. She didn't want him to keep apologising.

'It's okay. Let's just go.'

He said *Sorry* again as they arrived home, and Audrey said *It's okay* again.

Inside she washed the dishes they'd left in the sink.

'I'd never do what your dad did,' Nick said, standing behind her.

'I know that.'

He touched her arm. She started. The glasses skittered on the drying rack. Nick took a step back, bewildered.

'I can't help it,' Audrey said. 'I can't help it.' She couldn't believe how quickly it had happened, this new pain. She was twenty-four; it was seven years since her father had last hit her. Nick had only ever known her with a crooked nose, a break that had happened in the Wellington Street flats and never quite healed straight. Stringy blood in her throat and her eyes, but when she'd got in front of the mirror it was all coming from her nose and it wasn't as bad as she'd thought. Sylvie had wiped the snot and blood from her cheeks with a warm washcloth. Audrey was fifteen.

Nick knew the story. Audrey told him everything eventually.

In bed they took turns being still.

'How are you feeling?' Audrey said.

'Better than before. I just can't drop off. My body's so tired, but my head isn't.' He clutched the quilt to his chest. 'I shouldn't have come tonight. I should've stayed home and crashed.'

'How much did you do?'

'I don't know. Not that much. I just freaked out.' He rolled over, face to the ceiling. 'It's gone now. I can't feel it any more.'

The next time she glanced over he was asleep. His scratched, swollen hand lay on the pillow. It was purple. His middle knuckle seemed to have disappeared. It looked sick, not sinister.

Audrey remembered the scene in *A Clockwork Orange* when Alex's eyes are held open with metal claws. She thought about hair. Someone had told her it keeps growing even after you die. She thought about her infancy, herself and Irène as children. With their mother they were *mes filles* or *mes p'tites*. When Neil was home, they were *the girls* once more. They slipped in and out of their selves like hands in and out of pockets. At work now she knew the word for it: *hypervigilant*, she'd say, meaning children who slept with one eye open, little hardened invertebrates.

They'd kept a sickly rabbit when they were living in the New Street flats. It was allowed to hop around the apartment; it knew to shit in its box. Audrey and Irène poked bits of lettuce and broccoli into its anxious pink mouth, but Neil loved it most. It sat on his lap like a cat while he read. When he was a good drunk, mawkish and weepy, he'd stroke the rabbit's ears and bellow about man and nature, and the creature would cower on his knees. Audrey was twelve. She read in a library book that rabbits could die of fright. 'Winter gardens,' Neil would drone, 'were all part of that, showing man's dominance over nature, the triumph of the artificial over the *real wild*.' Audrey watched the rabbit, clenched and petrified in her father's lap, and imagined its heart beating furiously.

The rabbit didn't die of fright. It ate all the shredded paper in its hutch and blocked its insides. Neil buried it in the yard, out near the gaping drains. A neighbour came out to protest with a mug of tea in her hand. 'It's the state's land,' she said. 'You can't bury a fucken bunny there.' Neil leaned on the shovel for a moment, cigarette dangling from his lip, but said nothing. He was gentle with the rabbit. Its fur rippled in the wind. Audrey had watched from a distance.

She slid her feet between Nick's thighs. She thought of his wounded expression in the kitchen. He'd looked destroyed at the idea that he could frighten her. She heard the first train rattle towards the city.

It was still dark when he turned on the heating in the morning. Water streamed down the drainpipes. The gutters flooded. Audrey got up with a mind to go to the laundrette. She took two armfuls of washing out to the car, and came back inside dripping.

'It's really raining,' she said. 'The gully trap's overflowed.'

'Do you want me to come with you?'

'It's all right. I'll get the papers.' They stood on either side of the kitchen bench. Audrey put her hand on the coffee plunger and very slowly pressed down its head.

The laundrette was cold. Audrey sat on the wooden bench and shuffled her feet over the linoleum, made her instep line up with the diagonals of the diamonds. Last night Nick had said *You're not twelve now, Spence.* He'd said it to reassure her. She wanted to say, meanly, *How astute of you. Thanks for making the distinction,* but making Nick feel bad would have punished her, too. When she'd left the house he was on the phone to Emy already, still apologising.

Katy was the first person Audrey ever told about her dad. Adam next. They were young, thirteen or fourteen. They sat out on the windy oval, or huddled in the bike shed. Katy jumped hurdles, Adam captained the football team and then the school, Audrey always had runs in her tights. In Year 11 she read Raymond Carver for school, in Year 12 it was Toni Morrison. Katy made herself vomit every lunchtime for a year; she could do it quietly and efficiently.

Audrey would wait for her outside the stall. Once Katy said *I know I haven't got it anything like as bad as you,* and Audrey had shrugged, said *It's not a competition.* In the worst times Katy had vomited into a plastic container to assess the weight of it, so she could know what she'd thrown up. Eventually she stopped. Audrey wasn't sure if Adam ever knew.

They only ever saw the marks on Audrey's body. She couldn't make them understand that there were good times, too. Drives to the coast, Gippsland creeks where their parents had camped in a tent and she, Irène and Bernie had slept in the back of the station wagon, curled like dogs, their breath fogging the windows. The week before Christmas when they'd choose the tree. Her mother always wanted to get a small one, or a tree with a bald patch, in case no one else wanted it. Weekday mornings, her father grating carrots and potatoes for hash browns the size of the frypan. Sometimes her parents were so in love it was like a film. Sylvie was bright, an electric woman. She danced to 'Tusk' while she cooked dinner, showed the girls how to apply makeup in front of the speckled bathroom mirror, let Bernie wear her costume jewellery. Neil was charming. He liked taking photos. They had a lot of pictures of happy times. Katy and Adam never got to see them. Once they were smoking in Adam's backyard at night and Katy asked *Does your dad ever do—anything else?* and Audrey had been high and terrified but even then she knew it must have taken Katy some guts to ask it. She'd shaken her head over and over. *No. No. No. He's not a bad person. My parents are not bad people.*

The washing machine finished. Audrey heaved the wet sheets back into the plastic basket. She thought of Bernie pissing his bed, aged six or seven. She'd hurried to bundle the linen into the machine before their parents noticed, then to bundle her brother into her own bed. She thought of how much force it took to open up a wall with your fist.

Dinner at Irène's house that night. Nick said he'd drive. Audrey almost argued with him, but he was in a good mood. He'd fixed the skylight, stopped it leaking. He kissed her eyelids closed as if he were putting her to sleep. She let him.

They looked at each other reluctantly as they got into the car.

'We don't have to go,' Nick said. He adjusted the rear-view mirror. 'I'll call Irène and tell her you've got gastro.'

'No, because Bernie'll probably bail too.'

Everything was black and gold. The rain fell like snow under the streetlamps. Audrey wished she were driving instead of Nick so she'd be distracted. She watched the smeary droplets on the windscreen. The car inched onto the freeway. The rainbow sign above the factories read OUR MAGIC HOUR.

Audrey felt sick.

Nick was concentrating hard, but he turned to her when they stopped.

'You look a bit better.'

'I'm fine.' She started counting lampposts. It was what her mother had told her to do when she was young, when she used to get carsick. The rain had flooded the underpass. She couldn't ask him to pull over. The traffic began to move and she felt better.

'Are you still mad at me?' Nick asked.

'Of course not.'

'Well, what can I do? I can't read you when you're like this. I don't know what to do.'

'You don't have to *read* me.' She could barely see through the windscreen for the rain. Nick was driving twenty kilometres below the speed limit. Audrey lost count of the lampposts and started to sweat. She made the air go in and out. They turned off the freeway. She looked for the streets and markers she knew. She tried to think of things outside of this interminable car trip. The rain eased suddenly.

They pulled up in front of Irène's house. Audrey yanked the door open. Cold air rushed into the car. Her breath came in an ugly gasp.

'It's last night. It's my fault.'

'It's not your fault.' Audrey rubbed her face. 'I got a fright. Maybe I overreacted. I'm tired. I don't know.'

He leaned over and kissed her, hard. She stroked his neck. The terror was gone, the bile, the sweat. What remained was small and sickly. She wondered if he could taste it in her.

'I'm sorry.'

'We both are,' said Nick. He touched her hair. 'Come on. We're here now.'

Audrey didn't know if she could face her mother, but they pressed on through the gate.

Bernie was inside already. He'd brought Hazel, who was helping David pour drinks. She sat back down next to Bernie on the couch and answered Sylvie's incessant questions with a beatific calm, limbs folded neatly.

'It's getting serious,' Audrey said, watching the three of them. 'She's the first girl he's ever brought home.'

'Who'd want to bring anybody home to this?' Irène said. 'Listen to Maman carrying on. You'd think we were in a gulag.'

Audrey looked at her sister, but Irène would not lift her eyes. She worked the salad servers like oars.

At the dinner table:

'How was Perth, David?' said Nick.

'Remember that time the car broke down in Kaniva, and there was a mouse plague, and there were mice in the motel room...' said Bernie.

'We wanted to renovate the kitchen, but it'd need to be done before the baby arrives,' said Irène.

'I want to do physiotherapy, but I don't know if my marks'll be good enough,' said Hazel.

'Nick, you have worked today?' said Sylvie.

'Emy leaves for Chiba on Friday,' said Nick.

'It's really incredible to just be surrounded by that much old stuff. We did a tour of the Zapotec ruins,' said David.

'What do you want to do for your birthday, Maman?' said Audrey.

'Audrey, you drink too much,' said Sylvie.

Bernie smirked. 'Runs in the family.'

Audrey felt something give. She set her wineglass on the table. 'Fuck off, Bern.'

'Don't talk like that *à ton frère*.'

'Oh, nice,' Audrey said. Nick squeezed her thigh under the table. She turned to her brother with his idiot grin. 'I look after you. I cook you meals and pay your rent when you forget. Don't insult *me*, you shithead.'

'Hey,' Irène said, gesturing to Zoe, 'can you just calm down?'

Bernie shrugged.

Later he asked for a ride. Hazel kept saying *Thank you* as she and Bernie got out of the car. She stood on the nature strip, face politely turned, while Bernie tapped on the passenger-side window. Audrey rolled it down.

'I'm sorry.'

'Come on, Bern. You're not sorry.'

'I am,' he said. He shifted from one foot to the other. 'I feel bad.'

'You feel bad because I lost it in front of your girlfriend.'

'If I'd wanted to impress her with my acute masculine sensitivity, I would've apologised in front of her.' He glanced over his shoulder to where Hazel stood, still looking down the street. 'I wouldn't have said it in the first place. It was just a goddamn *quip*. I'm an idiot. I'm sorry.' He grimaced at the cold.

'It's okay,' Audrey said. 'Don't worry about it. We'll call it a night.'

'Thanks for the lift home. See ya, Nick.'

'Take it easy.'

Nick waited for them to wave from under the security light and disappear inside the house before he pulled away from the kerb.

'He really knows which buttons to press,' he said as they started up Punt Road. 'You never take the bait.'

'He doesn't get it.' Nick had the heat on too high. She wondered if she'd feel sick again going home or if that had passed.

In bed they fucked savagely, knocked tooth to tooth. Audrey pulled at his hair and bit his lip and felt something had given way. Afterwards Nick lay on his back and stared at the ceiling, and Audrey lay on her side and stared at him.

'Just tell me what to do,' Nick said at last.

'You don't have to do anything. It's all right.'

'Yeah, you looked all right when we were driving to Irène's,' he said. 'You were all white around the mouth.'

'I'm fine, Nick.' He shifted to face her. Their bodies mirrored each other. 'I wish I hadn't yelled at Bern,' she said.

Nick traced a finger down her arm, let it rest on her hip. She felt sharp and sexless.

Audrey caught the 86 tram to Nicholson Street when she finished at the office. She waited for Nick in the Carlton Gardens, opposite the hospital. She walked in slow circles around the pond. When he didn't come she sat on a bench and moved her toes in her boots. First he sent her a message to say he was running late. Then he called and told her not to wait.

'I don't know how long I'll be stuck here,' he said. 'Don't sit in the cold.'

She walked over to the university to meet Adam instead. He was waiting for her at the corner where the old Women's Hospital had been, bouncing from foot to foot, wearing a Christmas jumper and his spectacles. Audrey felt a rush of tenderness for him.

'You look well,' she said.

'I feel fantastic at the moment.'

They started walking without deciding on a direction.

'Have you seen Olivia this week?' Audrey asked.

'Yeah. I was a bit of a fuck-up last Tuesday, so I went back this morning. But we're making the appointments fortnightly from now on. She's pretty sharp. We cover a lot of ground.' He shifted his backpack. 'I don't know if it's sort of psychosomatic, or something? You know, I ought to feel better, since I'm spending all this money and time on a *mental-health plan*. Maybe I've almost tricked myself.'

'Do you think that matters, though? If you feel better?'

'You're probably right. Hang on, where are we?'

They stopped. They'd walked as far as the cemetery. On the other side of the road, light from the residential colleges glowed in yellow squares. 'Come on,' he said. 'Let's get something to eat. I'm starving.'

They ended up over his side of the city. It was almost like old times. Adam walked quickly, in grand strides; he was finishing his teaching placement, he'd gone out every night that week, he had lungfuls of stories to tell, he reached across the table to pinch a slice of pizza from Audrey's plate. Once he stopped mid-sentence, and she turned to follow his gaze. Bernie was standing outside the restaurant, waving at them through the window, hand-in-hand with Hazel. They stepped inside. Bernie made the introductions like a gentleman, and then they left.

'What's Bern doing looking so normal? And who's Hazel? You didn't tell me he had a girlfriend.'

'Yes, I did,' Audrey said, watching them through the glass. 'I don't know if they're really together. But she came to dinner at Irène's.'

'That probably constitutes togetherness.' Adam, too, watched their departing backs. Bern glanced over his shoulder, saw them looking, and gave a little fingery wave. 'He looks like you. It's funny, because you don't have the same mannerisms at all—he's getting bizarrely Warholesque—but physically, he could be your twin.' Audrey emptied a sugar sachet onto the table, and began tracing a fleur de lys with her fingertip.

'I was one of twins,' she said. She hadn't known she was going to.

'What? I didn't know that.'

'Well, there you go. Fun fact.'

'How come you're not a twin any more?' Adam asked.

'Just one of those things. Maman always said it was Darwin's theory.'

'What?'

'Natural selection or whatever. Some things are better adapted to their environments, and they outlive the things that aren't. The others just disappear. It happened way before I was even born.' She went on pushing the sugar crystals around on the tabletop.

She couldn't sleep.

At night, when Nick was setting up the coffee pot for the next morning, and the traffic noises dropped away, she felt that desperation start to set in, the plunging sadness.

When she did doze it was under a light and patchy gauze. She had strange dreams—of dead dogs frozen in the kiddie pool in the backyard; of making confessions in front of old high-school teachers; of kissing Nick and feeling his teeth crumble in his mouth—and she would lie awake for hours. She dreamed she was driving with her father. It was back when they were living in the New Street flats in

Gardenvale, and in the early mornings the rabbits were crouched by the side of the road. In the dream Audrey and Neil were driving, singing crazily, and then all the rabbits ran out from the grass and onto the road, and Audrey and her father killed them all.

'We should have Ben over,' she said to Nick. 'I bet he's missing Emy.'

It was an odd evening. The three of them were not quite familiar with one another. Audrey made soup. After dinner Nick washed the dishes, and Ben stood and excused himself.

'Do you mind if I have a smoke outside?'

Audrey put on a scarf and jacket, and they sat on the back stoop.

'Have you heard much from Em?' Audrey asked.

'She called me on Friday night. She was pretty drunk. Sounds like she's having a good time.'

'Her emails are amazing.' Emy's missives were sprawling, self-deprecating tales of her petty triumphs and failures. Audrey read them at work, and wanted to write something pithy back, but never knew what to say. 'She's clever, isn't she.'

'She's really smart.' Ben glanced at her. 'I don't know where that leaves me.'

'How do you mean?'

'I met her parents before she left. They live in this big house, all landscaped, staircase, big cars. They were nice.' He tapped the end of his cigarette lightly. The ash quivered, did not fall. 'I'm a cook, you know? I'm sort of waiting for her to realise I'm a boring dickhead.'

'That's not true, Ben. That's not how it works.'

'Thanks, mate.' He stubbed out his cigarette.

Audrey looked at his hands. They were big and able.

'I can't believe you met her parents,' she said at last, and corked his shoulder. 'You two don't muck around.'

'I've never done that before. Dinner. It was weird.'

After he left Audrey and Nick fucked on the couch with the lights down low. She could hardly see his face. His hips could have been the ocean or a horse beneath her.

Sleep Too Light For Dreaming

Audrey was awake reading when the phone rang, but it still gave her a fright. It was shrill, the wrong sound for five-thirty in the morning. Nick didn't move.

'Hello?'

'Audrey?' The voice was tentative, female.

'Yes?'

'It's Hazel. Dawson. Um, Bernie's girlfriend. I'm sorry to be calling so early...'

'We're awake,' Audrey said. 'Are you all right?'

'Bern's been up all night, sick.' She sounded very young and very frightened. 'Sorry to bother you, but I remembered Nick was an ambo. I thought he might know what to do.'

'What's wrong with him?'

'He hasn't stopped vomiting. I think he's got a fever. And just before he walked out into the kitchen—I was getting him a glass of water—and he passed out. He just went down. He's awake now, but he's raving. I can't get him to stay in bed.'

'Has he taken anything?'

'I don't know.'

'Hazel. Just say.'

'No, I really don't know,' the girl said. 'He was sick when I got here last night. I stayed over to look after him, but I have to go to school. I can't stay.'

Audrey pressed her fingertips to her eyes. 'We're both working. I can't get there before tonight.' Nick stirred. She lowered her voice. 'How sick is he?'

'I don't know. Maybe I'm overreacting.'

'No, I didn't mean that. He's lucky to have had you there with him. I'll come as soon as I can tonight.'

Audrey sat on the edge of the bed in the dark room, waiting for direction. She went to the kitchen and made a cup of tea.

She drove out to Port Phillip Correctional Centre to visit a client. She rehearsed her lines.

Mr Stanley, I've recommended that Maddie be placed in permanent care.

No use calling Irène and asking her to check on Bernie. Better not to tell their mother at all.

This means that your daughter will be raised by another family. She won't be moved from one foster family to another. She'll have a permanent family who will raise her as their own child. The family who has been caring for Maddie since she was removed have applied to care for her on an ongoing basis. This is the best possible outcome we could ask for, Mr Stanley. She's been with them since she was six weeks old.

She thought about the other questions she should have asked Hazel. Should have asked her to leave him with lots of fluids, have him take paracetamol. But Hazel was seventeen. Bernard was the boy she fucked around with. It wasn't fair to ask her to do anything.

You can appeal the decision, but if I'm being honest, it's very unlikely that she'll ever be returned to you permanently.

The traffic rolled and stopped, rolled and stopped. Audrey phoned Bernie, but he didn't answer.

At the security checkpoint she couldn't find her lanyard with her identification. She dropped to her haunches and scrabbled through her handbag. The blazer she'd worn specially, thinking it made her look bigger, more professional, felt foolish. She was clammy.

'I'll have to go back out to the car. It must have fallen out,' she said.

The security guard watched her. 'It's all right, love.'

She felt in her pocket. 'Oh! Got it.' Her things were all over the floor where she knelt, her feet slipping from her shoes.

Later, back into the city, back into the office.

'How'd it go, Audrey?'

'Oh—you know. I don't think he's going to appeal.'

Can I have a photo of her? he'd asked. He'd been too shocked to even consider disputing the decision. Audrey began to sift through emails from the morning. It seemed a long time ago. Her desk phone rang.

'This is Amal Ahmad calling on behalf of Mr Martin Stanley. I understand you're Maddison's case worker?'

'Yes, I visited Mr Stanley this morning—'

'I've just been in contact with him and he's decided to make an appeal. He wants access rights to his daughter.'

'I understand that, but it's unlikely that the decision will be over-turned. He has a history of sexual abuse and he—'

'I know his details. I'm just ringing to inform you that Mr Stanley has opted to go ahead with the proceedings.'

'Well,' Audrey said dully, 'thanks for letting me know.'

She hung up and went to her manager's office.

'Penny said you wanted a word,' she said from the doorway.

'Yeah. Do you want to sit down?'

Audrey knew, then, what was coming. She felt very tired. She closed the door behind her and sat. She looked at the pictures of Vanessa's kids.

'What's happened?'

'The Saaed baby died last night,' Vanessa said.

Audrey held on to the arms of the chair. 'Fuck.'

'I know how hard you tried. I'm sorry. It's not fair.'

'I'm sorry.'

'Audrey. You did everything you could have done.'

'There'll be another inquest, won't there.'

'We don't know that.'

Audrey pushed her chair back and stood. The floor was still there.

'I need to tell you about the Bennetts, too,' Vanessa said. 'Mum's run off and left the kids with Grandad for the second time this month.'

Audrey stared at her.

'He's a convicted paedophile,' Vanessa said.

'Thanks. For telling me. I'll get onto it.'

It was dark by the time she left the office. She called her brother again as she drove.

His lights were off when she arrived.

'Bern?' She made her way to his room. The house was freezing. 'Hello? Bernie?'

'Audie?' he croaked.

She knelt beside the stained mattress. His eyes did not follow her, did not focus on her approaching figure. Sallow face, dark hair matted with sweat, vomit congealing on the floorboards beside him.

'I'm so sorry. I'm sorry, Bernie.'

His hand jerked. 'What?' he said. 'You were working. It's not your fault.'

'Have you had anything to eat or drink since Hazel left?'

'What?' he said again.

She went and got him a glass of water and a wet washcloth. She sat him up. He was barely conscious as he drank. The water ran off his lips and onto his naked chest.

'I'm cramping, Audie,' he said. 'Everywhere. My legs.'

The room stank of vomit and shit. Audrey took him to the couch while she stripped and re-made his bed, scrubbed the floor, opened the windows. She called Nick.

'Bern's pretty crook,' she said. 'Do you know if that clinic near Adam's is open twenty-four hours?'

'Bring him into St Vincent's.'

'I don't want to wait hours for him to be looked at. He's so dehydrated he's cramping. I should have come and seen him this morning. I shouldn't have waited.'

'It's quiet tonight. You won't be waiting long. Sounds like he needs a drip. You don't know what's wrong, anyway. He might have taken something.'

She walked Bernie out to the car in three stages: first to the front door, where his knees buckled, then halfway to the gate, where he sat down on the concrete path, and finally to the back seat. They drove slowly, with Audrey making low, soothing sounds as if to a child or animal.

They sat in triage for three hours. Audrey folded herself into a plastic chair, and Bernie lay across a bank of adjoining seats. Nick came by early in the night. He looked over Bernie, crouched before him. He brought Audrey coffee in a polystyrene cup and sat there as long as he could.

The other people waiting did not sit near Bernie. He was frightening, pitiful. One of the nurses gave him a kidney dish, and he dutifully alternated between sleeping and retching.

Three hours for an impassive woman to say *acute gastroenteritis* and prescribe him some antibiotics. Another two before they found a bed for him.

'I knew I was sick on Saturday,' he said, 'but I wanted to go out, and I had a big night. I think I did too much MD, and Hazel had some really good coke.'

'Fuck, Bern.'

'Yes,' he said, 'it probably wasn't one of my better ideas.'

He slept. Nick's shift finished, and in solidarity he offered to stay the night, but Audrey told him to go home. 'Take the car,' she said.

'How will you get home?'

'I'll get a cab.'

'Promise?'

She spent the night in the vinyl chair beside Bernie. Early in the morning she touched his arm. 'Hey. I have to go to work,' she said. 'I'll come back later in the day. The nurse thinks you'll be discharged tonight. You should probably stay at ours.'

'Okay.' He closed his eyes again.

Outside the sky was a cold, smoky blue. Audrey wrapped her scarf around her neck and walked up Young Street. The cafés were just opening. She was fumbling for her coin purse before she realised she didn't want any more coffee. Her body was confused.

Nick was sleeping when she got home. For a moment she stood in the doorway looking at him, his throat white and exposed, one arm flung out across the sheets. He looked vulnerable, boyish. She opened and closed the drawers quietly, gathering clean clothes, and then she ran the shower. She sank down onto her knees and sat on the slate tiles.

The door opened. Nick stood there in the steam, rubbing his eyes. Audrey's clothes were on the floor, shed skin. He nudged them with his foot.

'You should have called me,' he said. 'I would've come and picked you up.'

'You were tired.'

'So are you,' he said. 'You look pathetic.' He pulled off his T-shirt and slid open the shower screen gently so it wouldn't jam on its metal runner. She thought *I can't, I'm so tired I feel sick*, but all he did was reach for the shampoo. He began to wash her hair. Audrey's heart loosened at the small kindness. She watched Nick's face until he said *Close your eyes*. His fingers scrunched at her scalp.

He threw her a towel, and she shivered in it.

'How's Bern?' he asked.

'He's all right. He can go home this afternoon.' She leaned forwards to fasten her bra. Nick sat on the edge of the bathtub.

'Spence,' he said as she towelled her hair, 'you should talk to your mum. You shouldn't have to look after him like this.'

Nick's mother had driven him to football practice, ironed the number onto his guernsey, cooked him roast chicken every Sunday night of his life. He'd never had to worry about his brother.

Audrey opened the cabinet over the sink and poked around, fishing through empty paracetamol cartons and discarded tabs.

'Don't we have *any* Panadol?'

Nick leaned over her and found an unopened packet.

'Here.' He popped two capsules into her palm.

'He's seventeen,' Audrey said. She tipped back her head. 'I can't just abandon him.'

'I'm not asking you to!'

'This is just how it goes,' she said. 'Maman can't look after any of us. She doesn't know how. She expects me to look after him. If I don't, nobody will. That's how it works.'

'What about your sister?'

'If I don't look after him, nobody will,' Audrey said. 'Nothing's changed. It's always been like this.'

'Right. Nothing's changed. And look at you.'

She turned and pulled a face at the mirror. 'Yeah, what a hag.'

'There must be an easier way of doing this. That's all I mean,' said Nick. 'All this running around and pulling all-nighters in Emergency. You don't even have a good story to tell for it.'

She yawned. 'I've got to go. I'm going to be late.'

'Come on,' he said to her retreating back. 'You can't go to work. We're still talking.'

She pulled on her shoes and tied back her hair. She kissed him. They clung to each other.

'Nick. There is nothing to talk about.' Her heart beat fast.

'One of the first times my mum met you, she said *Audrey's very contained, isn't she?*'

'What do you mean,' Audrey said, 'by telling me that?'

She was very alive at that moment. She felt her eyes wide and tired; she felt her body made of blood and bone and nerves and something else, something harder, like steel. She could have run for days.

Nick held her at arm's length, peered down into her face.

'Are you all right?' he asked.

Shy worry: Audrey was taken aback.

'I'm fine. It was just a long night.' She pulled away. 'I was thinking. I might see if I can get a prescription for some sleeping pills.'

'That's a good idea,' Nick said. 'You might feel better if you could get some sleep.'

'I'll see you tonight.'

He stood at the front door and watched her go. She wanted to make him feel better. She turned back at the gate, mimed an extravagant goodbye.

She called Nick to come and get her from the pub. She couldn't be there another second. It was only the girls from work, but she couldn't remember what to say. By the bar Chelsea said *You okay? You look knackered.* Audrey couldn't see faces any more. She tried to think about where Nick would be. Two minutes to put on his shoes and jacket and find his keys, ten minutes up Nicholson Street to Glenlyon Road.

He called when he arrived. She felt her phone vibrate in her hand. She said goodbye to the others, bent over to kiss their cheeks where they sat around the table.

Nick met her at the door of the pub.

'I'm so glad you're here,' she said.

He hugged her a long time. 'What happened?'

'I just got scared.'

'Weren't you with work people?'

'Yes.'

'I don't want to be an arsehole about it,' he said, 'but I don't get why it was so scary. Can you just explain it to me a bit?'

'I can't. I know it doesn't make sense.'

He'd parked in Edward Street, opposite the warehouses. Audrey stopped by the car. 'Can we just wait here a second before we go home?'

They sat down at the kerb, and she put her head between her knees.

'I wish I wasn't getting into a vehicle,' she said.

'Yeah, I wish you weren't, too,' Nick laughed, but he rubbed her shoulders while she spewed stringy red-wine vomit out the car door later, and undressed her, and gave her a glass of water. He said *You don't need to keep saying thank you.*

Irène arrived mid-morning with Zoe, miniature coat and backpack hanging from her elbow. The heels of her boots made a smart *clonk clonk* along the floorboards. She didn't have time for a cup of tea, wouldn't sit down. Her clothes were tastefully drapey.

They all stood in the warm kitchen.

'Thanks for doing this,' Irène said. 'She's had bronchitis. We've just about knocked it over, but she hasn't finished the antibiotics yet. She needs four mill after lunch. It's printed on the bottle, anyway. It's in a Ziploc bag in her backpack.' She fished around for the medicine. Audrey glanced at Nick. He was working to suppress a laugh. *'Tiens,'* Irène said, handing Audrey the brown bottle. 'Can you make sure she's rugged up? Sorry if I sound neurotic. She's just been a bit sick, haven't you, Zoe?' She turned to Audrey and Nick. 'Thank you so much.'

'No worries,' Audrey said. 'Happy anniversary.'

Irène left.

'Your mother,' Nick said to Zoe, 'is very intense.'

They drove across the West Gate to Williamstown, past the factories and shipping yards, past the Backwash. They sprawled out on the grass by the water. Audrey unpacked the picnic, plastic-wrapped salad rolls, and poured coffee from the thermos.

'What a Honey Homemaker,' Nick grinned. 'I'll have to pat you on the bum and call you *love*.'

Audrey pitched a mandarine at him. It hit him squarely in the chest.

'Ooh,' he said to Zoe. 'Punk's not dead.'

Zoe appraised the roll gravely.

'Audrey,' she said, 'I don't like tomato.'

'Doesn't matter. Just pick it out.'

'Here, I'll eat it for you,' said Nick, and opened his mouth.

Later he went to move the car, and brought his old Sherrin back with him.

'Here, Zoe, see if you can mark this. I'll do a big one.' He moved back and Zoe stood with her hands ready, fingers splayed rigidly. Nick booted the Sherrin, but it landed too high. It hit Zoe in the face. There was a moment of shock before she put her hand to her nose, and saw blood. She started to cry. Nick and Audrey ran across the grass.

'Fuck,' Nick said. 'I'm sorry, Zo. Are you okay?' There seemed to be a lot of blood. It was in her blond hair, down the front of her T-shirt, smeared with mucous and tears across her face. Audrey knelt beside her, digging around in her bag for tissues. She pressed them to Zoe's nose.

'You're all right. It's okay.' She turned to Nick. 'Here, have a look. Do you think it's'—she glanced back at the sobbing kid—'broken?' she mouthed. She took the tissue away for a moment. Nick looked at Zoe's nose, touched it gently.

'No.'

An older woman was walking towards them.

'Is she all right?' she asked.

'She's fine, we just had a bit of an accident with the footy.' Audrey was still trying to stem the blood.

'I saw,' said the woman. 'Do you need a cold pack? We've got one in our freezer bag.'

Zoe stopped crying. The three of them traipsed across the road and stopped in front of a gelato shop. Zoe took a long time to choose, peering seriously at the bright containers.

They climbed into the car again just as the rain started. They drove back across the bridge to the other side of the city. Zoe slept in the back seat. Nick and Audrey laughed the whole way home, imitating their own panic: Nick's childless exclamation—*Fuck!*— and Audrey's own clumsy face-cleaning skills. 'So much snot!' The clipped woman proffering her cold pack and child-rearing expertise.

'Is that what happens if you're a parent? Do you turn into that? Fucking—*cold packs*.'

'The amoxicillin's in a bottle in a Ziploc bag in her backpack.'

At home, Nick and Zoe played cards on the living room floor while Audrey made dinner.

'Let's get that T-shirt off you, Zo. I'll give it a wash in the sink before your mum arrives,' she suggested.

'Yeah, that's a good idea. I reckon it looks worse than it actually was,' Nick said. 'Snap!'

Adam dropped by before dinner and took the fourth chair at the table. He and Zoe looked curiously at each other. He spoke without tempering his language or topics. It all streamed on: his assignments, an article he'd read on sex trafficking, his parents, his latest session with his psychologist. He was calling her *Liv* now. When Audrey looked around the table, Zoe was listening with the rapt attention of a child suddenly counted among adults. Nick had tired eyes, sunken stones in wet sand. Once he started a thumb war with Zoe. Once he got up to change the record.

Irène and David didn't stay long. Audrey collected the clean T-shirt where it lay drying on the heating vent, the medicine bottle from the bench. She stood on the nature strip to wave goodbye. Her sister wound down the window and said *Thanks* again.

Audrey sat back down at the table.

'You didn't tell me Irène was pregnant,' Adam said.

'I'm sure I did.'

'No, you didn't. You don't tell me anything any more,' he said. He was cheerful, rolling a cigarette. He was poking fun at his own chattiness, the way he dominated conversation, but Audrey felt Nick's leg press against hers.

It was late by the time Adam left. The record was still playing, but the house had gone quiet. Audrey filled the sink with water and left the dishes there. Nick took the empty bottles out to the bin. Audrey heard the muffled tink of glass.

He came back in and stood with a hand in his hair.

'He's *so much*,' he kept saying. 'He's just *so much*.'

Something about his expression, like a man shell-shocked, tugged at Audrey's chest.

'Thanks for today,' she said. 'With Zoe.'

'It's family,' he shrugged. 'Anyway. She's easy.'

He fell asleep quickly. Audrey tensed her muscles and relaxed them one at a time, toes to jaw. She turned on the bedside light and read sixty pages. She plucked her eyebrows, humming to herself in the bathroom. She got back into bed and turned off the light. Nick woke and laid an arm across her.

'Enough.' He squinted at her. 'Stop fidgeting.'

'I can't sleep.'

'Put all your body parts to sleep, one by one.'

'I did.'

'Guess it didn't work.'

'Guess it didn't,' she echoed. He touched her face, but his eyes were already flickering closed.

Audrey imagined disappearing through the mattress fibres. She could feel something leaking out of her pores, ready to poison everyone else. She thought of how neat and private Katy's sadness had been. It had built up like the salt crystals they'd grown in school, climbing, climbing. She missed Katy. She was sorry beyond all endurance, against all reason.

She wanted to wake up Nick, but she had nothing to tell him.

At lunch Sylvie spoke for sixteen minutes without pause about her job at the bank. The waitress stood dumbly by the table, pad in hand, waiting for her to draw breath. Audrey could have got up and left, and her mother wouldn't have noticed. She had that cloudy look in her eyes.

For six minutes, Sylvie re-enacted a particularly spiteful conversation she and Bernard had shared the previous week.

For four minutes, she listed the side effects of the new medication that Dr Lawrence had prescribed her.

For nine minutes, she recounted a television program she'd seen on the ABC: '—you know, the man, he's married to Jennifer Byrne—'

'Andrew Denton.'

'Non, non, not him. This man's smaller. He wears glasses. He used to have a show doing interviews. He was always having interesting people.'

'Maman. It's Andrew Denton.'

'No, I know who is Andrew Denton, and it's not him…'

The food arrived and went cold. Sylvie's words tripped over one another in their hurry to get out. Audrey could not keep up. She saw her mother in static: head thrown back in exuberance; hands splayed in the middle of a frenetic sentence; fork waving in the air to punctuate a sentence. Audrey ordered another glass of wine. It was all theatre and pity. Sylvie was lonely. She didn't see her children enough. She was so happy to be having lunch with her daughter. Audrey knew these things, but it made no difference. She felt drained and guilty.

Sylvie picked up her wineglass as though preparing a toast. 'Happy birthday, *p'tit lapin*. Always a good girl. Even when you were a baby.' The wine splashed in the glass. 'Bernard was the trouble. Like he *knew* that he was an accident.'

'Maman. Don't say that.'

'I don't mean I don't want him, or something like that. I just remember him so much…wanting things. Always crying, crying, crying.' She jabbed a finger across the table. 'Don't shake your head like that. You don't know what it's like to have that, all the time, *Maman, Maman*, and knowing that you have to fix it, to make him stop. You and Irène were much easier. I remember, Audrey, I could leave you in your crib, and when I came back you'd still be there on your back. Even if you were awake, you didn't cry. Not like Bernard.'

'Babies are supposed to cry when you leave them,' Audrey said. 'They're meant to cry. It means they expect you to come back.'

'So I'm a bad mother because you don't cry when you were a baby.'

'No, I don't—I don't know. I'm not saying that. I'm sorry.'

At last Sylvie shook out her napkin and spread it over her lap. She looked at Audrey.

'*Ça va?*' she asked.

'I'm fine.'

Sylvie speared a mushroom and regarded it without interest. '*Je t'crois pas,*' she said. 'You look like you have some sort of... deficiency.'

'Let's just have our lunch.'

'I was only saying what I thought. Don't be so defensive.'

'Well, why would you say that? A *deficiency*. How do you think that's going to make someone feel?'

Sylvie was looking at the street outside, playing with her pack of cigarettes.

Audrey drove home along the freeway. The sky was pale and wide and she was thinking about university, a cold afternoon lying on the whiskery grass with Adam. Him, philosophy: pulling apart *Leviathan*, reading bits aloud to impress her, fistfuls of highlighters colour-coding his knowledge. Her, social work: John Bowlby and attachment theory. The Strange Situation. Identify child as being anxious–avoidant. Anxious–resistant. Securely attached. Disorganised. Learn the signs and signals. A flat affect, a lack of discrimination between mother and strangers. Seven black birds flying in formation, a message in a crossword puzzle, a shape in the stars.

Audrey's throat ached.

Her birthday fell on a Thursday. The women made a fuss. Vanessa brought her a coffee in the morning. Penny made an orange cake. The new inquest was announced in the afternoon. It was all anybody talked about. Audrey had supervision. Vanessa said *We'll both be subpoenaed, probably.* She said *Your case notes are exceptional.* She said *There's absolutely nothing more you could have done.* Audrey nodded.

She left work half an hour early, hurried up Rathdowne Street to the clinic. It was the fragile end of the day. She sat in one of the chairs in the corridor of the old terrace with her coat over her knees.

The doctor took Audrey's blood pressure first, asked her to step onto the scales, made her lie down on the narrow table. Her hands were cool and broad. She put them on Audrey's skin, pressed lightly. Audrey stared at the ceiling. It was a relief to lie still. All the while the doctor spoke in a low murmur.

'You're a student? Working?'

'I work full time. I'm a protective worker.'

The doctor's hands went all over, as though trying to intuit something through the skin. Audrey had forgotten the shame of medicine, it had been so long.

The doctor tapped at her computer keyboard as Audrey pulled on her boots. They finished and looked up at each other at the same moment.

'You can also try warm milk or herbal tea before bed. Go to sleep later. Make sure you're eating enough.' Audrey sat with her legs dangling over the edge of the table. The doctor smiled indulgently. 'All the things you know how to do.'

Nick was waiting for her in the kitchen, sitting at the table with a beer.

'Paddy was over,' he said. 'You just missed him. How'd you get on?'

'Okay. She gave me a script.' Audrey sat down and put the folded papers on the table between them. Nick looked at her for a moment, and reached for the prescription.

'Temazepam,' he said. 'Woo-woo.'

Audrey reached for his beer. 'How's Pat?' she asked.

'What'd you get a pathology referral for?'

'You can throw it out,' Audrey said. Nick went on looking at her, steady, but he did as she said.

They made love in bed first, while the sky turned grim through the window; then in the shower, everything edged with heat. Audrey fell into a sleep too light for dreaming. When Nick woke her she thought it was the middle of the night.

'Come on. I said we'd get there at eight.'

'Let's stay here. Nobody'd notice,' Audrey said.

'Reckon they might. You're the birthday girl.'

Audrey wanted to stay in bed, sleep for weeks.

Nick sat on the end of the bed and watched her dress. She met his eyes in the mirror. She couldn't remember why she'd let him and Adam organise anything. She didn't want to celebrate her first birthday without Katy, didn't want to go to those same pubs and see the same people. The Evelyn, the Backwash, the view from Ruckers Hill, the Curtin: they'd been poisoned for her. *None of us can go back*, Katy's father had said. Audrey bunched her stockings together at the feet so she wouldn't ladder them.

'Tell me about Sylvie,' Nick said.

'What, lunch yesterday? She was all right. Bit manic.'

'No, I mean when you were small.'

Audrey found some lipstick and applied it leaning into the mirror, the way her mother did. She faced him again.

'Once when we were living in the Menzies Avenue flats, she decided to cook rabbit, and I couldn't bring myself to eat it. I would have been about nine, Irène was probably thirteen. Bern was still little. I ate all my vegetables and only the rabbit was left. I took a bite and gagged on it, and Maman thought I was acting. She got really cross and smacked me, and made me leave the table.' Audrey went to the wardrobe and pulled out her coat. 'So later, *Hey Hey It's Saturday* was on, and there was some band playing. Irène and I were dancing, and I accidentally knocked over this beautiful vase that Maman's parents gave her. It broke into five big bits, and Maman thought I'd done it on purpose. She didn't yell. I felt terrible. I kept offering to glue it, then I just went to my room and sat there. Much later she came in and said she was going to bed, but she handed me a little card with a picture of some mountains on it. Inside was this Kate Greenaway poem about a mother telling off her naughty kid—something about not being able to kiss a teary face. Neither of us really apologised, but I knew she wasn't mad, and she knew I hadn't done it on purpose.'

Audrey picked up her scarf and stood waiting.

'That's a nice story,' Nick said.

'When she was a good mum, there was no one better. Irène and Bernie and I got a story almost every night. We learned to read really quickly.' She remembered something she hadn't thought of in years. 'When she undressed us for a bath, she used to pull our shirts over our heads and say *skin a bunny*. She must have learned it from Dad.' She said it the way Sylvie had, slipped in and out of the accent the way she always did when she mimicked her mother.

Nick ran his thumb along her hairline. 'I like trying to picture you as a child,' he said.

The pub was warm. A handful of her friends from work were standing by the open fire. They turned to her. Audrey tried to remember what to do.

'We were just talking about the Dillons. Chelsea has to do a visit on Monday.'

'Yeah, if Mr Dillon can stop shaking the baby long enough to open the door to me—happy birthday, darl, anyway—' If anyone had heard their conversation, they might have been appalled, Audrey reflected, especially romantics like Adam. She found him outside in the beer garden.

'What are you doing out here by yourself?' She sat down beside him.

'Happy birthday! Give us a kiss. Have you been here long?'

'Fifteen minutes. Are you all right?'

93

'I was on the phone. Are you coming to Minh's gig after? He's playing at the Tote.'

'All right.'

'All *right*! I'll call him.' Audrey realised he was waiting for her to leave. She raised her eyebrows. Adam blushed, and pulled out his cigarette papers. Audrey finished her drink. 'I'm going back in. It's too cold out here.'

Back inside Audrey looked for Nick and found Suze instead.

'I've slept with three people in the last year,' Suze said, 'and they're all here tonight. This town's too small.' She gave Audrey a squeeze. 'You look *great*, lady. Happy birthday.'

Audrey drifted away. She was alone again, she was dopey with heat and wine, she was a sleepy satellite. She saw Josie and Vanessa and Chelsea and Penny, the four cynics, still cackling by the fireside. She saw tall Nick standing with friends. He was telling a story, talking with his hands.

They all walked over to the Tote in a joyful cavalcade. She and Nick stood close in the bandroom, leaning against the bricks. Between sets the crowd shifted, moved into the courtyard or out into the front bar. Audrey waited in the bathroom. Her own small, dazed face flashed back at her from the dirty mirror. The two cubicle doors banged opened at the same time; a woman stumbled out of each, and they giggled.

Outside the bathrooms she met Johnny with a pint in each hand. He offered one to her. She shook her head and he kissed her on both cheeks. She held up her wrist to the girl at the bandroom door. She threaded her way through the room, hot with bodies, and found Nick.

The plastic beer jug was wedged between his feet on the carpet. He looked glad to see her, as though he'd been worried she'd disappear.

It was late when everyone spilled out onto the pavement. They all stood around in the shocking cold, sobering up and making fast farewells, pressing cheek to cheek.

Audrey looked around for Adam to say goodbye, but he was standing with a full-lipped boy. They were lighting each other's cigarettes.

Audrey turned to Patrick. 'I think Adam's got a thing for Minh.'

'Fuck, I've got a thing for Minh, too,' Pat said in a tortured voice, and kissed her hair. 'Take care, you good woman.'

Audrey took Nick's hands and they reeled across the road in a debauched waltz. From the other side of the street they waved to the cheerful stragglers left standing outside the pub, and started down the slope.

In the kitchen Nick leaned against the bench and slumped onto the floor.

'You didn't have a birthday cake,' he said.

'Don't need a cake. I had a lovely day.' Audrey sat beside him.

'I feel like things have been weird for a while,' he said clumsily. 'And I know it's probably just been everything that's going on…' *What has been going on?* thought Audrey. *There's no excuse for me.*

'I don't want to give up,' she said.

'Is that what we're doing?'

'I think we'd know about it if we were giving up,' she said. He smiled at that. Audrey grabbed his coat by the collar and pulled him close for a kiss. After a while she went to the cupboard, and pulled out a bottle of Hendrick's.

Nick stayed on the linoleum holding his woollen hat. 'Spence,' he said, 'I know we don't, but it's okay to talk if you want. We're not having a fight. You don't have to make a joke.'

Audrey handed him a glass. 'Here's cheers.'

'You'll chuck.'

'No I won't. Cheers,' she said again.

'Happy birthday.'

They staggered to the bedroom. Audrey stood in the doorway, stripping off her skirt, and Nick fell onto the bed. His spidery legs dangled over the end.

'Help me,' he grunted, 'can you pull my boots off?'

'Do it yourself, you lazy cunt.' They began to laugh. 'Did I ever tell you,' Audrey said, lying down beside him, 'that I had a twin?'

'No. What happened?'

'It died before I was—before we were born. Darwin's theory.'

'So it wasn't your twin for long.'

'No, only a couple of weeks, probably.' She must have sounded sad, because Nick stopped looking at the ceiling and put his arms around her.

They lay there on top of the sheets. Neither of them moved for a long time.

'Are you awake?'

'Yes.'

'I feel like you're going somewhere,' Nick said, 'and I can't come.'

'I'm here.'

'But I don't know what I can do. Tell me what's wrong.'

Audrey could only practise thinking hateful things about herself. 'I've been feeling pretty dreadful,' she said at last, 'and as though it's all very hard work.'

'I know,' Nick said. He was on his side now, facing her. Audrey had to go on staring at the ceiling in case any of the noxious black grief leaked out.

'I don't want to punish you,' she said.

'You're not. I just want you to come back.'

'I'm here,' she said again. She wasn't sure who should do the comforting, so she turned and kissed his neck, the hollow below his ear, and they settled like that. She felt Nick fall asleep, felt the rhythm of his chest change, and she rolled to the edge of the bed. She pressed her face into the pillow. Her breath made a dragging sound.

In the morning, while Nick was still sleeping, she wrote him a note in very small letters, tucked it under the coffee plunger and went to work. When she got home he'd already left for his shift, but he'd written a reply on the same piece of paper. In her hand, *I'm sorry for being a monster.* And in his, below: *We're all at least half machine.* She felt such a complete and terrible sorrow that she curled into bed before dusk and tried to find a new space between waking and dreaming.

Pillar Of Salt

Nick left in a little hurricane of movement. He ate his dinner in a rush, read Audrey her horoscope from the newspaper to make her laugh, swilled a cup of coffee, brushed his teeth, kissed her up against the wall. The screen door slapped shut behind him; the broken concrete pavers rippled as he wheeled his bike out. He made all the noise that afternoon. He was trying hard.

Audrey called Adam first, and then drove across the river to see him. She looked for the sign over the factories, the rainbow, OUR MAGIC HOUR. Adam's hair was freshly cut. Audrey was glad to see him fussing over his reflection. They half-watched an American television program about psychics investigating a murder. Adam smeared ricotta on fig halves. Audrey listened to his latest escapades and conflicts. He talked about Minh. He went to the bathroom to piss, and told her about his placement supervisor through the open door. He settled beside her on the couch and theorised about Emy and Ben's relationship. Audrey thought how suddenly he'd turned around. She couldn't remember if she'd stopped worrying about him because he seemed better or because she was dog-paddling to keep her own head above water.

'You lost weight, Spencer?'

'No.' Audrey gave him a Miss Universe smile. He pulled a face. He rolled a cigarette and smoked it while she watched the pictures on the screen. He picked up a crumpled napkin and pitched it at her.

'Oi. Friend,' he said, 'what's happened to you? I feel like we haven't spoken in weeks.'

'We talk all the time.'

'Yeah, most days, but I don't know what's going on.'

'Nothing very exciting. Work's been full on.'

They watched a soundless blender commercial.

'Audrey. It's like you've had some kind of bypass.'

'I've been feeling a bit flat,' she said.

'How come?'

'I don't know.'

Adam started on another cigarette, pinching the tobacco until it was spread in a perfectly even line.

'I fucked up at work,' said Audrey. 'A child died. One of mine. Ten months.'

'What happened?'

'Neglect.'

'Shit.' He nudged the filter. 'Just because it was your case doesn't mean you fucked up.'

'The safety of those kids is my job. It's my only job.'

Audrey got up to put the kettle on.

Adam didn't move from the couch. 'I bet Nick said the same as me.'

'I don't want to talk about Nick.'

'You are a pain in the arse when you're like this,' Adam said. 'I'd forgotten.'

Audrey carried the mugs back to the sofa.

'I'm being really awful to him at the moment. I can't seem to stop myself.'

'I'm sure you're not.'

'I don't know what's happening,' she said. 'Maybe I've got no resilience. I keep getting more scared of everything. When I go out to gigs I want to hide in the bathrooms. I don't know what to say to our friends. There's too many awful things. I can't stop it all from happening to people. I didn't look out for Katy. I don't know how to look out for Bernie or Maman. I don't know how to stop it from happening.'

'Oh, Spence. You can't.'

Audrey read something embarrassed and tender in Adam's face. She was ashamed. It had been years since he'd seen her cry.

Adam gathered her to him, spoke close to her ear. 'Your religion is other people's happiness. It's absurd.' He touched the bones of her neck. 'You'll be okay.'

Audrey wiped her nose. 'I'm fine,' she said.

They laughed. Adam kissed her on the lips.

'I'm sorry. I feel awful to have done that to you,' Audrey said.

'Don't be sorry,' he said.

'I *am* sorry. I don't know what else to say. I feel terrible.'

'I think you should talk to Nick. Or maybe someone else, if you can't talk to him. I think you'd both feel better,' he said.

'It's not up to you, Adam.'

'No,' he said, 'it's not.'

Audrey drove home late and waited for Nick. When he got home she was asleep on the carpet.

'Hey, babe.'

She opened one eye and looked up at him.

'What are you doing on the floor?'

'I went to Adam's, and…' She was cold. 'I don't know.'

He lay down next to her and picked up the book of stories she'd been reading. She watched him thumb through it.

'Do you reckon I'd like this?' he asked.

'Probably not,' she said gently. Reading was a chore for him, though he'd never say it.

'How come?'

'They're stories about very small things.'

She fell asleep again. It felt like only moments before Nick said *Come on. Let's get into bed.*

He was tactical. If he came home from work in the afternoon and found her asleep in bed he was frightened. He'd say *Let's go out for dinner. There's a gig on at Shebeen. Can you help me make those zucchini fritters? Come with me to the laundromat, I haven't seen you all day.* She waited for him to lose patience, to say *How come you can be normal at work but not with me*, but he never did. On a bad night, one of the worst, he propped her at the kitchen table like a corpse. He cut up her food for her. He'd made an omelette with things she liked. She was paralysed with grief. He said *Look at me* and she couldn't. He said *I miss you.* They both began to cry.

Emy was back for a fortnight. She phoned Audrey.

'Dad drove out to get me from the airport. It's kind of weird, with Ben. Long-distance is hard. We hadn't been seeing each other all that long.'

'I'm sorry,' Audrey said.

'Don't be. I still don't know. We're going out tomorrow night, so we'll see what happens.'

Audrey was still typing in the bleak kitchen light when Nick arrived home. She heard his boots on the porch, heard him drop his keys on the sideboard. The reckless noise he made told her he'd be playing the cheerful, dopey drunk. He stumped through the door and she lifted her face to him.

'Ponytail,' he said.

'It's getting long. I have to get a haircut.'

'A ponytail always means shit's about to go down.'

'Does it.'

'Yep. You're ready to phone your mum, or clean the windows, or help me write a submission. Tie those hairs back.'

'I'm doing a court report. Maybe you're right,' she said. 'How was tonight?'

'Good. We just went to the Napier. You should've come.' He picked up her cold mug of tea and tipped it down the sink. 'How much longer with the report?'

'Don't know. I'm almost done. Maybe I'll get up early tomorrow and finish it.' He moved behind her. He touched her shoulder blade; she felt that part of her tense. She stopped typing. 'Hang on, I can't work on two things at once.'

'Jesus, Audrey,' he said, and fell back. 'It's not meant to be work.'

'Oh, come on. You know that's not what I meant.'

He looked injured.

Audrey reached for his sleeve. 'Let's go to bed.'

'Something happened,' Nick said as they undressed. He stood in his shirt and socks looking like a solemn child. If his voice hadn't been so earnest Audrey would have smiled.

'Are you all right?'

'I did something bad,' he said. 'Outside the pub I ran into this girl I went to uni with, and we went for a drink, and we hooked up.' Audrey caught sight of herself in the mirror: black stockings, black bra, the ribs of a mean dog. Her chest made her think of the chicken they bought at the market. 'I don't know why I did it,' he went on. 'I'm not attracted to her. It was just really weird and intense. And I'm so sorry.'

'Nick. Stop.'

'Then I was coming back down Condell Street and this older guy stepped out of one of the houses, and I imagined what I'd do to him if he pulled a knife on me, and I was ready. This big *adrenaline* rush. I could have killed him.' He sounded as if he were about to cry. 'He just walked right past me. I felt sick that I'd even imagined it. And I don't know why I hooked up with Georgia. I'm sorry.'

The panic strangled his speech. Audrey almost didn't recognise him. His brows were drawn together; he might have been confessing a murder.

Sometimes when they fucked now she thought of other things. Not other men, but of fields and waves and streams. She felt as though he were humouring her, that he was touching her because he felt sorry for her or because he was daring himself to. The joy had gone out of their bodies.

'It's okay,' Audrey said. 'It's all right. I get it. You didn't fuck her, did you? You're wasted, you hooked up—I'm not missing anything, am I?'

'Don't say it like that.'

'Like what? I'm not upset, Nick. I get it more than you think. I know I'm not'—now she faltered—'You've been patient. I get it.'

'Oh, don't be bloody *sacrificial* about it.'

She threw open her arms. 'Well, I don't know what you want me to say. How should I react? What do you want me to say?'

'I want you to care! It's like you're saying *Go on, fuck whoever, I don't give a shit.*'

'Fuck you,' she said. She turned away. 'I resent that.'

In bed they tried to salvage what they could.

Audrey pulled the sheet up over their heads like a sail. 'When we were kids, we had this ratty orange canvas tent. Maman used to set it up in the middle of the living room. She'd let me and Irène eat lunch in there, bring our books and blankets in.' Their breath was hot under the cotton ceiling. 'You know how when you're a kid, you think you're invisible because you can't see anyone else.'

Nick stretched the sheet taut overhead, let it slacken.

'Sometimes you make it sound okay,' he said.

'We were happy most of the time.'

'I still don't understand it.' Nick went on pressing the sheet with his hand. A great fold fell between their faces. 'I still don't get what it was like.'

Audrey's phone sounded in the middle of the night but by the time she came to, Nick was already switching on the light, licking his lips, climbing across her body to answer the thing.

'Are you all right? Where are you?' he croaked. 'Listen, mate, it's not really a good time. Isn't there—'

Audrey felt everything stratify. *Adam.* She hadn't imagined he could go backwards, that this could start again. Nick was rubbing his eyes. She pulled on her jumper and waited. Those endless nights spent with Adam, chasing his grief around their kitchen table or his, all the late-night phone calls. She didn't know if she could weather a second wave.

Nick tossed the phone onto the bed.

'It's your brother,' he said. 'He's off his tits.'

'Where is he?'

'Out the front.'

Nick pulled on some shorts. Audrey followed him to the door. Bernie stood on the step dressed in a girl's school pinafore. In his hand he held a fluorescent-blue tube and a shaggy wig.

'The fuck.' Nick started to laugh. They stepped aside and Bernie staggered to the kitchen.

'Sorry,' he kept saying, even as he collapsed at the table, 'sorry, mate. I'm really sorry, Audie.'

'Where've you been?'

'I started off at this party in Carlton, one of Tom's friends. And we went for a walk, to get more drinks, but I sort of got lost from everyone else.'

'What's with the lightsaber?' Nick asked.

'Dress-up party. Guess who I am.' He held up the mass of synthetic hair, and slapped it on his head. The red fringe fell over his eyes. 'Chrissy Amphlett. You know, like, *Boys in Town*-era. This is my microphone.'

'So you got lost.' Audrey handed him a mug of tea. 'Then what?'

'Then I was smoking a doobie in a park somewhere, and this guy comes up to me and says *he's* going to a party, so I got on the tram with him and it went a long way. It went to fucken Thornbury. I didn't even know where that was. But when we got there, to the house, I realised it was a sex party, and I got scared.' Nick rocked back and clapped his hands together. Audrey looked at her brother, with his smudged makeup and his lopsided wig, and she was laughing, too, an early-morning delirium. Bernie drew the teabag up and down in the mug. 'So then I slept in a bush for a while,' he continued, 'and by the time I wake up the trams have stopped running and my wallet's gone and I can't get a cab.'

'How'd you get here?'

'Walked.'

'What, from Thornbury?'

'Yeah, it's taken a while, but it was okay. I didn't want to wake you up so I just kept walking. Figured if I got here, I could crash on your couch. I just can't make it back to St Kilda.'

Close to five o'clock he passed out on the living room floor. Audrey put a quilt over his body. She stood and watched him a moment.

In the bedroom she lay down beside Nick and opened *L'Assommoir*. Gervaise was losing her mind on a sidewalk, her entire existence confined to the triangle between the hospital, the abattoir and the railway. Audrey remembered the tragedy from years ago, when she'd first read it. Her father had been pleased. She remembered a conversation she'd had with Katy. Must have been when her father was dying, around the time of Sylvie's psychotic break. There were phone calls at all hours, there were long drives to and from the peninsula, there were false preludes to death. Sylvie's behaviour became ritualised in its weirdness. It was mostly too difficult to explain to people. Once Katy had asked *Do you ever get scared you'll end up like them?* Audrey said *No*, and Katy said *Sorry, sorry*, over and over again. *I should never have said that. You're tough, Spence; you've built up immunity. You're the synagogue, you're Gilgamesh.*

Still. Audrey had gone home to Nick. She said *What do you know about epigenetics*, and he might have laughed, but she was shaking. He sat up with her all night, reading about heredity as if they were studying for an exam.

Gervaise was in front of the slaughterhouses. They were being torn down, but they still stank of blood. Audrey closed the book and covered her eyes.

On Saturday night Audrey and Nick drove over to Malvern where Emy's parents lived, near the private hospital. The houses were monstrously large. Their lights were just coming on. Their iceberg roses trembled in the wind.

'Who lives like this?' Nick said as they stood in front of the cavernous driveway. Ben opened the door to them. His shoulders nearly filled the frame.

'Come in, I'll introduce you to Em's parents, everyone's out the back—'

The garden swarmed with people. They huddled under the big gas heaters. Audrey could see Emy, flushed and happy. She looked so alive that Audrey wanted to rush over and kiss her, but Emy was busy talking. Audrey watched the scene. The music hummed in her teeth. Her friend beamed. She thought of Emy saying *What's been happening with you.* She turned back to Nick and Ben.

'I might go and see if Emy's mum wants a hand,' she said.

It was quiet in the kitchen. Mrs Takemura gave her a colander full of snow peas and a knife. They worked side by side. Their conversation was gentle and meaningless. Audrey could see the party, the darkening sky, through the glass over the sink.

When the food was ready she sat between Adam and Nick at the long table.

'Feels like the last supper,' said Nick.

'Something's happened,' Audrey said to him in a low voice. 'Ben's moving back to Japan with her, or something.'

'You reckon?'

'I just have this feeling.'

Veiny leaves floated on the surface of the swimming pool. The air smelled of smoke and damp soil. Audrey looked at the faces around the table. Beside her, Adam was telling a story about an argument. His voice hurried to fill the air.

Audrey went to get her jumper from the car, and returned as Emy was standing up next to Ben's chair, tinkling fork to wineglass.

'The reason we're having this party is because I wanted to see you all before I go back to work next week,' she said, and gave a cough, 'but also because Ben and I got married yesterday.' She grabbed his hand and held it up as proof: one thick finger was bound in gold.

'Well, fuck me,' Adam said. He clapped a hand over his mouth.

'I'm still contracted in Chiba for another eight months, but Ben's staying here, so it'll be a bit tough, but we'll survive.' She glanced at Ben. 'Anyway, that's all, I didn't want to make a speech…' She sat down anticlimactically, and there was hooting and noise and applause.

'I thought they split up!' Adam said.

'Guess they got back together again.'

'They must've moved fast. Emy's only been back for ten days.' His gleeful eyes wandered to the head of the table. 'I'm going over to get the goss,' he said.

Nick shook his head. He looked sideways at Audrey. 'Wanna dance?' he asked.

She couldn't remember the last time they'd danced, but he took her hand and they crossed the shadowy lawn to the far corner where coloured bulbs were strung between trees. They swayed from side to side in the cold. Audrey watched the holiday lights quivering across Nick's face. He bent his head.

'Give me *something*,' he said. His breath made a warm puff of air in her ear. She looked up, smiled. She squeezed his fingers lightly.

'I'm sorry.'

'Just give a little,' he said. She put her head on his chest. They rocked back and forth.

In the morning they walked to work together down Gertrude Street. Audrey came with Nick as far as the ambulance bay. She said she'd buy his father a birthday card on her lunch break.

'What's on for you today?' he asked.

'I have to go out to Port Phillip again,' Audrey said.

'What, the jail?'

'Yeah.'

'Same client?'

'No, different. It's weird, I'd never done a prison visit before this year and now I've done it twice. It's like that thing where you learn a new word one day, and then read it in a book or whatever the next day.'

'Baader-Meinhof,' Nick said.

'What?'

'The Baader-Meinhof phenomenon. The thing with the new words. That's what it's called.'

He was smiling shyly, the way he did when he knew he'd surprised her.

Audrey stared at him. 'Nick Lukovic, font of knowledge.'

He grabbed her wrists, pulled her close. He tasted of coffee.

It was an access visit, a five-year-old strapped into the back seat of the work car, Audrey making quiet talk with him.

'He looks tired,' Penny had said. 'He might drop off on the way there.' But every time Audrey glanced in the rear-view mirror he was staring out the window, absently stroking his hair.

He held her hand while they stood in the line for security, while she relinquished her handbag and mobile phone and the rice crackers she'd brought for him, while they shuffled into the open walkway with the other strangers, all there to see different people. There were no concessions for children. They were herded through the series of barren chambers in the same frightening, humiliating way as the adults. The air whistled through the cyclone-wire walls. The other visitors peeled off into rooms.

In the family visiting room everything was bolted to the floor. There was a plastic slide for toddlers. There was a low circular table set on a supporting pole. The chairs were fixed to the ground. They could not be moved closer. Audrey saw that small bodies could never sit at a comfortable distance from their drawing, or whatever modest distraction was laid before them.

She felt exposed without her phone or handbag. The room was cold. She bent to zip the child's parka to his chin.

At last the father appeared, flanked by an officer. 'Joey. Mate,' he croaked. He reached for the boy. He was shaking. The child threw his arms around his father's neck. It was only the two of them in the whole world.

Audrey glanced up at the correctional officer, watching by the door. His face was blank, but she thought she detected a masculine sympathy, a current in the air.

· · ·

In the afternoon there was a team meeting. Audrey took the minutes. She was still wearing her coat. The cold from the visiting room was in her sleeves. When everyone filed out, Vanessa said, 'How was this morning?'

'All right.'

'Those access visits are shitty.'

'It's the most hopeless place. It could not be any more terrifying for a child. That poor kid today. I hope he forgets it,' Audrey said. 'I hope his memory destroys itself.'

Vanessa was sitting the wrong way on the chair, with her knees either side of the seat. 'Why don't you call it a day,' she said.

'I'm okay.'

'I didn't ask how you were.'

Vanessa looked down the table at her. Calm face. Audrey picked up the exercise book with the meeting minutes. She gathered her things at her desk. She sensed she'd made a critical error somewhere.

After dinner at Nick's parents' house Audrey went to help with the dishes, stopped short of the kitchen doorway. She heard Nick in there with his mother.

'There's just been a lot going on,' Nick said. 'Two infant deaths, one after the other. One of them was Audrey's. Her mum shoplifted four hundred dollars' worth of clothes last week. She's manic at the moment. Last night she phoned six times.' He drew breath. 'Bernie's pretty nuts. It's all been sort of unrelenting since Katy.'

'Isn't there anything else they can prescribe her mum?'

'She's on the same meds, she just doesn't take them. I don't know what to do.'

'Oh, darling.'

Audrey retreated down the corridor. She went back to the wall with its reassuring family photos. There was some destructive energy humming in her body. She thought of what Nick had said about expecting to be attacked by the man stepping out of a shadowy house. *I was ready.*

He wandered out from the kitchen.

'You all right?' he asked.

'Yeah, are you?'

They looked at the pictures together. Audrey pointed at the frame that held the two of them, three years ago, dressed as the Tenenbaums. Their posture now mimicked the picture.

'I don't think I should ever go blond,' she said, 'do you?'

He squeezed her hand. He didn't answer.

'Did you tell your mum I'm losing it?'

'I don't think you're losing it,' Nick said. 'I'm also not going to have a fight about it here in the hallway.'

'Okay. Let's find a corner.' They faced each other. 'I'm sorry,' Audrey said. 'I don't want to fight. I'm sorry.'

Driving home the roads were quiet. Nick wound down the window and pressed his face to the streaming lights as they crossed the Maribyrnong.

'It's seventy here,' he said finally, 'you can do seventy.'

'Oh—oh, shit.'

'It doesn't matter,' he said, 'I just didn't know if you realised.'

And then, five minutes later, as they turned on to Wurundjeri Way:

'Jesus, Audrey, why haven't you got the lights on?'

She pulled into the driveway of a factory, unlit for the night. She cut the engine and got out. They stood on opposite sides of the car.

'Could you drive?' she asked.

'What?'

'I'm sorry, I know we're halfway home, but I'm really fucked.'

'You didn't have anything to drink,' he said.

'I know that.' They stood looking at each other. She saw he understood.

'The temazepam?'

'I have to stop taking it. I hate the way it makes me feel.'

'I wonder if you could have a lower dose,' Nick said. They switched sides. Audrey pressed the keys into his hand.

'It's only ever meant to be a short-term thing, you know,' he said as they pulled into Charles Street. 'The Normison. It's a short–term drug.'

Nick went to the bathroom. Audrey listened to the messages Sylvie had left on her phone, four of them.

'My mum asked if you were okay,' Nick called down the hall. Audrey could hear the splash of his piss against the bowl. She heard him flush the toilet and wash his hands. She imagined him standing in front of the mirror. He was so tall that he had to bend down to see the very top of his head. 'I didn't know what to say. That's all.'

He appeared in the doorway, his lovely patient face. She sat on the end of the bed and watched him undress. Something about his chest, his stomach, made her want to cry. She knew how to make him shudder, but it had been a long time. Last night she'd told him *I feel completely unfuckable.* He had accepted that.

'I s'pose you don't want to come to Pat's tomorrow night?' he asked.

'I'm sorry. I can't.'

'I was just asking.' He went on folding his jumper. 'Don't feel bad about it.'

'I'm so scared,' she said. 'I just have this dreadful feeling some-thing's going to happen.'

'Like what?'

'I don't know. Something catastrophic.'

'It's already happened.'

'Something worse.'

'There's nothing worse,' Nick said. 'You're not going to sleepwalk off a cliff. What's the worst thing that could happen?'

'The other day I was driving back to work along Heidelberg Road after a visit, and there was a petrol tanker going in the opposite direction. And for a second after we'd passed each other I was sure it had drifted across into my lane and we'd collided head on, and I was dead. I was really certain. I know that's not how you're supposed to think,' Audrey said, 'but I can't stop it.'

'Get into bed.' She didn't move. Nick stepped towards her. He pulled her jumper over her head. *Skin a bunny.* 'You lie straight and I'll tuck you in.'

Nick made the bed with hospital corners. Audrey imagined that was how his mother had taught him. He tucked the sheets so tightly that Audrey was pinned. He sat on the edge of the bed to pull off his boots, and he lay beside her.

'If I'm getting like my mother, I don't want you to be stuck with me,' she said.

'Don't do that. Don't use that as an excuse.'

'It's not an excuse. If I'm losing it, it's not up to you. I don't want you to feel like you're stuck.'

'What do you want me to say? I'm on your side, Audrey.'

It doesn't matter, she thought; there are no sides, there's only up and down.

Audrey cut the camellia blooms from the garden and put them in empty jars around the house. She phoned her mother and listened for almost two hours, sitting cross-legged at the kitchen table. She felt her face grow slack and mild. Nick met her eyes from across the room, and he knew she'd tuned out. She left him funny notes. She went with him to trivia at the Dan O'Connell, made bright talk with his friends. Walking down Canning Street afterwards, he said *Thank you for coming* and *Was that okay?* and *You did good.* She wanted to weep at their emotional economy, but she kissed him instead. Dinner in their backyard, all their friends around the fire pit, faces aglow. Day-drunk in the Edinburgh Gardens, someone's birthday. Audrey stayed when she wanted to go. There was MD going around. It made things more bearable. She looked sideways at Nick as she rubbed the last grains on her gums, and he grinned as if some secret had passed between them. Her hair was tickling her face. *Maybe this is what Maman needs*, she said. *It's making me feel better.* Nick's eyes crinkled. *Pop a goog in her mouth next time you have dinner. Here, Sylv*—lithium's *not a party drug.* At home Audrey drew lipstick circles around her eyes. PBS was playing jumpy swing. She danced a Charleston for him and he smiled and said something about Marcel Marceau, but then he rubbed at the lipstick with his thumb and said *Can you take it off?* and his voice was sad.

He talked about when they were first together. *Remember that year at Golden Plains, remember when we went to Cradle Mountain.* He'd taught her how to drive in the new estates in the western suburbs, way out past his parents' place. The houses were still being planned and built. The lots were empty. The streets were new. They had names like Belvedere Crescent and Lexington Drive. At night they drove with the high beams on. They peeled the learner plates on and off the windscreen and drank cans of Sprite. The city shone from the highway: a milky cloud of light hung above it. *Remember those made-up suburbs? They'd be real addresses now.*

Audrey knew he was trying, just like she was, to reconstitute it all. Warm weather, knocking off work at three to see a film, grass stains on knees, the glow-in-the-dark galaxies on the ceiling of his childhood room. But none of it fit any more. When Audrey's phone vibrated on the kitchen table, and her mother's name was on the screen, Nick would wiggle his eyebrows and hum the Wicked Witch tune, and Audrey would laugh, but it was all different. He'd made the joke before. They were bloodless.

She came home from work and found Nick in the lounge room. At first she thought he'd decided to paint the walls. The furniture had been pushed into odd shapes, everything draped in bedsheets. When she got closer, and saw him kneeling with the quilt in his hands, she realised it was a fort.

'What are you doing?' she asked.

'Remember a while ago when you were telling me about you and Irène, how you had that tent?'

'The tepee.'

'Was it anything like this?' he asked. He held aside a corner of the quilt. Audrey crawled in, and Nick followed on his knees. He'd laid out some blankets on the floor. The coloured lights from the back fence were strung up inside.

'Oh,' Audrey let out.

Nick crouched beside her, trying a smile. She wanted to be graceful about it.

'Hang on, I forgot something.' He shuffled out again, and returned with two beers. They touched the necks of the bottles together. The glass tinked feebly. Nick sat back as though evaluating a great architectural marvel. The quilt ceiling sagged in the centre.

'How did I do?' Nick asked. 'Is it like the one you and your sister had?'

'This is bigger,' Audrey said. 'We never had beer.' She propped the bottle between her knees and began to kiss him very slowly, holding his face as though it might fall away from her. She stroked its shapes. She knew the planes of his cheeks, the hardness of bones under her fingers. They were in each other's arms, hanging from each other. They hadn't fucked in weeks. Her body was reluctant, but she wanted to do it for him. It was good to be the author of someone else's pleasure.

It seemed a long time before he came. Her face found the hollow between his neck and shoulder. She felt his breath in her hair; heard his lungs catch. They turned away from each other.

Dead Nature

Audrey was sitting on the porch when Ben came sweeping around the corner on his old Raleigh. She startled.

'Did I give you a fright?' Ben asked, leaning his bike against the fence. Audrey remembered him saying once that he was conscious of his size, of looking like a thug.

'No, no.'

Their cheeks touched: his warm with exertion, hers stinging with cold.

'What are you doing out here? It's freezing.'

'Nick made spaghetti before he went to work. The whole house smells like garlic. I'm trying to air it out,' she said. Ben laughed. It echoed in the dark street. 'Do you want a drink?'

'I'd love one.'

She left him sitting on the porch. The radio was still on inside. She'd been half-listening to it: Radio National, they were talking about resuscitation, about the visions people reported between death and revival. There was an American specialist talking to the pre-senter—*Actually beyond the threshold of death,* he said. Audrey switched it off.

Ben had a plastic bag between his feet. She handed him a glass.

'Chin–chin.'

'Cheers.'

Audrey tilted her head towards the shopping bag.

'What've you got in there?'

'A heap of books Emy said to return to you. She said she didn't manage to get through *Ragtime* before she had to go back again, but she liked it so much she bought her own copy so she could finish it.'

'She could have taken this one,' Audrey said, thumbing through the pages. 'How's it going without her?'

'It's all right, I guess. I don't know. We're sort of used to it. I'm going over there in November for two months. That's not too far away.'

'It'll come quickly.'

Ben fingered the stem of his wineglass.

'Do you know what my dad said after we'd all been to the registry? He said, *I hope you two have done the right thing.* And I'm pretty sure he was joking, but shit...' He threw back the remainder of his wine. 'I'd better get going. Em said she'd call at nine,' he said.

'Thanks for bringing the books over.'

'No worries.' They stood, embraced. The security light blinked on with the motion.

Ben wheeled his bike out of the gate, swung a leg over and looked back at the house. His face was like a skull in the weird light. 'Hey,' he said. 'Don't be out here too long, eh? It's bloody cold.'

She nodded and smiled. 'Love to Emy for me.'

She watched him pedal away, then went back inside. The leftover spaghetti was cold on the stove. She sat down to call her brother.

'Hello, Aud-rey,' he drawled.

'How did the SACs go?'

'Psychology was all right. No, actually, it was good. I answered all the questions. Hazel and Winnie came over on Tuesday and we had a study night. I was prepared.'

'Good on you!'

'Accounting wasn't so good,' he said. 'I walked out halfway through. I don't even know why I chose accounting. I'm never going to get how to do that checks and balances shit. I mean, I live on a hand-to-mouth basis. I've got about twenty bucks in the bank.'

'If you stopped blowing it all on pills—'

'Fuck off, Audrey, you're worse than Maman.'

'I'm not trying to moralise.'

'No, I'm sorry,' Bernie sighed. 'I didn't mean it. Anyway, I've stopped all that. Hazel's pretty into school, because she wants to do physio or speech therapy or something next year, so it's no more disco biscuits for me, either. I just hate exams. They're so intense. Hey, did you cop Maman's story about her fight with the mechanic? I'll do it for you.'

He made her laugh, turning on Sylvie's shrill voice; the way she pronounced *exploit* as *ex-plwat*. She was bereft when he hung up. She lay on the couch and watched the late news. She dozed, woke to hear the woman on the television say *Total ground frost*. She half-expected Adam to call, but he didn't.

Nick arrived home before dawn and found her asleep on the couch.

'How was work?'

'Pretty slow,' said Nick. 'How are you?'

'I had a dream I drove our car off the pier down near Maman's house. I didn't die.'

Nick looked upset. *You weren't in the car,* Audrey did not say.

She followed him into the kitchen, and leaned in the doorway while he wolfed down a piece of bread and peeled a banana. Still in his uniform, still wired from his shift, he looked very presentable.

'Was Adam round?' he asked, gesturing at the two glasses listing in the dishrack.

119

'No, Ben came over for a bit.'

'Ben?' He turned from the sink.

'Yeah, he was dropping off some books that I'd lent Emy.'

Nick's brow tightened. 'Do you reckon those two getting married was something to do with Katy?' he said.

'What?'

He took a bite of the banana. 'I mean—do you think they felt like they needed to do things faster, or something?'

'I don't know,' Audrey said. 'I don't know why they did it.'

Nick dropped the banana skin into the plastic container they used for compost. The light was leaving him.

The morning of the union strike, Audrey had a cup of tea with Nick and Tim in the St Vincent's Hospital cafeteria.

'We might need to re-do the windows,' Tim said.

'Get Spence to do it. She's got nice writing.'

The three of them stood by the ambulance on Gertrude Street. Audrey passed Nick her paper cup.

'What am I putting? I'm too short to reach.' They laughed.

We apologise for the delays you are experiencing under a Liberal government,' said Tim. Audrey reached up to scrawl across the window.

'And then here'—they moved to the back of the van—'*What's the difference between a large pizza and a paramedic's wage? A large pizza can feed a family of four.*' Audrey's breath hung in a cloud. She rubbed at a wonky letter. The chalk marker left a blue stain. 'You coming today?' Tim asked her.

'Depends on work. But I'm in the Lonsdale Street office today, so maybe.' She looked back at Nick. He was staring at the blue letters on the window. She couldn't tell if he wasn't listening or just pretending not to hear. His face was like a vacant house.

She moved to the front of the ambulance.

'What about the windscreen?' she asked.

'Nah. Not allowed.' Tim stood back to review her work. 'I reckon your job's about done, mate.'

She walked up to Trades Hall at lunchtime and stood across the road by the pub. There was a woman with a megaphone, a sea of red T-shirts and vests and flags. She glimpsed Nick's face between Tim and an older woman. They were standing on the steps in front of a television crew. Audrey watched the crew arranging their cameras and microphones. Nick and Tim were dicking around, pulling faces, tugging at their collars, but on the cameraman's signal she saw Nick's mouth begin to move. He spoke deliberately. She was thirty metres away, she couldn't hear what he was saying, but his face was full of purpose and intelligence. The cameraman shook his hand, they grinned at each other, Nick's lips said *Thanks, mate.* Audrey scanned the painted banners. IN SA I'D GET AN EXTRA 32K. IN VIC I'D NEED TO GET INTO PARLIAMENT. She looked back at the steps where Nick had been, but he was gone. She could have called him. He'd say *I'll come over to meet you,* and he'd be flushed with cold and resolve, kiss her, make a joke about being on television. Audrey remembered him tucking her in, saying *I'm on your side.* She thought about him on the Trades Hall steps. She realised they were in different climates. He could be a new person out here, away from the sad air in their kitchen. She turned from the building.

Adam phoned at the end of the day, before she'd left work.

'The gallery's open late tonight. Do you want to come?'

She got there first, and phoned Nick while she waited outside.

'I heard you're famous,' she said.

'I'm basically the Paul Keating of the union,' he said.

She laughed. 'Are you at the pub?'

'I came down for a few beers, but I reckon I'll head off soon. You home?'

'I'm actually at the NGV. I said I'd meet Adam here. We might get tea after. Do you want to come down?'

'Oh-h-h-h—no, it's okay. You two should just hang out.' Something had shifted in his voice. 'I'm actually knackered.'

'I'm not surprised. You only had about two hours' sleep last night.'

They had nothing else to say. Audrey sat down by the fountain. The air smelled of chlorine and car fumes.

Adam was almost in front of her before she noticed him. He hugged her very tightly, as though he were relieved to see her. His mouth was close to her ear, in her hair. She thought he was going to tell her something, but at last he pulled away. He winced. They linked arms walking towards the entrance.

Inside they drifted apart. Audrey was glad, standing in front of a wall of Louise Bourgeois drawings. She didn't want Adam beside her while she flinched at the red bellies and hands.

At the end she came to a great dark room. There was a ladder suspended from the ceiling, made of fibre-optic cables that changed colour. As she got closer, it seemed to stretch impossibly into the sky, and down into the ground. It was dizzying.

Adam was lying on the floor on his stomach like a child. Audrey lay down next to him. The dark, his warm body, the lit ladder reaching into the ceiling, its illusion of bright endlessness. Audrey thought she might cry.

'It's a mirror,' Adam whispered. 'See? There's one at either end.'

Audrey stared at the ladder, watched the colours change until the room around it melted away.

At last Adam stood, and she did too, obediently. It was like swimming up from underwater.

Out by the gift shop it was light again, and they both blinked.

'Do you want to get a coffee?' Adam asked.

'I think I want wine. Sit down, I'll get it.'

122

They sat for an hour in the gallery café, watching the people coming and going.

'So then Sean says *You need to think about the best interests of the child. He'll be less displaced if he stays with Dad.*' She affected a neanderthal voice, tucked in her chin, scratched her groin. 'And I said *I think it's in the child's best interests that he* not *remain in a houseful of smackies, and Dad's got two DV charges, you fuckhead.*'

'No you didn't,' Adam said.

'I didn't call him a fuckhead. But he is.' She watched Adam scoop the last of the froth from his cup. 'He's all non-interventionist when it's some bloke with a string of assault charges, but he's pretty trigger-happy when it's an ID mum or a Koori family.'

'Fark.' He glanced around. 'Hey, do you reckon we're the youngest people in here by about twenty years?'

'I'd say forty.'

Adam scooted his chair around so that he sat beside Audrey. He reached for her, and she settled into his arms. 'Do you know,' she said, 'we say *still life* but the French say *nature morte*?'

'Dead nature.'

When Audrey raised her head, Adam's face was crumpled.

'I feel like everything I say upsets you,' she said, 'and I'm sorry.'

'I'm not upset.' He touched her cheek, checked his watch. 'Come on. They shut soon.'

On the way out he bought her a postcard of a Louise Bourgeois painting. It was the red watercolour hands, reaching.

Walking home from the tram stop she passed the pub. They were packing up the outdoor furniture. There was music streaming from inside. The guy stacking the chairs said *Hey* to Audrey as she passed, and she said *'Night.*

At home she took the postcard from its white paper bag and tacked it to the fridge. She knew Nick would ask about it the next day. She switched off the lights.

Afternoon in court. Audrey arrived early and went to get a coffee. She walked to the Flagstaff Gardens. It was cold and hazy. She saw Katy standing by a park bench. She was smoking a cigarette, politely tapping the ash into a rubbish bin, wearing her navy work cardigan. There was sunlight in her hair.

Audrey stopped herself from calling out just in time. She had thought all that was finished, or at least faded.

She walked home afterwards in the thin sun. On the nature strip outside their house there was a dead possum, its blue guts blown open across the grass. Nick was sitting at the kitchen table eating a sandwich, flicking idly through one of her novels. She smiled when she saw him, and he held out the sandwich.

'Tomato,' he said, 'worthless white bread. Salt and pepper.' She shook her head and sat down beside him. 'You're home early.'

'I was at the Children's Court. Wasn't worth going back out to the office. How was your day?'

'I went for a big bike ride. Right round Merri Creek, down the CityLink trail and Footscray Road.'

'Must have taken you ages.'

'Five hours,' he said, and she raised her eyebrows.

'Impressive.' She took off her lanyard and set it on the table.

'How was court?'

'I don't know if I can do this job.' She looked down at her ID tag: her own face smiled back at her. 'It's really bad right now. There are too many people who weren't supposed to have children.'

'I don't think that's how it works.'

'What do you mean? Of course it is.'

'People don't think about whether or not you're *meant* to have kids.' Nick went to the sink and rinsed his plate. He spoke to her over his shoulder. 'They just do it. And your job is full of people who need help to do it better. Not everyone's like that. Nobody's "not supposed" to have kids.'

'There's this dream I have,' Audrey said. 'I'm walking down a street and I can see a baby, a toddler, coming towards me. No mother, but I figure she's coming, and I'm smiling at this baby. And then a few seconds later, the mother runs towards me and says *Have you seen my baby?* and she's panicking. I turn to point her the right way and this truck zooms past, and it's got a stroller hanging from its grille. And I just—I know what's happened, but I don't want to look down the street to see.'

'Spence. It doesn't mean anything.'

'Of course it does.'

Audrey went to the bedroom. She felt miserable and mean.

Nick leaned in the doorway. His hands were hidden in his pockets.

'I don't understand why you're doing this,' he said.

'Doing what?'

'It's as though you're saying *We're ending, something bad's going to happen, we're unhappy,* and we're not—but you go on saying it, so it becomes true. Fuck, Audrey.' He kicked the mattress in frustration.

'Fuck what?'

She sat down hard on the bed. Nick crumpled next to her. He watched the floorboards. 'I remember when we first started going out,' he said. 'When we started sleeping together I could see you processing. I felt so proud that I'd worked it out for myself. I always felt like I was doing the right thing by dropping back all the time, leaving you alone a bit.'

'You were,' Audrey said. Her eyes were leaking. 'You were the first person to get it.'

'But I think maybe it made me complacent, or something.'

'We have not been happy for a long time,' she said.

'Do you want me to argue with you?' he asked. 'All right, then.

All right. It's okay, Audrey.'

The screen door slammed behind him. She heard the car pull away. There was a sound coming from her that she didn't recognise, a groaning she hadn't known she could make.

She thought to call Adam. He'd come to pick her up. She crawled to her side of the bed, where she'd dropped her handbag. But when she found her phone, her fingers dialled her mother's number. Sylvie said *Here's what you're going to do. I'm going to tell you.* Her voice was calm and low. *And you're going to leave a note for Nick. He'll be worried if he gets back and you're gone.* Audrey was weeping.

Spring was coming, and everything was strange. Between Adam's flat and the office, Audrey worked to find her forward motion. She felt turned around, coming from the other side of the river. She could hardly remember what things had been like in the summertime. All open windows and love, enough of it to go around. Audrey thought she remembered blinding happiness, ciders in the Darling Gardens, gentle fucking in the hot night, but maybe she'd built a myth of it. She couldn't be sure.

She walked home from the station in the rain. The sky looked like something out of a painting, billowing pink clouds. She couldn't stop crying.

She slept beside Adam every night. They watched old films. In the dark they talked a lot about being younger. Audrey had expected him to fuss over everything, but he was surprisingly calm. When she sat at the bottom of the stairwell one evening and watched the sky flood blood orange, he crouched on his haunches beside her. He said nothing for a long time. They drove all the way out to Arthurs Seat, where the bitter wind felt like Vicks on their skin, and visited Sylvie on the way home. They caught the tram to the South Melbourne Market for fresh bread and cheese and fruit, and ate their feast sitting on the balcony, rugged up against the cold. Adam practised his freestyle rapping and made up songs about the *mad bitch* who lived in the apartment across from his.

Audrey went along with him to Minh's gigs. Bar Open, the Curtin, Cherry. They played sleazy cowboy rock. Wednesday nights they had a residency at the Espy. Audrey liked the view from the wide windows in the front bar, right round to the Newport power station; she liked the sober light in the bathrooms. She liked to see Adam's face. In the crowded rooms, at the foot of the stages, he was so full of helpless love. Minh might have been playing only for him. Audrey understood it when she saw him. Hair falling over his face, the clean angles of his cheeks, his shirt rolled at the cuffs. He played bass, standing at the side of the stage. He sang backing vocals but he never spoke. Audrey wished he'd seek out Adam and give him something, just eyes or a smile, just once. He never did. Adam was in thrall watching him. Afterwards they'd clink their gin glasses and step outside for a cigarette. They always went back to Minh's place. The three of them would stand on the pavement outside whichever pub or bar it was, Adam or Minh saying *Are you sure you're right to get back*, Audrey laughing and saying *Yes, yes*, and it only ended with somebody getting in a taxi. It felt wrong sleeping alone in Adam's bed, so she'd drag his quilt to the couch and lie with the television on until she fell asleep. In the morning her neck was stiff. The coffee plunger made too much for one person. She was afraid that she couldn't be alone.

She went to dinner at her mother's house. Sylvie made chicken. She played an old Pete Seeger record that had belonged to Neil. She talked about Irène while she stirred and chopped and smoked. Audrey listened. She opened the door of the budgerigar's cage wide enough to fit her hand in, and let the bird peck at her finger.

The two of them ate at the square kitchen table. When the record finished it was too quiet but Audrey couldn't stand to hear that music

127

again, those songs her father had sung, so she washed the dishes and covered the leftovers with plastic wrap. Sylvie served vanilla ice-cream and tinned peaches like she had for every dessert of Audrey's childhood. She said *Can you just eat a little, can you just try. You're skinny like a nail*, and somewhere between the butchered idiom and the sweetness in the bowl, Audrey started to cry. Sylvie took the spoon out of her hand where it was dripping sticky stuff onto the table. She put her arms around Audrey and kissed her cheek, her hair.

'*Mon pauvre lapin*. I never wanted you to be like this.'

Audrey was slack-mouthed with grief.

In the bathroom Sylvie ran the water. Audrey sat on the tiles and let her mother tie her hair into a knot. *Skin a bunny*, said Sylvie. She tugged Audrey's shirt over her head, just like Nick had done.

'Do you remember I used to do this when you were little?' Sylvie said. 'It's what my maman told me. What you do for children. They like to be in the water when nothing else works. You make a bath.' Audrey didn't want to shake her head, didn't want to tell Sylvie she remembered no comfort. She didn't want to make her sad.

Sylvie sat her in the bath. She began to soap her back and shoulders with a washcloth. The water smelled of lavender. Sylvie was saying *Ma pauvre petite, mon pauvre petit lapin* over and over again.

Fever Dream

Adam was dragging her out to the Green, Meredith's birthday drinks, where their friends would be. All day at work she had the cold sweats thinking about it. Adam phoned late in the afternoon, said he was having beers with Hannah or someone, he'd meet her there. Audrey raked her hair into a plait.

She got to the pub first, couldn't stand to see anyone she knew. In the bathroom mirror she saw herself: damp skin, shaking fingers, bulging eyes. She locked herself in a toilet cubicle and opened a book on her knees. She tried to work the words into shapes, to make sense of the sentences. She sat in the cubicle until Adam messaged her to say he'd arrived. He met her by the bar, hugged her close.

'You look relieved,' he said. 'You all right, Spence?'

'I think I might go,' Audrey said.

'I just got here!'

She wondered that he couldn't hear the noise she was making.

'Come on,' Adam said, 'I'll get you a drink.'

Everyone was crowded into the back room, squeezed onto couches, cross-legged on the floor. The windows were fogged with their breath. Meredith said *You made it!* and jumped up; she kissed

Audrey's cheek and squeezed her until Audrey remembered to say *Happy birthday.* She looked to Adam. He was sweeping their seated friends in greeting. *How are* you *doing,* Meredith said, and Audrey said *Okay, actually.* She hoped her smile didn't look sick. Her whiskey was gone. Johnny's face, his halo of blond hair, his rough cheek by hers, *Sorry to hear about you and Nick, how are you holding up?* Audrey had nothing to say. How many more condolences? All the friendly faces, more tender than before, *Sorry, sorry,* kind smiles with no teeth showing, *We should get coffee next week,* and all the while she was gulping down air. She went back to the bar and finished her drink quickly. Back to the bathroom. Same cubicle. She re-read the graffiti. She checked her watch. It couldn't last forever.

Ben was outside the bathrooms. He eyed her. 'Do you want to come for a walk?'

She would have gone with anyone. They started down the street. Ben stopped at a cash machine.

'Are you all right?' he said, punching in his numbers. 'I'm only saying this as a mate. You're looking pretty pinned tonight.'

Audrey thought the noisy breathing had stopped, but as soon as she opened her mouth her lungs heaved again.

'Sorry. I'm sorry,' she said. She was crying and she was ashamed. They sat down on the stoop of an unlit shop.

'Breathe through your nose,' Ben said. 'Do the out part slowly.'

She kept trying. He put a hand on her forehead as if he were taking her temperature, pressed gently. He counted to ten over and over again. Audrey made the air go in and out until she was done.

'Tell me what you need,' Ben said. 'What can I do so you feel safe?'

'I think I want to go home. I want to—not be conscious.'

'It'll pass, you know. If you can ride it out.'

'I don't think I can wait that long,' she said. 'I don't want to be here.'

'Okay. Let's get a cab.'

'You go back to the pub,' Audrey said. 'Please. I don't want them to know I've left. I don't want to make a fuss. Can you just go back?'

Ben was steady. 'I'll turn around and come straight back here. I just want to make sure you're home safe.'

'I promise I'll be all right. Please. Can you just go back.'

They stood.

'I used to get them too. When I started chefing,' Ben said. 'It fucking sucks.'

'I'm sorry.'

'Stop saying sorry. Nothing to be sorry for.'

He waved down a taxi, waited until she was buckled. 'Can you message me when you're home?' he said through the door.

She nodded. 'Thanks, Ben. I'm really sorry. Thank you.'

The cab driver made polite conversation with her. When they pulled up outside Adam's apartment and she looked at the meter, she saw it was only ten-thirty. She fumbled in her purse. A tram clattered by.

'You can hear the trains from anywhere in this city,' the driver said. Audrey handed him the money.

Adam came home early the next morning. Audrey was still in bed: not asleep, but looking out the window at the white sky. Adam sat beside her, offered her a bite of toast. She sat up. 'How was your night?' she asked.

'Good.' He kicked off his shoes. 'It was okay. I ended up back at Hannah's. I just wanted Minh to invite me home. He's so cool about it all. I'm scared I'm coming on too strong. But I'm jealous of his flatmates and the guys in the band. I want him.'

Audrey rubbed her face. 'You've got to stop thinking in terms of *possession* like that.'

'That's so typical of you to say,' he said. 'You've never been the one who loved more.'

'Oh, come on.'

They sat there in the grey light: Adam with the plate in his hands, and Audrey hugging her knees to her chest beneath the blankets.

'How are you feeling, anyway?' Adam asked.

'Better than last night.'

He nodded. He went to the kitchen. Audrey heard him drop the plate in the sink. He returned, dove belly-first onto the bed beside her. The mattress bounced. 'You got crumbs in the sheets,' Audrey said.

'I didn't. I wasn't even fucking *eating* up here.' He propped himself up on one elbow. 'Everyone was worried about you last night.'

'It's my fault, not Nick's. I was the one who called it off.'

'You know what I mean.'

'I don't know what's happening to me. I've never been a crier in my life. And I just can't stop at the moment.'

They were quiet. Audrey looked at the dead maidenhair fern by the door.

'I'm so mad this is happening,' Adam said.

'Well, you can be mad.'

'What does Nick always say to you when he knows he's right? *Remember the pneumonia?*'

'Don't, Adam.'

'No, I just mean—it's not going to be like this forever. I *know* that.' He lay beside her, his hands tucked under his head. 'Give me some blanket,' he said. He tugged at the quilt. 'I'm cold.'

Audrey made herself useful on the floor in Irène's house, surrounded by drop-sheets. The room was at the back of the house. Its window looked over the neat garden: daffodils, Zoe's scooter against the chook pen, jacaranda tree. It was good to do small, productive tasks; to concentrate on inches at a time. Audrey puttied holes in the walls, smoothed them over. She wore an old shirt of David's. Irène had a roller brush and a tray of paint. They worked in comradely silence. The little blow heaters sighed on and off.

'Have you spoken to Nick?' Irène asked.

Audrey was on her hands and knees rubbing at the skirting board. 'We spoke on the phone a few days after I went to Adam's. It was hard to talk.'

'When I broke up with Marty we went out for coffee. We tried to be civil about it,' Irène said, 'and we both just ended up bawling in the middle of the café. That really snotty, ugly crying.'

'Marty,' Audrey said. 'That seems like a different lifetime.'

'I was twenty-one.'

'And you had Zoe two years after that.'

'It seems nuts, doesn't it?' Irène toed the drop sheet. She set down the roller and picked up a smaller brush. 'So how's Nick taking it?'

'I guess he's okay.'

'Better than you?'

'I don't know.' The sandpaper made a rhythmic, chafing sound. 'I sort of don't know what to do with myself. It's like I've forgotten how to do normal things.'

'Like what?'

'I don't know. Like Nick. I don't know what I'm doing at Adam's. I don't think I can go back to my job right now. Everything sort of feels contaminated.' She sat back on her heels. Irène had stopped painting. She was looking at her from across the room. 'I'm going in circles,' Audrey said. 'This whole city.'

'Maybe you need a bit of emotional quarantine. You don't have to stay here. You can leave.'

'I can't. You know that.'

'Bernie's almost there. Maman isn't going to get any better or worse.'

'That's so easy for you to say.'

133

'No, don't *do* that. You're being…ascetic about it.'

Audrey stared at her. 'That is exactly something Dad would say.'

'We're talking about adults. Maman's gas isn't going to get cut off the second she forgets to pay the first bill. Bernie can feed himself. You're spent. Maman's worried about you.'

'I don't want anyone to be worried.'

'How could we not?' Irène said. 'You're ridiculous. We could stick you in the middle of the Pacific and you'd start swimming. I remember when you had the cheekbone fracture. That whole side of your face was a mess, and you were trying to make Dad feel better. That's why it's scary.'

'That's not resilience,' Audrey said. 'He hit me so hard I needed plates to hold my eye socket together. Making him feel better wasn't resilience. That's how abuse works.'

'I know. I was there.'

'I'm sorry.'

'But that's years ago,' Irène said. 'It's finished. It can't happen again.'

Audrey smelled something chemical. She realised she'd knocked over the jar of turps. 'I can't talk to you about this any more. You look—*maternal*. That was another life.'

Irène had the paintbrush between her teeth. She pulled her hair into a knot.

'You just need to keep going,' she said at last.

'I know that.'

'Do you want a sandwich?' Irène asked.

'I'm okay.'

'Come on,' she said. 'Let's take a break.'

After lunch they climbed into bed without talking about it. Irène held out her arm for Audrey.

'You're so little,' she said. 'I always forget. Spider sister.'

'It feels so indulgent, being in bed in the afternoon,' Audrey said.

'I've been doing this every day. It's my routine at the moment.'

Audrey remembered exactly how it felt to be held by Irène. Four years between them. How many nights crawling into each other's beds, how many times falling asleep on Irène's lap in the back seat of the car.

'Remember when we'd go camping and Dad used to squish the mattress in the back of the van? And it never fit, and we'd always be rolling into the centre towards each other?'

Irène was still. 'I don't remember that much,' she said. 'Not like you. I don't really have any memory of anything before I was about seven or eight. I used to worry about it, but I guess it's okay now.' She shifted. 'My adult memory's great. I know my Medicare number by heart.'

'I don't know how true any of it is,' Audrey said. 'Sometimes it's hard to trust yourself.'

But she was sure of what she knew, of the residue of their childhood. The long grass by the drainage canals where she and Irène had thrown stones and bottle-tops. The smell of chemicals from the photo-processing shop near the Menzies Avenue flat. It went out of business like the video shops and milk bars. The snooker complex where she and her sister had waited for what felt like hours, crouched against the wall with cans of soft drink sweating into their palms. In her mind it was at the intersection of a highway, set back against a field. For years she'd wondered where it was or if she'd invented it altogether—though she *knew* the look of tired, smooth faces beneath the pool-hall lights, because when she sometimes saw her friends playing clumsy billiards in pubs, the familiarity rushed at her like a king tide; and she *knew* how women's hair looked under that light—and then one day she'd found it by accident out near Dandenong, by the bread factory and the railway.

'You know what I remember?' Irène said suddenly. Audrey had thought she was asleep. 'Maman and Dad had a tube of KY in the bedside drawer. I used to check if they'd used it, to see if they were still fucking.'

Audrey laughed. 'They fucked *heaps*! I walked in on them so many times.'

'I know. I heard them. But I used to check when they fought—I didn't get that you could fight like that and still want to fuck afterwards.'

They went quiet again. Audrey felt Irène's breathing slow. She wriggled to the edge of the bed. 'Do you want me to shut the blinds?' she whispered.

'No, leave them. The light's pretty this time of day,' Irène said. 'Oh, but can you set my phone alarm so I wake up in time to pick Zoe up?'

'I'll get her.'

Irène reached for Audrey's fingers and kissed them. Audrey watched her sister fall asleep. It happened quickly. Her face turned younger.

Audrey walked to the primary school and waited on the bitumen outside the portable classroom. There was a series of painted lines on the asphalt, a four-square box, a hopscotch square. Audrey remembered having to line up for assemblies on cold mornings, turning to face the flagpole to sing the national anthem. The windows of the portable were up high, above eye-level. There was coloured card tacked to the glass inside.

The children came out in a stream of thick legs and enormous backpacks. Audrey watched Zoe drop her sunhat once, twice; watched her scanning the line of parents for her mother. Audrey stepped closer, waved at her. Zoe came running.

'Audrey!' She turned her cheek for a kiss, threw her arms around Audrey's neck. 'Where's Mum?'

'She's at home. I thought I'd surprise you.'

'Is Nick coming?'

'Nope. Just me. Have you got your reader?'

'N-n-n…yes I do.'

They started across the oval towards the back gate. The grass around the cricket pitch was flattened and muddy, edged with clay.

'Who'd you play with today?'

'Veshalini and Jaclyn at playlunch. Why are you wearing that funny shirt?'

'I was helping your mum paint. I needed to wear something old.'

'Did you bring my scooter?'

'Nope. Sorry.'

'My legs get tireder when I walk,' Zoe said, 'than when I'm on a scooter.'

'I'll piggyback you if you get tired.'

'I'm already piggybacking my schoolbag.'

They pushed through the chainlink gate, stopped at the crossing. Zoe's hand found hers obediently.

At home they stood side by side in the doorway of the white room. Irène was kneeling beneath the window. The skirting board was painted along two walls.

'I said I'd do that,' Audrey said.

Irène held out her arms for Zoe. 'Be careful,' she said. 'It's all wet.'

'Why can't the baby sleep in my room with me?'

'He'll wake you up all night.'

'I won't mind,' said Zoe. 'I can look after him. He won't even know if you're the mum, or me.'

Irène glanced up at Audrey, standing in the doorway with the schoolbag slung across her shoulder. 'Do you want to stay for tea? David's getting pizza.'

'Thanks, but I'd better go. Adam—um, I think he said he's got something.'

Five years old, standing in the dark corridor at an hour she wasn't supposed to be up. She'd woken from a bad dream but her parents weren't in their bed. She was almost in the kitchen doorway before she was awake enough to know it was a bad fight. She made her feet line up with the heavy shadow. She was scared to look into the kitchen. Her mother was saying *You make me sick, you're bad for me,* but she was speaking in French and her voice was muffled, like she was under a blanket, and Audrey knew her father wouldn't be able to make out the words. There was a yelp, heavy stumbling, wheezing. She knew if Irène were there, she'd tell her to keep her eyes shut. Then a thud, and the shattering of ceramic on tile. Sylvie must have hit the cupboard where they kept the plates and cups. Audrey wanted to look but she couldn't move. She was sure the whole cabinet must have fallen on top of her mother. She pictured her legs sticking out from underneath it like in *The Wizard of Oz.*

Her father's face was above her in the doorway. He was breathing like he'd been running. Audrey's limbs were stone. She felt a hotness on her calf and realised she was pissing. Her father looked at her feet, at the feeble pool on the lino. Audrey was sure he'd kill her right there. But he was looking at her face again, and then he was hitting his head against the doorframe. His eyes were squeezed shut. The banging was rhythmic, like the sound of the headboard on her parents' bed against the wall when they fucked, only slower. He kept going even after his eyebrow split open.

Audrey slipped past him. Sylvie was awake. She was sitting with her back against the fridge. There was a worm of blood from her ear to her collarbone. She had a bag of frozen peas pressed to her eye. She wouldn't let Audrey see. *Go back to bed. You'll cut your feet. C'est moi qui va nettoyer tout ce foutoir.* The tiles around her were covered in pieces of broken plates and cups.

In the morning she lay beside her sister. Irène said *Are you sure you didn't dream it? You don't smell like pee.* But there was blood on the doorframe, dried, with a few grey hairs sticking out of it. The kitchen tidy was filled with destroyed crockery. In the afternoon Sylvie took them to the Salvos to pick out new plates. She tied a scarf around her neck.

I was five years old, Audrey wanted to say to her sister, and *Why don't you remember.*

She took a week's leave, then went in to meet with her manager. When she stood between the cubicles saying fast hellos to the others, the familiarity washed over her. It felt safe, and she almost faltered. But she'd thought about what to say in Vanessa's office. She was calm and certain.

Vanessa reminded Audrey of every high-school teacher whose class she'd dropped—German, physics, biology, media—who'd wanted her to keep going. *But you're so good at it! But if you hadn't missed the outcome on thermodynamics, you'd have all As! But if you just had a bit more confidence!* And Audrey, sixteen, hair falling from its plait, eyes sliding to the door.

'I haven't felt competent for a very long time,' she said. Vanessa asked Audrey to think it over. She said *I'm so sorry you've been feeling like that* and *Are there things I could have done to support you more?* and Audrey said *No no no, it's nothing to do with you. Truly.* It was easier than she'd expected.

'When you interviewed me, when I was still finishing uni,' Audrey said by the door, 'you mentioned the turnover rate in child protection. You said something like *They get in and get out.*'

'I said that to everyone I interviewed. Anyway, it's true.' She was smiling.

'I really wanted to stick it out,' Audrey said. 'I thought I was going to.'

Vanessa was looking at her closely. 'You know what you could do,' she said, 'is apply for unpaid leave. Do something else, short-term.'

Audrey nodded with a hand on the doorknob. *Yes. That's a good idea. Thanks for being so good about this. Sorry. Sorry. Sorry.*

Outside the day had turned hazy. Walking near the hospital she saw a man with a boy on his shoulders. As they passed beneath a tree, the child reached up his hands to shake the leaves hanging overhead, fat with water. It rained on them only.

She saw Nick at a gig at the Workers Club. She turned her head and there he was. Perhaps he'd seen her first. His face, unsurprised, flashed at her under the lights. They looked at each other for a long time.

She turned to Adam. 'Nick's here. I'm just going to go over and say hullo.'

'Are you sure?'

'It's okay,' she said. She drifted away.

Nick raised a hand in greeting, in defence.

'Look who it is,' he said. He opened his arms to her. It was a heavy hug.

'How have you been?' she asked.

'Oh—all right.' Audrey looked back to the stage, where a girl was singing, her eyes closed, her hands suspended in the air as the music crashed and fell around her. It was a Jonathan Richman cover, but it sounded like a prayer. Audrey was seized with longing. It was the sound of her infancy, of driving home from the promontory on a Sunday night, lying on the back seat with Irène. The bush fell away from either side of the car in streaks of dark scrub through the windows. The high-beam headlights caught the reflective road signs and beamed them back in emerald flashes. Her sister would be asleep, heavy adenoidal breathing, but Audrey would watch the film reeling on in the front: her mother's wild hair, her father's unbuttoned shirt; casual hands stroking thighs across the centre console and warm rain on the windscreen. They'd be talking their bastard talk, lightning French and English. Her father singing along and her mother watching his profile with the kind of love that Audrey had no words for in either language.

Jonathan Richman would always sound like the end of the holiday. Now the chanting, over and over again— it was too much under the throbbing lights, too charged.

Audrey turned back to Nick. He was waiting.

'Let's get out of here,' she said.

'Yeah, it's a bit intense, isn't it?'

He finished his beer. Audrey looked for Adam, and sent him a signal. *It's okay.* He gave her a thumbs-up and turned back to his conversation. Nick and Audrey pushed out of the bandroom, past the bar, onto Gertrude Street. They walked slowly, Nick wheeling his bike, Audrey with her arms crossed against the cold. The magnolias were out. Audrey missed living here.

'How is it with Adam?' Nick asked.

'It's good.' They passed the second block of flats, and Audrey stopped. 'Look,' she said. 'Someone's having a party up there.' Nick looked up: on the very top floor, one window flashed coloured lights. They stood there a moment, looking at the little square blinking pink and green, and kept walking.

'It's a bit suffocating,' Audrey said, 'but he means well.'

'He would.'

'He makes me chamomile tea before bed. He runs me baths. He bought me a voucher for a meditation class. Mindfulness. You know.'

Nick glanced at her. 'Mindfulness,' he repeated. 'I really cocked up, didn't I? No wonder it all went to shit. I was doing it all wrong.' They stopped at the lights and faced each other. 'I was kidding,' he said, 'I was only joking, Spence.'

'I know. I know you were.'

The house was cold. Nick poured wine. The gentle hollows under his eyes were blue.

'Are you hungry?' he asked, and Audrey shook her head. He made toast anyway, and cut up some oranges. They ate sitting on the carpet.

'How's your mum?' Nick asked.

'Pretty loopy.' Audrey saw his patient face reflected in the television screen. 'Last week she turned up at Irène's place virtually naked except for her dressing-gown. They were having David's parents over for dinner.'

'That's fucked.'

'Yeah, but Irène doesn't help, either. She was threatening to take her to the Peninsula triage.'

'Let her. They won't admit her.'

'I know.' Audrey brushed her hands together. 'What about yours?'

'Everyone's good. Will's still in Amsterdam. Mum's worried he's not coming home. She keeps asking about you.'

'Remember me to her.'

Nick looked up, his mouth twisted into a strange smile.

'What?'

'Such an old-fashioned way of saying it,' Nick said. *Remember me to her.*

They were already forgetting each other.

Audrey threw the orange skin into the compost bin. She finished her wine standing by the kitchen sink. Nick staggered down the hallway to the bedroom. 'I'm rooted.' Audrey followed him, but stopped in the doorway. He sat on the bed, unlacing his boots, and he looked surprised when he saw her standing there at the threshold, still in her coat.

'What are you doing?'

'I didn't think—I don't want to—'

'Christ, Audrey, I don't want to, either. Just get into bed.' He turned around while she undressed. She stripped to her stockings, and pulled on an old jumper of Nick's. It fell to her thighs in slack folds. She felt ugly and small.

They faced each other on the mattress. Cold space between them: they were not enough to fill the bed.

'I read your book,' Nick said.

'Which book?'

'*L'Assommoir*, however you say it. The French one you've been re-reading. I went to the library and got it in English.' Audrey stared at him. 'Here,' he said, reaching for the paperback. Its pages were age-softened and discoloured; it smelled fusty and dank. She opened the book and unfolded all the turned-in corners before she said anything.

'How did you find it?'

'Fucken long.' He rubbed his eyes. 'I don't know if I'm just a dickhead, and I know your dad loved Zola, but I didn't get it. I didn't get what his big message was.'

'At the time it was all science and reason. They thought everything was hereditary back then. You know, if you're born into—'

'No, I get that, but what's the point of it? If you're fucked, you're fucked, that's it, and you can't do anything about it?'

'Maybe.'

'I don't think it's true,' he said. Audrey put her hands to her face. Her fingers smelled like oranges. 'Spence? I don't think it's true. That was a hundred and fifty years ago.'

Audrey didn't answer. They curled like babies and sleep swarmed in.

In the early morning they sat on the back step looking out at the fence. The sky was wide and chalky. The magpies sang. Audrey's bum was cold. She kept passing her hands through the steam purling from her tea.

'Remember that time we both got that lurg after Christmas, and we didn't leave the house for a week?'

'Yeah,' Audrey said. 'It was so hot, remember?'

Nick had come down with it first, a virus that made him sweat and shake and vomit. Audrey dampened washcloths under the bathroom tap and made ice cubes from orange juice and kept the blinds drawn until she was sick too, clammy and aching. Every morning they got up and changed the bedsheets, and collapsed again, swaddled in their sickness. They joked about painting an X on the door. One sweltering night just before New Year's they sat in front of the pedestal fan watching *Twin Peaks*, and Audrey fell in and out of fever dreams about red rooms and mountain roads.

'You working today?' she asked.

'Not till tonight. You?'

'No, I'm taking a couple of days off. I've got a lot of time in lieu.'

Nick nodded. He stretched out his legs so that his toes touched the weeds poking through the cracked pavers. 'Wanna go and get breakfast?'

'I'd better not. I've got to go round to Bern's and give him a driving lesson. His test's coming up.'

Nick tipped his tea down the gully trap. Audrey stood to leave. They were done.

Audrey tried to make a routine. She got up, ate breakfast with Adam, walked to Barkly Street for coffee, then came home and settled to a day's work. She was full of steel. She applied for positions with migrant aid centres, palliative care facilities, out-of-home care organisations. She was diligent. She wrote painstaking responses to dozens of selection criteria, made adjustments to her CV, hunched over drafts of cover letters. Sometimes when Adam came home he'd look over her handwritten list of jobs or proofread an application. *It looks like a lot*, he'd say. When Audrey talked about finding her own

144

place or overstaying her welcome, he brushed her off. *You can't leave. I'll be lonely without you.*

Vanessa was kind. She sent messages. *Trapeze called for a reference. Peter Mac called. Odyssey House called.* There were a few interviews. Audrey went along in too-formal clothes, feeling like a fraud.

Some afternoons she filled Adam's bathtub and lay there to read. *What you do for children, you make a bath.*

Adam's key in the lock. She half-expected Minh's voice, too, but it was all quiet.

'You home?' he called.

'In the bathroom.' The door swung open. She scrambled to cover herself.

'Relax. I don't want to bloody look at you.'

'Are you going to piss? I'll get out.'

'I'm not going to *piss*,' he said. He slid down the wall to sit beside the tub. 'What book?' he asked. Audrey held up the cover. 'Read me something.'

She read half a page, uncertainly. The story was about a Belgian man on a train. Wartime. Rolling hills and young love and danger everywhere. It was a skinny book, so Audrey was persevering with it.

'Westmead called today,' she said. She set the book on the tiles.

'The hospital in Sydney?'

She nodded.

'I didn't know you'd applied there.'

'They had a position in the paediatric oncology ward.'

'Kids with cancer,' Adam said, 'that'd be heaps more uplifting than your old work.'

'Well, they offered me the job.'

'Good on you! That'll make you more confident with the others.'

'I think I want to take it,' Audrey said.

Adam picked up the book and thumbed through it. 'Is that a bit rash?' he said.

'I've thought about it.' He glanced at her. 'Irène said something a while ago. Bernie's almost done with school. Maman doesn't really need me like I think she does. There's nothing keeping me here. And I can't explain it, but there are so many places I can't stand here since Katy. And Nick. It's like I've wrecked them all.'

'You didn't wreck them,' Adam said.

The water had turned tepid. Audrey was cold. 'I can't live here with you forever,' she said.

'I didn't mean to sound negative,' Adam said. 'I just want you to do it for the right reasons, not because everything's gone to shit.'

'I'm not. I want a change.'

'Okay. Then it's great.' He stood up and passed her a towel. 'I've got a couple of friends in Sydney. I could see if they know anyone who needs a flatmate.'

'Thanks, Adam.'

He was leaning against the sink, back to the mirror. He gave a small smile. He said *I love you*.

Yusra phoned to see if Audrey was coming to Tilly's birthday, made it sound casual. 'I told her you had a bit going on.'

'Thanks,' Audrey said.

'And actually, I'm pretty stuffed this week. I don't know if I'm up to it, either. Do you feel like coming round here?'

Yusra cooked fish. Audrey sat on the bench and watched her. When she sliced the onions, her eyes wept so much she was blinded. She said *Oh—it's a really bad one* and put down the knife. Audrey offered to take over, and then they were both bent double, pressing palms to their eyes, laughing. Yusra's mascara had run down to her chin.

'We look miserable,' Audrey said.

'You know what I need,' Yusra said. She disappeared into her bedroom, and emerged a moment later wearing swimming goggles.

She struck a pin-up pose in the doorway.

Adam came by late, alone, halfway to drunk. He'd walked from the train station, and Audrey felt the stinging cold on his cheek when she kissed it.

'I've got some K,' he announced.

The three of them climbed into Yusra's bed and sat shoulder to shoulder against the wall, wrapped in blankets.

'I don't think I want any,' Audrey said.

'Go on,' Yusra said. 'It'll just make everything go sideways for a bit.'

It didn't make things go sideways; it only made her sleepy. She dozed between their warm bodies. She heard Adam say *I thought the music had been going the whole time.* She heard Yusra say *Don't do any more yet.* Before she fell asleep properly, hot in the heart, she heard Yusra say *I don't want you to go.* It was so much like things had been with Katy, the three of them curled beneath a doona, that she had to think very carefully about where she was.

Audrey borrowed Adam's car and drove over to Charles Street.

'You could have just let yourself in,' Nick said.

'I thought you were working today.'

'Not till tonight.' He stepped aside. The house still smelled like their house. Dust motes floated in the hall.

She turned to face him. 'I'm just coming back to get some things,' she said. 'I got a job in Sydney.'

'Sydney. Congratulations.'

He stood with his hands in his pockets.

'So it's okay if I—I'll just be in the bedroom—?'

'Yeah, knock yourself out.'

She worked efficiently, packing her clothes and shoes neatly into bags. Nick helped her cart boxes of books out to the car. Afterwards they stood on the pavement.

'Thank you. Thanks for helping me with my stuff.'

'That's okay.'

She wrapped her scarf around her neck. Nick's face lightened; he gave a strange laugh.

'You've sort of stopped looking like a person wearing a coat,' he said. 'You look like a coat with a person in it.'

'I'm sorry. Don't be sad.'

'You want me to be the bad guy.'

'That's not true.'

'I can't make you feel better,' Nick said. 'Do you understand that? So don't, don't apologise.'

Audrey nodded at the footpath, arms folded across her chest.

'I'll write. Let you know my address up there.'

'Yeah, let me know.' He stepped towards her and they hugged sharply, bone and bone. 'Take care, Spence. Look after yourself.'

'You too.' She touched his arm. 'See you.'

Badlands

In Sydney the light was strong. Audrey's shadow was more certain. In the days before her job began, she walked the streets as a tourist. She sent postcards home with pictures of the glittering harbour. In Glebe she found a book of Marjorie Barnard's short stories. It had been raining and the sky was greenish. Audrey paced back and forth in front of the bus stop and looked down the streets that sloped to the city. The glass of the tall buildings turned gold and winked, then the windows became hundreds of lit squares, and the weird mushroomy clouds pitched and rolled.

She sat on a crowded train on another rainy day. The girl opposite her was reading: her head bent forwards into the book, her serious brows drawn together. She had milky skin and thick arms. When she stood to get off the train, their legs brushed, smooth, shaved knees, and Audrey could have shuddered: longing rushed into her pelvis. She felt savage. She was surprised when anyone spoke to her.

She moved in with Adam's friend Claire for the first few weeks. Sweet, languid Claire, who welcomed her wholeheartedly, who boiled eggs and made cups of tea in the morning. She and Adam had met in a hostel in Byron Bay—*We were in a four-bed dorm, and the other two people started fucking one night, and we had to evacuate,* Adam had explained, though Claire told it differently. There were always friends calling by the house. Audrey was grateful for the noise. For three weeks she occupied the bright room at the end of the hallway. Claire's son, Elliott, six years old and clever, slept in the room opposite. Audrey heard him moving around in there at night, turning lights off and on, singing to himself and reading aloud, shuffling down the hall to his mother's bedroom.

The Redfern streets were sleepy in the mornings. The train to the hospital took half an hour. Just before Westmead there was a mason with a sign that said MONUMENTAL MEMORIALS and sometimes Audrey chanted the words to herself like a skipping rhyme while she walked. The big hospital was a terrifying, brutalist building. It seemed to take up the entire suburb. The Children's Hospital was at the end of the road, orange and terracotta coloured, opposite flats and motels. It was quiet in the mornings, but by the time Audrey left for the day, there were kids on the play equipment out front and people smoking by the entrance, waiting at the bus stop. Everyone wore crabbed, hesitant smiles.

The Camperdown ward staff seemed surprised when she said she'd come from child protection. They all said how young she looked. Audrey worked to remember names and answers to questions. She tried to summon up things from the only hospital placement she'd ever done, years ago. That first week was a deluge.

On Friday afternoon she walked to the station with one of the other workers. They passed the university, the grim strip of shops, the sign in the window of the Westmead Tavern that said LUCKY LOUNGE, making small talk.

'You must be buggered,' the woman said. 'Anytime you start a new job it's like that. Trying to suss out who's who in the zoo, take it all in as fast as you can, not muck up. You'll be right.'

Audrey felt a flash of gratitude for her. She couldn't think of her name when they said goodbye. They waved at each other from different platforms.

Claire went out with a friend and Audrey offered to look after Elliott.

'Let's go down to the sea,' he said. They buttoned their jackets and caught the bus to the beach, where they took off their shoes and waded in the cold water. Elliott collected shells and bits of glass in a leather purse that had once belonged to Claire. His face was set in a determined grimace against the wind. Eventually he relaxed and told stories and joked with her. Audrey was glad for the company.

After a while Elliott wandered further up the beach. Audrey sat on the sand and took out her book. When he came back he was grinning.

'Do you know,' he said, sitting down beside her, 'there's a man up there having a wank.' Something split inside Audrey and laughter came flying out.

'If I say *You're very suave*,' she said, 'do you know what that means?'

'Nup.'

'Sophisticated. Cool.'

'Charming?'

'Yeah, charming, too.'

Elliott inched his small bum closer to hers. 'I'm going to tell Claire she's suave.' He fiddled with the frayed strap on his purse. 'I always want to live with Claire,' he said. 'I'm going to live with her forever.' His long lashes flickered in earnest. Audrey smiled at his devotion.

It was late afternoon by the time they caught the bus home again. The wind was cold and dry. Elliott examined his bag full of sand

and shells. Audrey watched the grey sky through the window.

'Hey Audrey?'

'Yes?'

'Is your mum beautiful like Claire?'

'She's different to Claire.'

Elliott thought about it. 'Claire's the kind of beautiful that if she does a handstand and her legs go in the air and everyone sees her undies no one cares.'

'You're probably right.'

They made it home. Elliott sang all the way. He hurled his body around the footpath as he sang, giddy. He liked to test Audrey. *Do you know where that train's going? Do you know when Claire's coming home? Do you know*—as they crossed the park on Louis Street with its brick-wall mural of the Aboriginal flag—*what that painting means?*

Claire came back at teatime with a tall man whose head was bent into the collar of his jacket. His hair was covering his eyes and he looked surly, but he softened when he saw Elliott.

'Hello, mate.'

'*Hola*, Julian. Hi, Claire.'

'Hey, Rambo. What'd you do today?'

'Went to the beach.'

'The beach?' shrieked Claire. 'But it's fucken c-o-o-o-ld!' The three of them pushed into the warm kitchen, where Audrey was making soup. Claire introduced everyone with flapping hands and a smile that showed her teeth.

'Audrey, this is Julian. He's Elliott's dad. Julian, Audrey. She's up from Melbourne.' They waved. Claire leaned over the stovetop. 'That smells good.'

'How can you be hungry after lunch?' Julian asked.

'It always smells good when you don't have to cook it yourself.' Their conversation ricocheted sentence for sentence. Audrey felt a twinge of longing.

Julian hoisted himself onto the bench and poured a glass of wine.

'So how long are you in Sydney for?' he asked.

'I've taken a job here,' Audrey said. 'I'm just staying with Claire until I find a place.'

'You're kidding.' He faced Claire, incredulous. 'Thanks for telling me, you peanut. You know we've been looking for someone to take Sam's room.'

'I wasn't thinking.' She and Elliott were engaged in a complicated handshake. Julian watched them while he talked to Audrey: he would not meet her eye. She turned away and began to slice the bread, speaking to him over her shoulder, to make things even.

She went to see his place the next weekend. It was bigger than any house she'd lived in, set on a corner. In Coogee all the houses had names like Rosedale and Beach-Lynn and Rosaleen Flats. The streets slanted down to the sea.

Julian answered the door. He was barefoot, less churlish than he'd seemed the other day. He left Audrey in the kitchen while he went to get the others. *This is Pip, and this is Frank.* They made cheerful conversation, asked her what she did, handed her a cup of tea. 'Oh, you've been living with Claire! The best girl!'—to Julian—'She must be a good egg, if she's staying with Clairy.' Pip looked right into her face. Audrey smiled. She felt as if she were auditioning.

Julian walked her through the rooms.

'This'd be yours,' he said. 'It's a bit smaller than the others, but it's cheaper and there's good light.' He laughed at himself, a sudden, gunfire sound. Audrey started. 'Am I doing a good job? I feel like a car salesman.'

The room overlooked the backyard. It was paved in concrete, filled with wild green. Audrey could hear the hum and hiss of the powerline. A knobbly frangipani tree stood beneath it.

She followed him down the hall. He was talking about the block of land being worth heaps, how none of them knew how it was still being leased except that it was an old house, something about fibro–cement.

'What do you reckon?' he said at last.

'It's a great place. I love that room. But it's a long way to work,' she said.

'Where's that?'

'Westmead.'

'Yeah, it would be. Hang on, come in here a sec.'

They were in the front bedroom, his, with its window over the ocean. It was impossibly beautiful. The open water made her think of Nick in the surf down at Fairhaven. *I'm pretty rubbish at it. It just feels really good.*

'Do you like swimming? There's the baths just across there, if you're into that.'

The white August light poured in. 'Anyway,' Julian said, 'have a think.'

Audrey got hot walking back to the bus stop. She peeled off her jumper while she waited in the sun, and immediately felt the sweat chill her shoulders. She'd never lived with strangers. When she first moved out of home she was still in school. It was an emergency, it was her father with his fist and a glass-topped table and a cut that needed stitches. She stayed with Katy's family for a while in the house on the hill. Then she lived in Preston, in a bungalow at the back of a house owned by one of her teachers. She paid rent out of the money she earned working at a newsagency after school, but it was charity: fifty dollars handed over in a white envelope each week, and both parties felt as if they'd wronged the other. Mr MacPherson's wife taught cello, and Audrey used to listen to the gentle sawing from her window while she did her homework. Mr MacPherson drove her to school every day with his kids in the back seat. Sometimes she took them to the playground on Jessie Street in the afternoons. They accepted her presence happily and without pity, and they ran around until the air was cold and it was time to go home. Mr MacPherson's wife always asked if Audrey wanted to eat with them. Audrey always said no, politely.

She lived by herself in Flemington for a while when she started university. The landlady kept trying to sell her pills. The hot-water system broke in June and took three weeks to be repaired. The couple next door shrieked and swore. Audrey felt very far away from everyone. The year that Adam went travelling, Audrey and Katy moved in together. They tried cooking complicated meals and watched entire television series and slept in each other's beds most of the time. At that time Katy was still obsessed with changing her body. There was an athletics track near their apartment and early in the wintry mornings they walked around it, Katy in her expensive leggings and runners, Audrey mostly in her flannelette pyjama pants, their breath making clouds in front of them. They must have walked thousands of circles on the rubbery red turf.

And then she moved into Charles Street with Nick. They walked to the Abbotsford Convent; they walked around the river, and down along the tourist drives in Yarra Bend Park, sometimes as far as the Thomas Embling Hospital. Audrey loved the way the rows of houses and warehouses and breweries dropped away into green at the end of those streets. You could imagine you were in the country. Their little house, where everything had happened in the bedroom and the kitchen, and a car out front meant someone was home.

In the afternoon she lay on her single bed. Maybe it would be good to have other people around. She thought of the sea, the hilly streets, the grand houses. She wanted to make herself new.

Elliott was singing in a soft, high-pitched stream in the other room.

. . .

155

She moved into the house on Neptune Street. Julian came to pick her up and loaded her things into his station wagon. He kept saying *Is this it?* as though there ought to be more bags, more possessions. 'Do you need anything from Ikea? We're over this side of town.' Audrey said *Thank you* so many times he laughed at her. It was sunny, blustery. He drove with his music very loud and his windows down so that people turned at traffic lights. He spoke quickly, then not at all. He reversed into the driveway recklessly, stood at the front door, hollered for the others to come and help cart everything inside, even as Audrey said *It's okay, it's okay, I can do it.*

She sat cross-legged on the bed and assembled her clothes racks, one, two, and a bedside table. She worked quickly, instructions spread before her.

She could hear the others downstairs, but she didn't want to intrude. They seemed so at ease together. She laid her quilt across the bed and tried to stop the flow of adolescent insecurities. She was eight, an ugly child, always watching. She was twenty-five, and just as timid.

But they were kind people. There was always someone to talk to. The kitchen was never empty.

She went to the beach every night. Sometimes she walked all the way to the clifftops around Gordons Bay. She struggled over the soft sand. She wanted to make herself a new hard body.

Occasionally somebody accompanied her. Pip regaled her with stories, and Audrey could be attentive and passive beside her. Julian was good company: he and Audrey could chat or fall to pleasant silence. Frank was a gentle gossip. When he and Audrey ran out of things to talk about, they would sing in tuneless companionship, bodies bent forwards.

Mostly she walked by herself. At night the streets smelled sordid, all aviation fuel and overripe fruit and the ocean.

· · ·

She visited Claire at the flower shop in Balmain. She was working on an order for a wedding, masses of peonies and gardenias. She gave Audrey a handful of the white blooms, wrapped in wet tissue, for her room. She disappeared into the back of the shop, and returned in a clean shirt dress and pair of heels: Audrey went *Woo-woo* when she saw them. Claire lifted her apron over her head and said *Do you want to come with me to deliver these?* Audrey had nothing else to do, and the two of them drove across the harbour in the van full of flowers. *This is a rich-person suburb,* Claire said. She'd kicked off her shoes to drive. She was talking about Elliott, a house in Katoomba, coal power stations, her parents, the possum in her roof. Her conversation moved strangely; she latched on to things Audrey said in reply or in passing, and refracted them.

'When Julian and I split up, and I moved out with El, blokes kept coming on to me,' she said. 'It felt as though they hadn't in years, and then all of a sudden—it was as if they *knew*. Like I was releasing some sort of sadness chemical.'

Audrey tried to imagine how loneliness pheromones might smell, but the air in the van was sweet. The gardenias in her lap were electric white.

The guilt crept in at night when she stopped moving. She and Nick waiting at the laundromat, trying very hard not to laugh when a man forgot to put his washing in the machine before he started it—'Oh, shit, oh shit,' he'd muttered, staggering to and fro. Audrey had thought she would explode, biting back hysterical laughter. Nick did the impersonations for months afterwards when something went awry, hunching and fretting, *Oh shit, oh, oh shit.*

She hoped Nick wasn't lonely. He was still the person she wanted to call most. At night she took the blame cowering under the bedsheets.

She wrote letters home, to her mother, to her brother and sister, to Adam. Adam's letters and phone calls were cautious. He was infatuated with Minh, but quiet about it. *I'm all right*, Audrey wanted to say, because she knew he worried. *I'm happy you're happy.* He was being careful not to upset her, but the censorship of his new grand love was worse. Audrey missed his honesty.

She went to a film. She could have asked someone else to go with her—Claire would have said yes without hesitation, maybe brought Elliott if there was no one to mind him. Julian probably would have liked the film she'd chosen. But she straddled her bicycle and realised the purpose of seeing the movie was to pass time: she couldn't bear to do nothing. She rode to the theatre. When the film finished she didn't want to go home, but it was late and she had nowhere to go, so she pedalled back to the house where everyone was asleep. The night was airless, different to the damp Melbourne cold. She flicked on the blow heater and stripped down to her singlet and tights.

She called Nick. Her own voice answered.

'This is Audrey and Nick.'

'And you have really bad timing, because we're not here—' His voice, laughter. She remembered recording that message sitting on the floorboards by the bed. '…Or maybe we are here but we don't want to talk to you…'

'It's your turn to talk now,' she heard herself say. 'Leave a message.'

Lying in bed, she was sure she could turn to iron, to something harder. She practised being very still. MON–U–MEN–TAL–ME–MOR–I–ALS.

Nick wrote once, after Audrey sent him her new address. *Everything's the sameish here*, he said.

The other day I was called out to a cyclist who'd been hit by a tram and gave her 6x the right dose of fentanyl. I'd been on for 13 hrs, but there's no excuse. I realised after she'd been admitted. Everything was ok. I couldn't believe nothing happened. Dicko didn't even caution me.

He'd seen Bernie once, riding his bike down Johnston Street. Nick was wasted, too wasted to be driving, and when he'd stopped at the lights he'd seen Bern's pale face bobbing outside the car window. Nick's mother asked after Audrey. How was her new job? *Take care*, he said.

They knew how to write to each other. Audrey had always left little notes and drawings for him. It started because they sometimes slept in shifts, and continued out of habit.

Five degrees overnight, no wonder we were cold.

Dinner, pinned down by two pears and a thick sandwich.

Your dad called round today, seemed surprised you weren't here. We had coffee. Told him you finish at 6. He asked if you'd call him. Said it's not urgent. (I think he just wants to know what to buy your mum for mother's day.) Love love love, with a little drawing of a middle-aged man, stooping, as very tall people often do. It was a picture of his father. It was a picture of an older Nick.

Audrey's family wrote, her friends wrote, Katy's parents wrote. Nick sent just the one letter, a gentle turning away.

After work Audrey and Pip sat in the kitchen. Audrey was cutting a pear.

'Such a nonna way of doing it,' Pip said.

'What do you mean?'

'That's how my nonna cuts up fruit.'

Audrey looked at her hands. Fruit in her left palm, knife blade coming in towards her, pear flesh falling away in pretty cheeks. She had never thought there was another way to do it.

Julian arrived home talking about snow chains. He and Pip had weekend plans. Audrey rinsed her plate and knife. The other two argued about which car to take, whether they could knock off work early on the Friday afternoon. Audrey was only half-listening. Pip said *It's only half an hour on to Perisher anyway.* Her phone rang and she left the room. Julian looked to Audrey.

'Do you want to come? Jindabyne. Pip's parents live up there, but they're in Tassie this week. We usually go earlier in the season, but there's still snow.'

'I can't ski,' Audrey said.

'What, you never went as a kid?'

'I've never seen snow.'

Julian shrugged. 'You can learn. Come if you want.'

'Come!' Pip said from the doorway, phone cradled between her ear and shoulder.

There was kindness in the offer, and Audrey was love-hungry. She packed a bag.

They stopped in Cooma for petrol. Julian went to piss. Pip walked half a block with her pack of cigarettes. Audrey could smell it on her when she got back into the car, and she could only think of her mother then, and of Katy, and Adam, and home.

Audrey sat wedged beside Julian's pack and a slab of beer. The other two chattered on pleasantly in the front. She put her face to the window. Cows with steam puffing from their nostrils in the cold afternoon. Three jet trails in the darkening sky, like a snail's gluey track. There was no air in the grass, no wind in the trees. They sped on through the small towns, bakeries, Chinese restaurants, rest stops, motel rooms with a security light above every door. The paddocks began to look ashy. Ahead, twin red tail-lights winked and disappeared between bends. The first snow was dirty, clinging to the sides of the hills. Audrey fell asleep with her head on Julian's pack. When she woke she saw water through the windscreen, pinpricks of light around the lake.

Pip and Julian got up early to leave for Perisher. Audrey heard them in the kitchen, quiet voices, running water, the front door opening and shutting as they carted their gear from the house to the car. It was seven o'clock. Audrey pulled the sheet up over her face. The light was still grey. The bed smelled different: of other people's houses, of a room that wasn't often slept in. At home-home Nick was usually the first one awake. He was cheerful in the mornings. He'd make the tea, bring it back to bed. Sometimes he'd sing *Let's get up and brush our te-e-e-th!* Sometimes it was *Good morning girl.* Audrey missed that body. It was a grief she hadn't expected: she missed touching skin. Even when they hadn't fucked for weeks, and when she couldn't look at him in bed at night, Nick would still roll over and hold her. They sought each other out in their sleep.

Audrey went to the kitchen with the doona around her. She fiddled with the gas stove, couldn't find matches, poked around Pip's room gingerly looking for a lighter. She made coffee. In the portable CD player someone had left a Springsteen CD. She played it while she drank her coffee and read a month-old copy of the local paper. She stood by the window and watched two birds on the carport roof. She moved around the house and tried to imagine Pip growing up in its rooms. There were photos of her and her brother by the television, primary-school age, with missing teeth and straggly haircuts. By the door to the laundry there was a strip of wall with names and heights and years marked in pencil. In the toilet, a Leunig calendar; a framed cross-stitch by the bath; a laminated poster that read *DID YOU KNOW??? About 1,800 L of blood passes through the kidneys each day. No other organ gets as much blood as youre kidneys! MICHAEL ALESSIO 3C*, illustrated with a light-faded texta drawing involving complicated anatomy. Audrey thought of Katy. She would have laughed. *YOUR KIDNEYS!* she would have bellowed, trying for a nine-year-old boy's authority. It would have become a joke or a catchphrase, somehow.

Audrey drew a bath. The steam fogged the mirror over the sink. She left the bathroom door open so she could still hear the music. She held her breath to sink below the surface. She watched her knees turn pink with heat.

She walked to town. She sat with her book in an Italian restaurant and ate a bowl of salty mushroom linguine. It felt good and hot in her body. The only other customers in the restaurant were two men arguing about a car. Audrey thought they might have been brothers. There was a television mounted on the wall playing an old Harrison Ford film.

At the newsagency she bought three postcards: one for her mother, one for her sister, one for Adam. The sky was heavy and dull. There was an op-shop set up in the Uniting Church. Audrey poked around the used books. They were mostly pulp romance novels, but she found a biology book from the fifties. She opened it to the page on symbiosis. *Symbiosis occurs when two or more different organisms have a relationship in which they depend on each other. There are different kinds of symbiotic relationships, including mutualism, commensalism, amensalism, or parasitism.* There was a helpful illustration of a hermit crab and an anemone. She read about parasites.

'You right there, love?'

His smile was benign. Audrey dropped the book as if it were burning.

She walked down to the water. It all seemed very quiet. She sat on a rock and tried to think about the lake being artificial, but she couldn't imagine what had been there before.

She phoned Adam. He didn't answer. She watched an older woman struggle by with two schoolchildren, all of them bundled into ski jackets. The woman huffed a greeting. Audrey smiled at them. Her nose was running. When she walked back up to the road, all the cars had their headlights on.

Pip and Julian came back late in the day. They were tired and laughing.

'What did you get up to?' Pip asked.

'I read. Went for a big walk. It was nice.'

They went to the pub for dinner. Audrey borrowed an old parka that was hanging in the wardrobe. It was enormously thick, lined with tartan fleece.

'Nice eighties-soccer-mum aesthetic,' Julian snorted. 'I reckon you might pick up tonight.'

'I thought it was more, you know, early Dana Scully,' said Audrey.

She was glad to have them back.

The pub was at the edge of the lake. It was a bright country sky. The moon on the water reminded her of an ultrasound image.

'I'm already sore,' Julian groaned.

'Wait till tomorrow. Your body repairs itself overnight,' Pip said, 'you'll be fucked.'

'I won't be able to walk.'

The pub was crowded. Julian explained something to Audrey about it being a party town in the snow season. The music was loud. Audrey wished she'd bought the biology book.

They clinked their glasses, shed their coats.

'I can't have gin,' Pip said. 'It makes me depressed and spewy.'

Audrey was laughing. 'Whiskey makes me sin but I can't say how.'

'*Sin,*' Julian said. 'What a word!' Audrey wasn't sure what had made her say it. They started talking about funny things that had happened all day: the lift operator, the woman at the petrol station, Julian falling over. They were saying it in a way that involved Audrey.

By the bathroom, after dinner, someone offered Julian some speed. 'It might have been fun,' he said when he got back to the table. He and Pip tried to out-do each other with stories. Audrey had a flash of Katy's face, eyes swimming, joyful and dancing. It wasn't a story she could tell. It had no punchline. She stood to get another round.

Someone started talking to her while she waited at the bar. He was a slow speaker, nondescript. He wore a fleece sweater. Audrey was bored, but only in a dim way: she was drunk, he was going on about snowboarding, it was bearable. She looked back at their table. Pip and Julian were still talking. The guy in the fleece sweater wanted to buy her a drink. They sat at the end of the bar. He touched her back, down low. Audrey tried to remember what to do with her body. In the bath she'd touched her own skin, pretending it was someone else's hands. Now the hands were here they meant nothing. Audrey finished her drink. She smiled and made to thank him, to excuse herself, and he leaned in. His mouth was soft. She wanted to want it.

'I have to go,' Pip said over the music. She was leaning against Julian. 'I'm spent. This always happens when I'm tired and I drink.'

They were both grinning at her.

'You guys go on,' Audrey said. 'I can meet you at home.'

Pip raised her eyebrows.

Julian spoke close to her ear. 'Be safe.' Audrey felt him squeeze her arm through layers of clothing. He and Pip left, arms linked. Audrey watched them push through the doors.

'They friends of yours?' the guy asked.

'My housemates,' Audrey said. He nodded, as though the topic were exhausted. He kissed her again. She put her face to his neck. She wondered if the spasm would pass.

'What are you doing?' he said. He scratched his head. 'Do you want to come back to mine?'

His motel room was cold. Audrey already knew it was a mistake. He handed her a can, rum and cola, and they sat side by side on the edge of the bed.

'You wanna take your jacket off?'

Audrey shook her head, put the drink on the bedside table. He began to, he began to, he began—

'Hey,' she said, but her voice sounded like someone else's. 'Stop. I'm sorry. I don't want to.' His face was too close for her to see it properly. She breathed in rum and beer and that cold motel smell. And woodsmoke: it made her think of the fire pit at Charles Street, of Nick, of that house. 'Stop,' she said again. He went on kissing her neck. 'I'm serious.' She pushed his hands down, away from her face, but he was finding his way under her shirt, one hand on her wrist. Audrey was suddenly frightened, pinned up against the bedhead. All she could think was not to lie down. His face swarmed over her. His lips were making soothing shapes, he was smiling, his hair was hanging over his forehead. She wondered if she should just let him do it, wait for it to be over. His eyes were yellow.

She swiped out. Her hand hit the brick wall. The bedside lamp crashed to the floor, taking the phone with it.

'The fuck are you doing?'

'Fuck off. I said *stop*.' Audrey clambered to her feet. The phone cord was caught around her wrist. There was a thudding at the door and then Julian was in the doorway. He grabbed Audrey's wrist roughly, yanked her from the room.

'Listen, mate—'

'You stay away from her,' Julian said. He grabbed the other guy by the neck of his shirt. The three of them stood there as if suspended. Audrey looked at the two men, grunting and struggling in the freezing night.

'For God's sake,' she said. She turned and walked away.

She'd left her scarf back in the room. Her chest was cold. Julian caught up with her halfway across the carpark.

'What's wrong with you?' he said.

'I'm sorry.'

'Your hand's bleeding.'

Audrey looked down at her hand. Her knuckles were grazed.

'It's not bleeding,' she said. 'How'd you know where I was?'

'Pip told me to follow you. She had a feeling about that guy.'

Snow was falling, tiny flakes gathering under the floodlights.

Audrey stopped walking. Her arms were shaking. *Fight or flight*, Nick would have said. She realised her shirt buttons were undone but for two. 'I'm sorry. I'm sorry. Thanks,' she said. She wrapped her jacket around herself, zipped it up, pulled the cuffs down over her hands. 'I thought he was okay.'

'Didn't your mum teach you about stranger danger?'

'Don't talk to me like I'm a child.'

'Don't act like one.'

The blood was rushing in her arms. 'Fuck you. I can hold my own.'

'*Hold my own*. God, you're a loose unit.'

They stumped back to the house. It seemed a long way. Pip was waiting in the kitchen, three mugs set out.

'Everything okay?' she asked. She looked from face to face.

'Fine,' Audrey said.

After Pip had gone to bed Julian and Audrey sat at the table.

'Did you ever argue with your mum or dad and then go out to pick a fight?' Audrey asked. Julian looked at his mug of tea. 'I mean, you knew you were in the wrong, but instead of apologising you tried to get your head kicked in. Then you could feel like you'd copped the punishment without having to think about what it was for.'

Julian said nothing.

'Forget it,' Audrey said. 'I don't really know what guys do. Sorry.' She left the mugs in the sink, left Julian at the kitchen table. They didn't talk about it again.

The fog hung low when they drove home on Sunday. Pip fell asleep. Julian tuned the radio to an oldies station, volume down. Audrey dozed, too, in the back seat, but somewhere near Goulburn she jerked awake when she heard it: Springsteen singing 'Badlands'. She said to Julian, 'I was just listening to this yesterday.'

'What, Bruce?'

'Yeah, at the house, it was in the CD player.'

He turned it up and sang. Pip lifted her head and said, irritably, 'Don't be a jerk, Julian, I was asleep.' She settled back into her seat. 'My mum loves the Boss. This reminds me of being at home.'

Audrey looked at the poplars, the paddocks, the bleached-skull trees by the roadside. 'There's this sign in Melbourne near the city,' she said. 'Near the river. It's on top of one of the factories. It's this rainbow that just says OUR MAGIC HOUR.'

'"Our magic hour". That's nice.' Pip yawned. 'What made you think of that?'

'I don't know,' Audrey said. Julian met her eyes in the rear-view mirror. She looked away.

At home she left her bag and washing, and walked down to the beach. She phoned Adam again. She was so relieved to hear his voice. He said *What's wrong, you sound weird*. She told him about Jindabyne.

'I don't know if he was going to do anything. I don't think he was a bad guy.'

'You told him to stop and he didn't,' Adam said. 'Are you okay? Do you want me to come up?'

'What? Don't be silly. I'm fine. You know, it just gives you a fright.'

A flock of gulls took off nearby. Their wings made a sound like paper rippling.

'I keep waiting to be punished,' Audrey said, 'but it never comes.'

'You've done nothing wrong. Spence? Are you crying?'

'No!'

'You have to care about yourself enough to be safe. You're behaving like a very depressed person. This risk-taking shit, it's textbook. You know that.'

'You can't just pathologise people. It wasn't risk-taking. I didn't know it was going to happen.'

Adam was silent. Scabs had formed on her knuckles, and they itched.

Gritty Underfoot

When children died at Westmead, it was at the hands of some terrible division of abnormal cells, not a parent who knew no better or was too stoned to care. It was Audrey's job to make the families comfortable, to offer taxi vouchers, food vouchers, emergency housing, support. She no longer visited houses where syringes lolled on stovetops and dog shit laced the floorboards. Still. It was a shock the first time one of the kids died. It was the first time she'd really hated the commute: she only wanted to be home, closed off from everyone, but it was the train to Central, then the bus across the city. She sat in the window. The streets were green with growth, the bougainvillea was out. At Randwick the horses were being walked around the track. Everyone sang out *Thank you* when they got off the bus. Meningioma tumour, neglect: they were just different kinds of defeat. Audrey wondered when she'd build up the muscles for it again.

The front door was open. Audrey went to the kitchen to find a beer. Julian was in the living room playing a car-racing video game. He said *Hey* without looking up. A furrow of concentration snaked across his forehead. Audrey was halfway to the stairs before he said it—'Hey, could you transfer the money for the internet?'

'I did it the other day.'

'Oh'—irritation in his voice—'well, can you tell me next time?'

Audrey stood looking at him. At last he threw down the console in sudden frustration and turned to her.

'Yes,' she said. 'I'll let you know.'

There was a string of missed calls on her phone. She sat on the floor to play the messages. Three from Sylvie, one from David, one from Bernie: Irène had had the baby at four o'clock that afternoon, a boy, seven pounds something, it was very quick, everyone was fine. Bernie's message was like a performance piece for radio, an impression of Sylvie. Audrey laughed until her eyes were streaming. She missed him.

She called her mother. Sylvie was still at the hospital.

'I wish *ton papa* could see him,' Sylvie said. 'You remember how happy he was when Zoe was born?'

Sometimes Audrey wondered if they recalled the same man at all. There were a few photos of Neil holding Zoe as a baby. He'd been sick by then. He'd ended up in a palliative care facility on the peninsula, near the golf course, not far from the home all the children had escaped. The roads were poorly lit. Audrey hated driving there at night: tired, she'd hallucinate ragged figures or animals by the side of the road, lurching out from behind trees.

There came a time when Audrey was no longer afraid of him. He'd suddenly become as harmless as a plant. He changed quickly. His body bloated, the shape of his face changed. He was an old man and in pain.

When he was close to the end, Audrey had submitted her final essay for her Masters and drunk a glass of wine by herself somewhere on Elgin Street. She'd phoned Nick from her sunny window seat. At home there'd been a surprise party: all her friends crowded into the front room of the Charles Street house, bunting on the wall spelling out BRAIN PARTY, confetti and champagne in her hair, Nick kissing her in the kitchen. She remembered Katy shrieking *You brilliant woman!* Audrey was unshowered, in a sloppy shirt, sleepless from the night before. Yusra poached her an egg on toast and they drank Veuve, then Yellowglen, and then beer. She remembered a spirited 4 a.m. clean-up, Paddy singing *Many hands, make 'em light.* Giggling at the clatter of the bottles in the recycling bin outside. Katy wiping down the benchtop. Dustpan and shovel for broken glass. Audrey and Nick stood on the front step to wave the last of them off.

Sylvie had phoned the next morning. *Your papa is gone.* Audrey sat on the couch looking at the wall opposite where the bunting had come unstuck overnight. Relief and sorrow were already grinding against each other. Nick asked if it felt like the end of an era. He was trying to understand. Audrey hadn't known how to explain that it was just a fresh mystery. She might never have simple feelings about her father. A week after his funeral she'd already begun to forget his face, and she wondered if maybe he hadn't meant as much as she'd thought.

After she'd spoken to Zoe and Irène, Audrey sat on the floor for a long time, on the bright rug Katy had brought her back from Mexico. The coarse fabric still smelled of somewhere she'd never been, even after all the years she'd had it. She saw herself in the mirror by the clothes rack she'd assembled the day she'd moved in. Shirt unbuttoned to the chest, handbag puddled beside her on the floor. Untidy hair, crooked nose. Bare face, a look of mild astonishment, as though she couldn't quite believe she was seeing herself there.

Claire suggested the bookshop to her. It was on Oxford Street. It must have been a home or boarding house in another lifetime, an old terrace whose rooms divided the genres, with a café at the bottom. It was out of the way, but Audrey had time to waste. Her weekends were empty. She was still working out the city. She still paused to examine bus routes.

She stood upstairs in front of the shelves. She was holding the book close to her nose. A man—a boy, he was younger than her—made to squeeze past. He had a teapot and honey in his hands. Audrey realised he was an employee. She was embarrassed about how distracted she'd been, standing in the passageway. She stepped back. The boy said *Sorry, darling* as he passed. Audrey felt old for the first time in her life. She paid for the book downstairs, reeled out of the shop into the thick afternoon. She guessed her way to the Botanic Gardens and lay on the grass to read, but it began to rain in sudden, fat drops. Her feet slid in her sandals. She stood in a greenhouse and waited for the weather to ease. She paced up and down the brickwork between the staghorn ferns and the cyclamen. Her parka was wet and cold. She thought about the fastest way to get home. She was stunned with loneliness.

She looked after Elliott the next morning while Claire worked. At the door, Claire squeezed her fingers and said *Thanks for doing this at the last minute.*

Audrey and Elliott sat on the carpet and cut pictures out of magazines for collages. She was amazed at how long the task held his attention. They took racquets and a shuttlecock to the big park, but it was windy and hard to play, and Elliott was irritable. Audrey took his sticky hand and they walked home across Chalmers Street. He rolled the shuttlecock between his fingers.

'It looks like a lady in a long dress,' he said, 'or a vampire.'

'We could dress up when we get home if you want.'

'It's okay,' he said. He balanced the plastic feathered thing on his palm. 'Do you like living with Julian?' he asked.

'He takes my food and won't let me change the TV channel, but he's all right. I don't see him all the time.' Audrey thought about it. 'What made you ask that?'

Elliott shrugged. 'I want to live with him again. Me and Claire did before, but I was a baby, this big'—he spread his hands to demonstrate—'and I don't remember.' He shook his head so his hair fell across his little face. 'Do I look like him?'

'I suppose, a bit.'

'Claire says I've got his mouth, but the rest of me looks like her.'

Audrey studied his features. She could only see Claire's angles, her pale hair, intelligent brow.

'I *wish* we could all live together again!' Elliott said. His face lightened, darkened with the shadows of trees and houses.

'Sometimes you can really like someone, but you just can't live with them. Claire and Julian are probably like that. It's good they still get along.'

'Yeah.' He was unconvinced.

Claire was later than she'd said. Audrey didn't mind. It was good to be needed, even in small ways. But she was tired when she got home. The wind had turned light and warm. Music streamed from one of the nearby flats. The cicadas were just starting up. She met Julian at the gate: she was coming, he was going.

'Pip's copulating very loudly in there,' he said. 'I'm going to have a beer. Wanna come?'

They power-pedalled up the rolling streets, Audrey following Julian, to Randwick. They stopped by the cinema, crossed the road to a narrow bar with BAT COUNTRY in thin capital letters over the entrance. They sat in a booth. The light was fashionably dusky, the menu full of complicated drinks and craft beers.

'I looked after El today,' Audrey said.

'Yeah, Claire's got that funeral on tomorrow, hasn't she.' Julian was sorting his coins into piles. 'She'll be busy.'

'He was talking about you. About when you still lived with him and Claire.'

'He romanticises it. He was three when Claire and I split up. He couldn't possibly remember,' he said, but tenderly. 'There were five or six of us all living where we are now. I'm the only one still left. We used to have a lot of parties. Cheap meat and crap wine. Sometimes we'd have slab days.'

'I don't know what that is.'

'Everyone brings a slab and then you have to plough through it all. Anyway, Clairy and I ended up together for a few years, and then we had Elliott. We were ridiculously young. Claire was twenty, I think. When we split up, we thought we could go on living together, but *being* separate, you know? We were such hippies!' Audrey said nothing. 'Eventually El started to piss people off. He was pretty precocious, and nobody was used to having kids around. So he and Claire moved out.'

Julian pushed over his coin piles, and began restacking them in size order.

Audrey watched his hands. 'You don't talk about him.'

'I see him all the time,' Julian snapped.

'All right,' said Audrey, 'I wasn't having a go.'

He looked like he didn't believe her.

Audrey went to the bathroom. The walls were papered with pages torn from old magazines, and for a second she forgot where she was, reading, toilet paper bunched in her hand. She wiped herself and saw she was bleeding. She was surprised. It had been a long time. She'd almost forgotten that was how bodies worked.

She sat down opposite Julian again. He'd bought her another beer.

'This is funny,' she said. 'It feels like we're kids skipping school. Killing time.'

174

'We're just hanging out,' said Julian.

Audrey ran her hand over the brick wall. It reminded her of the one in the motel at Jindabyne. She was still embarrassed about it, about Julian being there, thinking she needed to be *reined in*, maybe. She pushed her glass around with her finger, tied her hair into a knot.

'What, are you on speed or something?' Julian snapped. 'Stop moving.'

'What's the matter with you?'

'Nothing's the matter.'

Audrey waited for him to tell her. She could feel herself bleeding into her jeans.

'I had a big fight with Claire,' he said. 'About Elliott. That's probably why she asked you to look after him this morning, instead of calling me.'

'Oh.'

'She says I only see him on my terms,' he said. 'But I work. We both work. It was her choice to move out. We never wanted to do that "weekends with dad" bullshit. He's still mine.' He dropped his head. 'I'm embarrassed now. Don't tell anyone.'

'Okay.'

Audrey left him there while she went to get another drink. Her hands were sticky with heat. When she sat down again, he was calm. She handed him a schooner. Beer sloshed onto the table.

'Sorry,' she said, reaching for a napkin.

'No, I am.'

They fell silent again. Audrey watched the bartenders mucking around.

'Are your parents still together?' Julian asked after a while. 'Mine are. It's sort of nice. I mean, they hate each other, but they're pushing on anyway.'

'My dad's gone. They were still married when he died, though.'

'I'm sorry.'

'It's okay. He died of cirrhosis. We knew it was coming for a long time.'

'Liver failure?'

'Yes. He was an alcoholic.'

'So was Churchill. Bukowski. All the big names.'

'Fuck off, Julian. He was abusive.'

Julian gave a short laugh. 'Sorry. I didn't realise. I didn't mean to offend you.'

'I'm not offended.'

When he looked at her properly, when he wasn't hedging or turning from her, she saw a flash of something like defiance.

'I just want to *crack* you,' he said after a while, and Audrey thought *What about you, the way you swing from charming to shitty.* When they finished their drinks they stood without speaking and rode home, single-file, the way they'd come.

In November the days were longer and the baths stayed open until seven. Audrey started swimming every night after work. She was not confident enough for open water, but the sea baths were kind. There was a chalkboard by the entrance that read BLUEBOTTLES: NONE TODAY and PLEASE KEEP AWAY FROM THE NORTH WALL AT HIGH TIDE. In the change rooms the older women stood naked, talking and laughing and wringing out their hair. Their bodies were sun-ravaged and healthy.

Audrey had the idea that she was not particularly graceful, but she toiled away, stroking slowly but neatly, the way Nick had taught her. She tried to keep in a straight line. Things shone pearly on the rock floor, beamed their milky light up at her.

Afterwards she'd sit on the rocks with a towel around her to get her breath back before she climbed the steps to the change rooms. She liked watching the other swimmers. The older men nodded at her. Sometimes they'd ask *How is it, love?* or say *Evening* on their way in.

Some nights she sat out on the front stoop while she ate dinner. She read or watched passers-by. If they sang out *Hullo* as they went, she called back. She'd never gardened before, except for some straggling plants back in Melbourne, but she bought a second-hand book and planted a few things. Her tomatoes flourished, her azaleas died. She took her victories where she could.

Once a week she phoned her mother and sister. Conversations with Irène were splintered by dinner or the crying baby. Audrey always called at the wrong time.

Sylvie sounded different, several hundred kilometres away. Audrey was more tolerant. She felt ashamed when she thought of how she'd had to work up the energy to call her mother, brace herself for a quick visit. She thought, again and again, of Sylvie putting her in the bath, soaping her neck. She mentioned it to Irène once. *That sort of sums her up*, Audrey said. *She's always got all this drama going on, but when it's someone else's crisis, she knows exactly what to do.* Irène with a shrug in her voice. *Aren't all mothers like that?* Audrey let it drop.

She said she'd come down for Christmas. She said she'd stay with Sylvie.

In the house on Neptune Street, the windows and doors were always open. The beach towels hung out to dry, flapping brightly on the washing line. The rooms smelled of the sea and clean laundry and beer. The old floorboards were gritty underfoot with sand.

She tagged along to parties, mostly with Julian. He stayed too long, but she was getting better at sticking it out. She could remember the paralysis, trying to attach reason to her emotions, so infected with sadness she was frightened of passing it on, but she told herself she'd left it in Melbourne. She told herself she was getting tough again, building up muscles. She could swim more laps than before. The nights blended into one another. Arrive. Make small talk. Stand with whoever Julian introduces you to. Get a drink. Stand alone. Relax. Relax. Relax. It's just people. Finish your drink. Talk to someone. Talk to the sweet boy stuck in the never-ending post-graduate degree. Talk to the girls you meet in the bathroom. Talk to Julian. They're all kind. They'll talk to you. You might make them laugh, because sometimes you're funny. They all say: *You remind me of someone. You're exactly like my sister* or *friend* or *girlfriend.* The everywhere girl. Have another drink. Go outside. Smell the cigarettes. It smells like Sylvie, like Adam. Dance to whatever music is playing. Get stuck in a photo. More conversation. Getting drunk. More listening, less talking. The Getting-To-Know-You Game. Sit in a circle. Take it in turns to ask questions. What is your middle name. Who was the first person you talked to tonight. Who was the first person you slept with. Ever, not tonight. Have you ever hit anybody. What's your favourite film scene. Make up the answers to most of these questions. Probably everyone does. Party begins to end. Taxi back home, streaming street-lights out the window, hot head. Make a cup of tea. Talk. Re-enact scenes of twenty minutes ago. Impersonate yourselves. Laugh, laugh, laugh. Collapse on the couch. Watch a voluptuous late-night European film. Crawl to bed. In the morning you will laugh about how you crawled to bed because walking was too demanding.

Once Audrey and Claire lay out on someone's dry lawn, sweaty and exhausted from dancing, and laughed until they couldn't breathe.

Once they took Elliott to see a burlesque show in Newtown, where a friend of Claire's was performing. For weeks afterwards he drew bosomy ladies on napkins and hummed sexy trumpety music.

Once there was a violent thunderstorm. The sky went grey-green before it split open. Audrey and Frank sat outside collecting hail in plastic cups. They couldn't hear each other speak over the rain.

Once Pip and Julian had an argument that lasted for six days. It climaxed in a note on the fridge that read *Just because we live together, doesn't mean we have to be friends.* Julian laughed so hard and so meanly when he saw it, and Pip got so shitty and twisted, that eventually they just made up because it was simpler than being angry.

Once a colleague of Audrey's, a paediatric nurse, was late to work. Her twenty-two-month-old son was undergoing tests. They found a tumour along his spinal column. He died very quickly, very peacefully, after complications from unsuccessful surgery, in the ward where his mother worked. The whole climate changed: the grief was oppressive, they were all breathing it. Audrey's debriefing appointment was almost a week after it happened, at the end of the day. When she left the shadows were falling. She couldn't believe everything outside the hospital was the same, that there were things going on beyond its ruthless walls. On the train she sat with her handbag on her lap and looked for the anchors, the things that meant she was on the right line. Parramatta Park on the left, the cemetery on the right.

At home she lay on her bed in her dress and sandals. The plastic venetian blind tapped against the window. When Julian came home he passed by her room and looked in at her.

'What are you doing, you weirdo?' he asked. 'Are you all right?' She sat up. She started to explain, but by the time she'd told him the worst of it, she said, 'I don't really want to talk about it any more.'

'Shit, mate, that's the pits,' said Julian.

'It's the pits for Sangita. It's not mine to be sad about,' Audrey said. 'I'm just in a funny mood.'

'Yeah, but it's fucking rough. Don't underestimate it.' He scratched his head. 'Can you chuck a sickie tomorrow? Get out of there for a bit?'

'I can't just flip off work. There's too much to do. Anyway, that's embarrassing.'

'Go on. I'll do it too. We can hang out.'

'And do what?'

'Fuck, go to the aquarium, it doesn't matter.'

He made things simple. He did things for reasons she didn't understand.

She did call in sick, and so did Julian, and they did go to the aquarium. They moved through the blue tunnels, not speaking much. Once Julian said *I bring El here sometimes.* Audrey turned to look at him, the shadows of light through water passing over his face. He was watching an enormous stingray with rapt, uncomplicated attention.

A postcard with a picture of the Yarra on it, printed in Bernie's immaculate uppercase:

Dear Audrey, you might even be in Melbourne by the time this arrives, because today is Saturday, and I'll probably forget to post it on Monday, and then who knows what could happen? It will probably get lost under all the shit on the kitchen bench. Meanwhile you could have turned into one of those people who jog on the beach with their labradors and join book clubs and rollerblade. Keep it real.

Things are going swimmingly here in colder climes, which are actually hotter than yours at the moment. Yesterday Hazel and I went Christmas shopping together which is relationship suicide. I like Hazel quite a lot but I don't give a fuck what colour beach towel her dad gets for Christmas. The whole thing really killed my holiday spirit.

O and my Year 12 art has been selected for Top Arts, which means it will be exhibited in the gallery in at Fed Square for the world to see. I'm very honoured, it's all very smashing, etc, etc. The day they told me, I bought some goon and a pet rabbit to celebrate. Hazel named it Cher. It bites you on the ankles and pisses on your legs. We should have called it Sylvie. Har, har.

Hope you're well, have a surfing lesson because I hear that's what they do UP THERE, and also speak French and pretend you're a tourist (I did the other day and I got a free beer), love as ever, Brother Bern

He sent photos. *Now that school is done I am terrifically productive*, he wrote, *and I went through my art things and found these. Thought you might like them?? I don't know how you feel about it. Send them back if you don't want them—don't chuck them out—B.*

Audrey spread the pictures out on her bed to look at them. They were all mixed in together. Bernie, sixteen with pinprick pupils, in the backyard at Charles Street. Audrey holding her toddler niece on her hip, Zoe's hair a blond cloud. Audrey and Sylvie a few birthday lunches ago, both wearing black.

Frank knocked at the open door.

'Is that your curry in the fridge?' he asked. Audrey shook her head.

Frank nodded at the photos laid out in a grid on the quilt. 'Getting into decoupage?'

'My brother sent them,' Audrey said. Frank stepped closer, stood over the pictures. He scratched his neck. He pointed at a photo of Audrey and Katy at a music festival a few years back. They were grinning, standing on dry grass. Katy in a sundress, a rockabilly Venus; Audrey braless in a shirt that could have been Nick's. Dusty ankles, arms around each other.

'You look happy there,' Frank said. 'Look at how you're smiling, both of you.'

Audrey thought he was going to ask about Katy, but she heard his feet on the stairs.

. . .

Early morning, already warm. Pip in her T-shirt and underpants, standing in the kitchen doorway.

'I think I'm going to have a beach day,' she announced. 'Does anyone want to come?'

'Oh, yeah,' said Frank. 'I might call Tessy.'

'I'll come with,' said Audrey.

Julian grunted his assent, already halfway up the stairs.

Audrey and Frank made dozens of sandwiches standing at the kitchen bench. They told each other stories.

'...and all he said was *I'm a Yuggera man* and they carted him off.'

'He sounds amazing.'

'He was. I don't really remember him. He died when I was little. He was sick a long time, and Mum and Dad used to visit him without me. I think they thought I'd be frightened of all the hospital stuff. They just wanted me to remember him as, you know, my grandad.'

Claire and Julian must have reached a ceasefire, because she arrived with Elliott and an armful of shopping bags. Elliott sat on the linoleum, right by Frank's feet, and listened to the conversation. Claire made scones like it was nothing: 'It's just flour and milk and sugar and cream. You chuck it in there, and beat it like it owes you money.'

They spiked the lemonade. They left the dirty dishes in the sink and traipsed down the hill to the main beach, Julian with the cricket bats and plastic stumps under one arm, Frank and Tess hauling the esky between them. Oleander the colour of musk sticks behind the fences, grimy frangipanis on the footpaths.

At the beach they spread out their things. Claire rubbed sunscreen all over Elliott's back. He sat obediently, gnawing on a piece of watermelon, in a floppy black hat of Claire's.

'You look like Bob Dylan,' laughed Tess.

'I've got extra,' Claire said. She turned to Audrey, hand cupped. 'Here, let me do you.' Audrey held her hair out of the way while Claire smoothed the stuff over her shoulders. She did it like a mother, moving the straps of Audrey's bathers to the side to make sure nothing was missed. Frank and Julian had already gone for a swim. They ate dripping all over the sand and their towels.

After lunch Elliott and Julian went off with their bodyboards. The conversation turned sporadic and drowsy. Audrey ate watermelon lying on her back looking up at the sky. The juice ran into her ear. She wiped it with the back of her hand.

Propped up on her elbows, Claire admired the boys hurling their bodies into the waves over and over again.

'I'm glad they're spending time together. Elliott really misses him, but Julian's a fair-weather friend. He always gets to choose.' She rolled over onto her belly, rested her head on her long freckled arms. 'I can't remember things being easy with him. I can't remember what he was like before we had El.'

Audrey pulled her hat down over her brow. She hovered lightly above sleep, strange visions. A field on fire. Shadows over a skylight. She dreamed she was living in the country, a town on a river, with a group of friends. Katy was there; it was her sister who was dead. Audrey was wearing the same perfume Katy's sister had. All of their friends were working in shifts to sleep beside Katy and take care of her. When it was Audrey's turn, she upset Katy with the perfume, and it started a fresh onslaught of grief.

Audrey lurched awake. Sweat was running down her ribs in the sun.

Claire smiled at her. 'It's called a hypnic jerk, when that happens,' she said. 'When you're almost asleep and you think you're falling.'

. . .

183

Julian brought a woman home from the consultancy firm where he worked. The two of them finished off the wine cask Audrey had bought, and ate the rest of the picnic leftovers.

The girl was gone in the morning. Julian ate fistfuls of cereal from the box, looking pleased with himself.

'How's your lovelife?' Pip asked.

'Get fucked.'

'I was *joking*.'

Audrey had the impression she'd missed something between them, another tiny earthquake. Julian and Pip fought like siblings.

Julian shoved the cereal packet back into the cupboard. He grabbed his keys and called over his shoulder:

'I can be prickly, too. Be friends or don't be friends.'

They listened to him stump out of the house.

'O-o-o-o! He's in a real *shit*!' Pip said, and clapped her hands.

It had been years since Audrey had lived with someone whose moods she could not trust. She'd almost forgotten about those roads with the hairpin turns.

You Were So Alive

At Tullamarine Audrey picked at her cuticles, shuffling from the plane to the terminal. She was hungry for the bay, the suburbs she knew.

Adam ran to her across the carpeted floor. She dropped her bag and caught his embrace.

'Fuck it's good to see you,' he said.

His face was pressed against hers. She was suddenly, surprisingly knocked for six. She said *I missed you.* It was hard to get the words out.

The city came into full view as they crossed the Bolte Bridge. Everything shimmered through the car fumes.

'—and I'd always imagined Minh to be sort of hard and inaccessible somehow,' Adam said. 'You see him playing a gig and he looks like he's having a good time, but he always stands up the back—when we first started hanging out I thought he was so restrained, so cool about everything. But he's not at all. And neat, the little prick; he's always picking up my shit and putting it away, and then I can't find it. Like Katy used to.'

Audrey's head snapped sideways, but Adam's hands were relaxed on the wheel. He could say her name without flinching!—She triggered in him a tender memory! '…neither of us can cook, so I got mum to make a ratatouille the day before and I zapped it, and his parents thought I'd made it from scratch!'

He laughed, and Audrey did too, the sound peeling away from her.

He took her to a new place in South Melbourne. It had appeared where an old pharmacy had been in the time she'd been gone. They sat for hours. Adam was boisterous and flirtatious, the way Audrey always thought of him. She could barely remember him as he had been in March, a husk of a man.

She wanted to speak about the things they never spoke about on the phone. She wanted to say something about how change had beat away at him since she'd moved. She wanted to tell him about hypnic jerks, spider tumours, symbiosis, artificial lakes. She wanted to ask when Katy had passed from a friend to a memory.

But there were no spaces for those things in his conversation. She was afraid that she could say Katy's name aloud and Adam wouldn't blink.

They scanned the bill standing by the register. Audrey looked up to see their images in the mirror behind the counter. Her own face, impassive. Adam, serious only for a moment, hairline receding slightly.

'You going to call Nick while you're down?' he asked as they fumbled for change.

'Adam—'

'You could be friends. Heaps of people are friends.'

Audrey swung the café door wide. She tilted her face to the dry afternoon.

'It got pretty ugly,' she said. 'We haven't really spoken since. Come on, let's go for a walk. I've missed this.'

Adam kissed her smackingly on the cheek.

． ． ．

He drove her all the way to Sylvie's that night, through the suburbs along the beach. Warm air at the window, caravan parks, ti-tree. Audrey felt nostalgic for something she'd never had, suburban delirium and fast car rides at night, soft-serve summers. She propped her face on the window.

Sylvie was waiting on the porch, cigarette between her knuckles. She was barefoot and coltish. Her hair tumbled from its knot.

'P'tit lapin,' she said when she saw Audrey. She stood to embrace them both. 'Come in, Adam, how are you? Do you want some coffee?'

'Thanks, Sylv, but I have a hot date.'

'How is your mother?'

'She's good. My dad had a triple bypass about a month ago, but he's doing well now. Mum can't wait to get him out of the house, she's going insane. She's taken up painting.'

'Men, they are all the same,' Sylvie said with a congenial eye roll.

'Thanks for driving me all this way,' Audrey said.

'No worries. I'll call tomorrow. We'll go out.'

'I want to see Minh.'

'I'll phone. See ya. Au revoir, Mrs Spencer.'

Audrey put her things in her room. She opened the wardrobe. There was an old jacket hanging there, dark green, hooded. She could almost hear Katy's laugh—Oh yairs, very narce, it's vai-r-r-y nineties teen witch—coming from the part of her brain that had still expected Katy to be waiting at the airport beside Adam.

It was a kind of doublethink, the bargains and lies she'd been fashioning since Katy had gone. If Audrey always switched off the bedside lamp with her eyes already closed, Katy might reappear. If she could guess the seconds left on the microwave until her coffee was finished reheating. If she could hold her breath for half a lap of the pool, if she could make it home without seeing any brown cars, if there were no messages on her voicemail at the end of the day. The superstitions were crushed as soon as they proved untrue, but she invented new ones each day.

She sat down on the end of her bed, smoothed the bedspread. Everything was covered in a thin layer of dust. The evening light streamed in.

Sylvie leaned in the door. 'How are you?' she asked.

'I'm good. It's nice to be home. I didn't realise how much I'd missed it.'

'You're thin.'

Audrey looked at the mirror. 'I've been busy.'

'Do you have a boyfriend?'

'No, Maman. I'm just taking things as they come.'

On the dresser was a glass case with a painted figurine of Jesus on a cloud. 'That's new,' Audrey said.

'It's from when I was a little girl.'

'I meant—' Audrey meant *It must have been in hiding all this time*, since her father would never have allowed it, but she stopped herself.

Sylvie nodded and shifted. 'Let me get you a cup of tea,' she said at last.

'*Merci,*' said Audrey. Sylvie left the room. Audrey lay back and put a hand over her mouth.

When she got out of the shower she could hear the television on—evening news, bushfire alerts—and Sylvie talking to the budgerigar in French. She sat at the kitchen table with her towel around her shoulders. She watched her mother prepare dinner. It was almost nine o'clock. Sylvie had been waiting for her.

'How's work, Maman?'

'I received a promotion,' Sylvie said. 'I'm a team leader now.'

'That's fantastic! You didn't tell me,' said Audrey. 'When did that happen?'

'Last month.'

'Congratulations. You should've said!'

Sylvie's back was to Audrey. Her knife went *slock-slock-slock* over the asparagus.

'You all probably thought I wouldn't even keep the job,' she said.

'Nobody ever said that.'

Slock-slock-slock went the knife.

Audrey watched her mother's neck; she watched the muscles working.

'Don't sit with wet hair,' Sylvie said without turning around. 'You'll catch a cold.'

After dinner they hauled the grey water outside to pour over the garden beds.

'I've started gardening,' Audrey said.

Sylvie seemed pleased. 'How is it?'

'I haven't planted much. Just a few tomatoes, some azaleas.'

'*Ben*, anyone can grow tomatoes,' Sylvie said dismissively.

Audrey reached down to tug a withered flower head from its stem. It fell away in her hands, dry and without perfume.

'A gardenia,' her mother pronounced. Audrey let it fall.

She'd almost forgotten Sylvie's turbulence. She felt that skin forming, that hard outer shell: the part of her she needed to weather it. Audrey lay on her bed and looked at her watch. She'd been home for two hours. She opened the window, changed into her pyjamas. She read for a while, and when she went to the kitchen to get a glass of water the lights were off. Her mother had gone to bed. But coming back up the hall she heard Sylvie call out for her.

Audrey went to her room. Sylvie was propped up in the double bed. The room was dark but for the television. There was a black-and-white film on. A man and a woman standing in a ballroom or a parlour. The subtitle at the bottom of the screen read *You're thinking of someone else.* 'Come here,' Sylvie said, and held out an arm. Audrey tucked herself in its curve. 'Do you know this film?'

'I don't think so.'

'It's *Last Year at Marienbad. L'année dernière à Marienbad.*' Sylvie looked younger in the dim room, her eyes fixed on the screen. 'Your papa took me to see it once at the Astor. It was screening for a festival. He loved it. I thought it didn't make sense.'

Sylvie's skin smelled of rose-scented talc and cigarettes. She stroked Audrey's hair in an absent way, held her close. It was everything Audrey might have wanted as a child. The subtitle read *You were so alive.*

Audrey took her brother's old bicycle out of the shed, pumped its tyres and pedalled to the beach at Balnarring. The hardy families were just getting to the beach, setting up their sun shelters, toddlers with fat legs tugging at their hats. Audrey watched the surfers, the big breakers. She liked the uncomplicated camaraderie they had, going in and out, *How's it today, mate*; their healthy bodies beneath their peeling wetsuits, their dripping hair. Audrey waded to her chest. Nick had taught her how to recognise riptides once. Already it felt strange to be in the water here, uncertain in the surf, when she'd stroked away safely in the sea baths.

Riding home in the shade the sweat cooled on her neck. Sylvie had left for work. Audrey phoned her brother. He was at home, he said; he'd be home all day.

He looked the same. That mop of dark hair, that thin face that shone at her when he opened the door. He gave her a quick hug. They examined each other: it seemed longer than a few months since she'd seen him. They hustled down the hall and into the kitchen, where they sat and spoke greedily. Bern told her about his exams, about the parties afterwards, about Hazel, about Irène's family and the new baby. Audrey listened, leaning forwards on her elbows.

At last he got up and set the kettle boiling. He went to the cupboard.

'Don't tell me you've got food in there,' Audrey said, and Bern affected a housewifely pose, biscuits in hand, one leg bent upward at the knee, eyelashes fluttering.

'Iced VoVo?'

Audrey laughed. 'Listen, do you mind if I have a look at your art?'

Bernie dropped his head.

'I didn't mean to put you on the spot. You don't have to show me.'

'No, it's not that,' he said. 'They're just…nothing special.'

She followed him into his bedroom, whose walls were lined with canvases: their family in oils. Audrey was stunned.

'I don't really know what I'll do with them yet,' Bern said. 'Only one painting's going on display at the Ian Potter, and that's not until April or something.'

'They're amazing, Bern.'

He blushed. 'I was getting quite prolific there for a while.'

Sylvie occupied three rectangular canvases. She stared vacantly, cigarette in hand; she leaned back in her chair; she was savage-eyed, hands swiping the air. Audrey recognised her own face with a shock. Her image smiled hesitantly, as though she'd just looked up.

'I was trying to get that whole Princess Di thing you do,' Bern grinned, giving her a nudge. 'Oh, little *me*, I'm so *demure*.'

'Fuck off. We can't all be Nick Cave.'

She couldn't meet her own eyes. It was her likeness, but it was not familiar. She was used to the bump in her nose, the lines of her body, but something in her welled up in protest. She tilted her head at the canvas.

'It is weird,' Bernie said. He cleared his throat. 'It has to be weird to see yourself, or a…representation of yourself, like that.'

Audrey looked at him. 'I guess it is.'

'One afternoon I was having a really bad time of it, and Hazel came over for a smoke. I should've known, because I don't like weed. But I had this complete dissociative thing, where I couldn't see myself in the mirror. I felt like I wasn't my body.'

'Bong on,' Audrey said. She instantly wished she hadn't made a joke of it. She wanted to tell him about that night at the Brunswick Green when she'd looked at her reflection in the bathroom cubicle and hadn't recognised herself, or the time she'd been driving and had sensed a divergence, sure the petrol tanker had collected her car, certain she was dead.

She turned from the painting. 'Is it weird sleeping in here, with all of them?'

'It's sort of nice,' Bern said. 'They're keeping me company.'

The final canvas depicted their father reclining on a sofa chair. Audrey recalled the image from an old photo taken several Christmases ago. Bern had made him disarming. He looked like a simple man, a minor character from a play. 'That was the one that NGV wanted to exhibit,' said Bern, 'but I asked if they'd show the family portrait instead.'

'Where's that?'

'Painting room. They've taken over the house.'

Audrey followed him. The largest canvas occupied almost an entire wall. Sylvie the matriarch sat squarely. Her face was regal and serene: only the cigarette between her fingers hinted at anxiety. Beside her sat Irène, whose hard face was relaxed into a smile. In the back, Audrey and Bernard. Bern with a sheepish grin, leaning on Sylvie's chair. Audrey laughing openly, unexpectedly. They were a family.

'I've never seen anything better than this,' Audrey said. She couldn't stop staring.

He was bashful. 'I'll go and finish the tea. You can look around, if you want.'

She went over to the desk by the window and opened one of his black folios. The entire process was detailed, from its inception to the final toilsome stages. Digital photographs of the paintings at various stages in the process had been pasted in, altered, painted over, annotated. Bern's handwriting spilled over the pages.

> Maman was the easiest to paint. She's so animated ALL THE FUCKING TIME, which makes her an easy subject. I didn't notice it until I started watching her more when I was preparing this folio. You can look at her at any given moment, and she'll have some incredibly expressive face on. Irène was okay once I captured that intense motherliness. This year I felt like she stopped being my sister, now she's really just Zoe and Lucas's mum, but that's alright, I was never that connected with her anyway. After she had Lucas I went to visit her one day and her tits were leaking—I would really have liked to paint <u>that</u>, but she would have been offended by it. She thinks she looks frumpy, but I'm happy with the final product…

How invasive it seemed, Audrey thought, how clinical, that this had been inspected and marked. She flipped through more pages. Photos of her: a few with Nick, some miscellaneous family shots, a few ballpoint pen sketches of her own face.

She closed the folio and retreated to the kitchen.

'You're pretty clever, Bern.'

'It's just art.' He turned from the sink and handed her a mug. 'Don't get excited.'

It was a long way back out to Tyabb without a car. Audrey hadn't done it since school: she couldn't believe how far she'd commuted those months before she'd left home. Train to the end of the line, then the sporadic bus, then the phone call to come and pick her up.

Sylvie had huffed—*The schools are all the same, you will meet the same friends at school here, it's ridiculous, this travelling,* hein, *you sleep in your friend's house more than at home*—but when her father picked her up he was kind. Those were Audrey's gentlest memories of him. It was winter when they moved out there. It was usually dark by the time she called. She'd wait for the car in well-lit spaces, under shop awnings or in phone booths. She pulled the sleeves of her rugby jumper over her hands, hopped from foot to foot. She only felt safe when the slowing headlights belonged to her parents' decaying Holden Commodore. When it was her father behind the wheel he'd lean in for a kiss (shocked, every time, by her cold cheeks) and blow a hot breath in her ear. Sometimes he'd stop at the servo and buy her a bottle of orange juice or a bag of chips. He respected her stubbornness, her tenacity, in making that stupid trip.

She caught a cab home. Sylvie was there, skirt and flesh-coloured stockings and the bank's garish black-and-yellow shirt, watching the evening news with the captions on.

Audrey sat on the arm of the couch.

'How was work?' she asked.

Sylvie pushed her lips out and made a little *putt* sound. 'Just the same. What did you do today?'

'I rode to Balnarring and went for a swim first thing this morning. I must have just missed you. Then I went to Bernie's. I saw his art.'

'If he spend as much time on his schoolwork as he spend painting,' Sylvie said. Audrey waited for the end of the sentence but it didn't come.

'I don't think it matters about his score,' she said. 'The course he wants to do, they don't care what he got for accounting. It's about his art.'

'You always defend him.'

'He's smart in the ways that matter,' Audrey said.

'*On verra.*' Sylvie fiddled with her earring, trying to unscrew the back. The tiny pin fell away, and she swore. Both women dropped to their hands and knees, looking for the piece of metal. Audrey pinched it between her fingers. *'Tiens.'* They faced each other, sitting on the rug.

'How were you swimming?' Sylvie asked.

'What?'

'You said you went to swim this morning.' Sylvie sounded suspicious. It was such a funny thing to mistrust that Audrey had to suppress a grin.

'Yeah, at Balnarring. In Sydney my house is close to the sea baths, almost across the road. I've been trying to swim every day.'

Sylvie sat back on her heels. 'How did you learn?'

'Nick taught me. Ages ago.'

'It's a good thing to know,' Sylvie said. 'I wish I learned.' She had lipstick on her front tooth. Audrey felt a pinprick of sorrow.

'I could teach you,' she said. 'I'm not very good. But we could try.'

'I'm too old now.'

'Fifty-three isn't old. You can learn.'

'I'm embarrassed,' Sylvie said.

'We can go early in the morning before anyone's there,' Audrey said. 'Only if you want to, though. I don't want to fight you about it.'

'I want to,' she said. 'But not in the sea.'

'Okay. We'll find a pool.'

Sylvie turned the earring over in her fingers. In a second she'd get up and find her cigarettes. *We can do it*, Audrey wanted to say.

Adam phoned. The outdoor cinema was showing *Mulholland Drive*. They had a few beers in the courtyard of the Standard, then walked over to the old convent. Adam stopped to piss in an alley near the train station and Audrey hissed *Shush, can't you do it quieter? The whole of Collingwood can hear you taking a slash*, and he hollered *Do you hear the people sing, singing the songs of angry men*, and Audrey started to laugh helplessly. They marched over to St Heliers Street arm in arm, picked their way to a pair of seats, clinked their bottles of cider together.

'I saw Bern yesterday.'

'How's he doing? When does he find out about uni?'

'Not till January. I think he's put VCA down first.' Audrey dug at the label on the bottle with her thumbnail, tried to peel it off cleanly. 'I saw his paintings. They were unbelievable. I was a bit thrown.'

Adam glanced at her. 'How so?'

'I don't know. He's just always been the baby, this artsy little shit, you know, making zines and taking photos. But he's actually *good*.' The sky was darkening. She watched two bats arc from one tree to another. 'He just seems so old and so together since I went to Sydney. But it hasn't been that long.'

'Maybe I should buy up now,' Adam said, 'if he's going to be the next Brett Whiteley.'

It was still warm when the film finished. They walked over to the grounds so Adam could have a cigarette. From the top of the hill the city seemed close. Audrey looked at the patterns the old factory chimneys made. She paced back and forth, walking the line where the paved area finished and the garden began. There was a small sign warning of snakes in summertime.

'You know that scene with the opera singer, where she falls over and you realise it's been a tape all along?' Adam said. 'It just terrifies me. I always sit there waiting for something awful to happen. There's something really sinister about it.'

'I know what you mean. It's sort of—emotionally gruesome.'

Adam nodded, grimaced. The breeze blew light and hot, but Audrey saw him shiver. She thought of Nick.

Audrey chose an indoor pool in Hastings. They went on a weekday evening, parked in the lot between the recreation centre and the foreshore. The day had been overcast. The floodlights were already on. It was a bleak foreshore, gentle and grey, no waves. The boats barely moved. Sylvie looked out at the jetty through the windscreen. Her mouth was set.

Audrey worried she'd pushed her into it. 'We don't have to do this,' she said.

'I want you to teach me.'

'Okay.'

The air inside the complex was warm and chemical. In the change rooms Sylvie sat on the bench, towel around her like a shock blanket, while Audrey shrugged out of her shirt and jeans.

'I brought you some goggles,' she said.

'I need to put them—?'

'You don't have to put them.' Slipping into Sylvie's speech patterns. 'You don't have to put your head under at all. It's up to you.'

The pool was almost empty. The swimmers at the far end made it look like calm work, stroking in the roped-off lanes. The water fell away from their bodies cleanly.

The water was chest-high at the shallow end. Sylvie lowered herself to her chin. She kept her mouth above the water. Audrey watched her testing it out.

'Come and hold on to the edge,' she said. They stood side by side. Their knuckles made a mountain range. 'Take a big breath, and blow some bubbles. You don't have to go right under. Just like this.'

'Like a crocodile,' Sylvie said. She didn't smile. She took a lungful of air, put her mouth to the water and exhaled.

'Good—you're doing good. You can put your nose in. Nothing bad will happen. The water won't go up.'

She made Sylvie kick her legs out behind her, still holding on to the edge. 'Just be calm. You don't need to kick that hard. You don't want a big splash.' Her mother's body was tense and determined.

'Do you want to try floating?' Sylvie wiped her nose with her wrist. 'Come on, it's good. I'll be next to you. You can stand up here, anyway.' She flailed to right herself the first few times her feet left the pool floor. Audrey kept saying *Relax, just try to relax*, even though she knew it was impossible: she remembered the terrifying feeling of imbalance. She put a hand under the small of Sylvie's back, another hand under her skull.

Sylvie smiled up at Audrey, suspended and weightless.

'It's good, isn't it?' Audrey said. 'You're doing a good job. Can I let go? You'll be okay by yourself—' She took her hands away very carefully, one at a time. Sylvie floated by herself for a moment. Then she turned her head and water rushed in at her mouth and nose, and she panicked. Audrey grabbed her under the arms.

'*Laisse-moi, bon sang.*'

'It's okay if a bit of water goes in your face. Your mouth was closed. It's okay.' Sylvie clutched the lane rope. Audrey could see her standing on her tiptoes. She tried to remember how Nick had taught her, what he'd done differently. All she could think was how safe she'd felt. 'I'm sorry, Maman. I'm sorry you got a fright. Maybe I'm not the best person to teach you. Maybe we should get proper lessons.'

'You're a good teacher,' Sylvie said. 'I'm old and trying to learn. It takes me a lot.'

'I won't let anything happen to you.' They stood, warm water to their necks. 'Do you want to try putting your head under?'

'Okay.'

'Then we can go home. Let's hold hands instead of the side of the pool. We'll go under on three, okay?'

Sylvie nodded. Audrey counted and they sank below the surface, gripping each other's wrists. Audrey saw her mother's face through a swarm of bubbles: eyes shut tight, mouth sealed, hair streaming in the blue chemical space like an effigy of the sun king.

There was a funny English word Sylvie used to describe Australian Christmases—*uncivilised*, Audrey thought, or maybe *barbaric*; she couldn't remember. It was funny when Bernie mimicked her, but the actual conversation was tedious, and they'd had it a thousand times.

Audrey heard Sylvie moving around the house at six in the morning on Christmas Day. The air was already settling warm in the rooms. The white cloth was on the dining table, the good cutlery set out.

She went to the kitchen. 'Merry Christmas, Maman.' Sylvie was alight, smiling, her hands stained with beetroot juice. She pushed her hair back from her face with a flexed palm. The bench was littered with ingredients and objects that did not match. The room smelled of coffee and rosemary. 'Can I do anything to help?' The cutting board was floured. A tray of vegetables sat, sliced and seasoned, ready for the oven. The turkey was defrosting in the sink, water rolling off its plastic skin. Sylvie broke eggs into a bowl.

They took turns to shower. Afterwards Audrey sat on the edge of the bathtub and let her mother plait her hair into a crown on top of her head. When Sylvie was finished they stood before the mirror, Sylvie behind, with her hands on Audrey's shoulders, inspecting her handiwork. *'Voilà,'* she said, pleased, 'like a *déesse*.' Audrey thought that her face was too exposed, but she kept it to herself. She squeezed Sylvie's fingers.

Before lunch Zoe taught her father how to play Go Fish, and Irène watched them. Audrey sat on the couch, watching Irène. Bernard turned up Elvis Presley's *Blue Christmas* and crooned along with deadpan sincerity, swivelling his hips for Hazel. Sylvie put together the feast in the kitchen. When Audrey offered to help, she didn't seem to hear. Her hands worked neatly; she counted and mumbled to herself as she arranged the food. Audrey tried to cut the turkey in elegant slices, but it came away in shreds and thin wedges.

'I'm doing a shit job of this,' she said. 'What do you want me to do with the stuffing?'

'I'm going to have to toss these ones,' Sylvie murmured. She was mixing pretty vegetables, broccolini and beans and asparagus and potatoes in butter and parsley. She pitched the spoon at the sink. '*Putain*, I've forgotten the bread rolls. It shouldn't be taking this long. Put the plates and we can serve. Which one for Zoe?'

They sat down at last.

Irène turned to Sylvie. 'Did you forget the ham.' They did not look at each other, mother and daughter. Sylvie pushed back her chair with the furious shame that only women recognise. Her napkin slid to the floor. *Doesn't matter*, everyone was saying. *We don't need the ham. There's plenty of food here.* There was nothing for Audrey to do but she went to the kitchen anyway, stood beside her mother so that the others couldn't see her from where they sat at the table. Sylvie's head was bowed.

Audrey reached for two plates, washed two serving forks, unwrapped the package of ham David had bought: it was sliced ham from the supermarket, meant for packed lunches, not Christmas lunch. Sylvie set the plates on the table. Audrey stared at her sister, but Irène was inscrutable.

Sylvie held the baby and beamed as everyone unwrapped her gifts. They were lavish: she gave Audrey a cashmere jumper, an enormous box of lotions and creams, a thin gold bracelet. Audrey was confused by the excess. She thanked her mother over and over again. She saw Bernie, Irène and David glance at one another. Sylvie was smiling.

In the bathroom Audrey washed her hands with a heavy feeling of unease. Nick used to laugh at her for jumping at small noises, at always expecting the worst, but growing up she'd divined her parents' moods preternaturally. Sometimes she just knew. It helped to navigate what was coming. And yet she could not decode whatever she'd just seen pass between her brother and sister. She wondered if Sydney had dulled her senses.

Irène stepped in and shut the door. 'You need to talk to her. I can't. I'm going to say something awful. She's been borrowing money from us since October.'

Audrey was still holding the hand towel. 'What do you mean?'

'Since she lost her job.'

'She told me she got a promotion. She's a team leader.'

Irène looked up at the water-stained ceiling. 'A team leader,' she said. 'It's not really funny, I guess. But almost.'

'She goes to work every day. She wears her shirt and name badge.'

'She's not going to work, Audrey.'

'Okay. Don't—yell at me. I had no idea.'

'I'm not yelling.'

'Don't *speak* to me like that. It's not my fault.'

'I'm sorry.' Irène's arms were crossed. 'She says she's doing more volunteer work at the hospital. I don't know if she's looking for another job. I just thought she might listen to you.'

Audrey thought of Sylvie pinning back her hair every morning in the hallway mirror. Sylvie on the couch in her stockings, fiddling with her earring. *How was work, Maman? Just the same.*

'Please,' Irène said, 'please.'

Audrey found her mother in the kitchen making coffee.

'Those were really generous gifts, Maman,' she said.

Sylvie kissed her forehead. 'I like to make my family happy.'

'I know. And we're really grateful. But we weren't expecting anything this year.'

Sylvie spilled sugar across the bench. '*Qu'est-ce qui t'as dit?* Who told you about my job?'

Audrey went to get a sponge.

'It doesn't matter. I wasn't trying to make you feel bad, it's nothing to be ashamed of—'

'I'm not ashamed. Don't be patronising to me.'

'All right. I'm sorry. I didn't mean to upset you. I was just saying thanks. They were generous gifts.'

Sylvie fell back against the pantry door, arms folded.

'Let's just enjoy the rest of the day, all right?' Audrey said. 'Forget I mentioned it. I'm sorry.'

Her mother wiped her hands on a tea towel. She had a look in her eye, a mindless cruelty that was not really hers.

'Nick has a new girlfriend,' Sylvie said. Audrey's pain was acute and fleeting. She felt her arms go weak. Steady, recover, all in a matter of milliseconds.

'Does he.'

'Mm,' Sylvie said, sawing the tea towel between her fingers, 'Adam told me.'

'Well. As long as he's happy.'

'I'm surprised you didn't know. Adam didn't mention it?'

'No. He didn't.'

The coffee was made, the cups lined up along the bench. Audrey looked at her mother's face for a very long time, and was frightened by the absence of anything tender or regretful. She excused herself and went outside. She walked to the far end of the property and leaned against one of the big peppercorn trees. She had to put her fist to her mouth so she wouldn't howl.

She stayed at her sister's house that night, curled on the fold-out sofa. She read a Bruno Schulz book from Irène's shelves, battling through pages and pages and unable to recall in the morning a thing she'd read. The baby cried out after two o'clock. She saw the light go on in Irène and David's bedroom, heard their drowsy voices.

She was sitting at the kitchen table when the sun came up, drawing with Zoe's textas. She could see the blooming sky through the French doors she'd opened onto the backyard and through the skylight above her. *Red sky at night, sailor's delight; red sky in the morning, sailors take warning.* The air was sweet. Irène came out in her thinning dressing-gown and drank a glass of water standing by the sink, holding the baby. He was awake but not crying. Irène sat down next to Audrey.

'How did you sleep?'

'Good, thanks.'

'Could you hold Lucas? I need to get his bottle.' He squirmed slowly, moving his legs, opening and closing his fists. His eyes focused on Audrey. His hair smelled milky.

Irène took Lucas in her arms. He guzzled at the rubber teat.

'He just wouldn't take the breast,' she said, and Audrey made an empathetic noise in her throat, the noise of someone without children, who did not care. 'I fed Zoe until she was eighteen months old.' Audrey watched her sister expertly cradling the baby. She picked up the black texta. She added birds to her picture, crude dilated Ms hovering above the trees.

'Is it good to be home?'

'Yeah.'

'Yeah, what? There was a *but* coming.'

'No, there wasn't. I like Sydney.'

'You like the anonymity,' Irène said, shifting the baby to her shoulder. Audrey was surprised. Her sister gave a small smile. 'You forget we grew up in the same house. I'm sorry you were stuck for longer, but I was there, too.'

'No,' Audrey said, 'I don't forget that at all. But how do you—' The right words fell away from her. 'I'm happy, but I don't understand how you stop thinking about it all.' She put the texta down.

'It's hard,' Irène said. 'Maybe Zoe helped. You have to not be so self-centred. You can't have bad days. You work it out.'

Audrey had thought her sister understood.

'Of course,' Irène added, 'it was toughest for you. I just got out as soon as I could. Bernie's such a selfish shit, he doesn't know how much time we spent looking after him. You didn't want to leave Maman. You didn't want to leave Bern. And you didn't want to leave Dad, either. You felt like you had to stay.'

'No, I didn't.'

'Yes, you did,' Irène answered. 'You told me.'

Zoe thumped sleepily into the kitchen.

'Morning, blossom.'

'Morning.' She settled herself on the chair beside Audrey, leaning over to see the picture.

'That's really good,' she said.

Audrey laughed. 'Thanks, Zoe.'

'You're an *artist*.'

'Sell it to you for fifty cents.'

'I have thirty-six dollars,' Zoe announced, 'from the tooth fairy and also pocket money from Mum and Dad. And ten that *Mamie* gave me yesterday in my card. And she gave me a cooking set and a cardigan, and two pet fish. They have to have French names.' She slid off the chair, ran from the room.

Irène propped the baby on her lap, one hand under his chin to support the weak stalk of his neck, the other rubbing his back rhythmically.

Audrey cleared her throat. 'Irène, I felt sort of scapegoated yesterday.'

'I wasn't trying to scapegoat you,' Irène said. 'I just thought she might listen to you. You handle her better.'

'That's not true.'

'It is. And I know it's not fair, but I'm so mad at her lately I can hardly look at her.' She held the baby out to Audrey again. 'It was harder after Lucas. You know, you stop working, you stop seeing people. I felt like my world was very small. I don't want to exaggerate it. I love my kids so much. It's not that.'

There was a desperation to her that made Audrey look away. 'You don't have to justify it,' she said.

Irène's mouth was a hard line, like in Bernie's painting. 'I just wanted Maman to be a normal mother. I just wanted her to ask. "*Ça va?* Is there anything I can do? Can I look after him for a couple of hours?"' Her mouth trembled, and tightened again. 'I mightn't have even taken her up on the offer, but she's my mother. I just wanted her to ask. She didn't even come around. And you can't resent it, or her, because it's not her, it's the chemicals.'

Audrey squeezed her sister's arm. 'I'm sorry that happened.'

'I am happy,' Irène said. 'Don't mistake this.'

David appeared then, holding Zoe under one arm, joking about cooking her in a pot for breakfast. She was shrieking and Irène was hissing *Sh, sh*, but they were all laughing. The day had started without warning.

She went out with Adam for sangria at a rooftop bar, compared notes on Christmas. Adam's garrulous extended family, the house on the farm, made for cheerful talk.

Audrey shook her head when he asked about her day.

'Well, it must have been pretty fucked if you ended up at your sister's,' he said at last.

'It just sounds so petty in the retelling.'

'Go on. I live for this stuff. You know that.'

She gave him an abridged version. When she got to Sylvie in the kitchen, spilling sugar, spitting *Nick has a new girlfriend*, Adam pulled his lips back like he was watching a gory crime show.

'Sorry, Spence.'

'Don't be sorry. He can do what he likes.'

'You know what I mean. I'm sorry Sylv told you like that. I should've said something, but—'

'Did she call you?' Audrey asked.

'Yeah, she did, actually, before you came down. I sort of thought you might have asked her to do it. I thought maybe you were uncomfortable talking to me about it.'

'I'd never do that.'

'I *know*. It was just weird that she still had my number.'

Audrey picked a slice of orange from the bottom of her glass and sucked on it. It tasted faintly medicinal.

'Anyway,' Adam said, '*Girlfriend* is definitely a Sylvie term. I think they're just seeing each other.'

'It's all right. That's just Maman. Passive-aggressive is what she does.'

'I'm sorry.'

'What for? I just wanted to know she wasn't making it up.'

'How mature. Good on you, Spence. Fuck 'em all.'

Minh came by later and made Audrey laugh until she was weak. They ended up at an afternoon gig, drinking Pacificos underground in a narrow bandroom while the support act played. There was barely anyone there, only slow sexy music, a man singing *Take me home, you know me*, so breathy and low it was hard to hear. The three of them danced together right in front of the stage. Audrey could not help but think of Katy, the way the three of them had danced together so no one was left out. Minh's shirtsleeves were buttoned, and every time he raised his arm to spin her around Audrey watched the fabric strain upwards over his thin wrists. They reached for one another, grinning when the yellow stage light flashed over their faces.

Between songs Audrey slipped to the bar. She looked back at the two of them. Everyone in the room was watching; even the bass player was smiling at them from under her hair. Adam had his back to Minh, but their faces were close. It was almost too intimate a thing to see.

When Audrey returned to her sister's, late afternoon, her texta picture of the woods was stuck to the fridge.

Irène had invited their mother for dinner: an act of daughterly courtesy, a peace offering. Sylvie would not shut up. Audrey played dress-ups with Zoe in the backyard. They put scarves around their heads like bandits, they dressed as bride and groom, they were belly dancers with jangly belts.

Sylvie stood and smoked by the back door.

'Did you find something at the sales today?'

'Not really,' Audrey answered, unwinding a feather boa from her neck. She was residually drunk. 'I hung out with Adam and Minh. It was so crowded.'

'That's why I never go. It's disgusting, all these people.' She tapped ash into a clay bowl, a makeshift ashtray. She stepped forwards and touched Audrey's face. 'You've got some sparkle on your nose.'

'Thanks.'

She wished Sylvie would stop touching her, stop talking to her.

Zoe was trying to fasten an apron around her waist, but her small clumsy fingers got in the way of themselves. Sylvie reached down to help her.

'Thanks, *Mamie*.'

Audrey stopped to watch them, Sylvie squinting as she looped the strings, cigarette between her lips. And the way she had a thousand times before, she thought: *Let's start again.*

· · ·

They went back to the indoor pool. They kicked their legs. They blew bubbles together. Audrey showed her how to push the water back and forth with a flat hand, how to dog paddle to keep her head above water. She'd bought her some private swimming lessons for Christmas, but she doubted Sylvie would ever use the voucher. She tried to teach her as much as she could. Once Sylvie said *I want to see you do it.* She sat on the edge, knees tucked to her chin, while Audrey swam a lap.

Afterwards Sylvie floated on her back. She clutched a foam board to her chest in supplication, Audrey standing beside her like a doctor or a priest.

Sylvie drove her out to Tullamarine. They arrived an hour too early, and sat in a café watching the planes through the plate-glass windows.

'*Ça va*, Audrey?'

'*Ça va*, Maman.'

Sylvie folded her arms. '*Qu'est-ce que t'as?*'

'Nothing. I was just thinking.'

'*Chuis ta mère.* I know when something is wrong. *Dis-moi, ma p'tite.*'

It took you years to work out Dad was hitting us as well as you. You never know when you're sick. You didn't know I was dropping acid back when I was sixteen. You didn't know Bernie and I used to steal your Endep when we were still living in your house, when Dad was alive. How could you not have noticed it was missing? You didn't know when Nick and I were splitting up. You didn't know when Irène was stuck in that happy house of hers with two children and a sick head. How could you know?

She reached across the table for her mother's hand.

'Nothing's wrong, honest. What are you doing for New Year's?'

Dry Swallow

In Randwick the church sign still said *Wishing you a white Christmas!
May your sins be as white as snow.* The poinsettias were still out.
Audrey read for hours in her room, in the backyard, in the reserve
at the end of the street. She went down to the baths every night. She
and Pip lay on their towels at the beach and indulged in pointless
conversation. It was high summer, long daylight hours. They got
sucked into an Irish crime series, watching it at night on a laptop
huddled together in Pip's bed. They flinched at the noises of the
settling house, glanced at each other.

They had a New Year's Eve party. There seemed an impossible
number of people in the house, all friends or friends of friends, and
nobody was bothering to ask names. The windows and doors were
open. The house groaned with the weight of so many feet. Bicycles
littered the yard. The kids leaned against the fridge and slipped ice
cubes down one another's shirts.

Audrey felt the blood in her fingertips. She danced until she was
sweaty; she sat down, breathlessly happy, and talked to Claire's
friends. She drew pictures with Elliott, who had started to document
All the insects in the world in an exercise book. His tongue pushed its

way between his lips as he coloured. With a fine-tipped black pen Audrey drew a rudimentary spider.

'There you go,' she said, 'a daddy-long-legs.'

'Those spiders,' Elliott said, inspecting it critically, 'have more poison than redbacks. They just don't know how to release it.' Audrey looked at him. He bared his teeth. 'Can I have a sip of your drink?'

'No.'

'*Mazel tov,*' he said under his breath, as though it were a curse. Audrey laughed. She picked up her glass and went out to the backyard.

Julian was by the side of the house on his own. He offered her a joint. She shook her head.

'No,' Julian said, 'you wouldn't.'

She watched him exhale. She leaned against the fence with her arms crossed, one foot crooked against the warm bricks. The party sounds and music were muffled from where they stood, surrounded by bamboo and hazel trees, lurid hibiscus.

Just before midnight Claire pressed a fifty-cent piece into Audrey's hand. *It's luck,* she said. *You're meant to hold a piece of silver when the clock ticks over.*

They crowded around the television to watch the fireworks. The room smelled of gunpowder, party poppers. Everyone sang 'Auld Lang Syne' without knowing the words. On the screen the coloured stars shattered over the harbour. Explosions of red like sequins; flares that lit up the night. Pip turned to Audrey and gave her a kiss. It left a bruise of lipstick along her cheekbone. Claire shut the door of Audrey's room and sat on the floor to crush a diamond-shaped pill on the back of her work diary. She looked up at Audrey helplessly, holding her Medicare card. 'I wasn't thinking,' she laughed. 'It's all gone in the fucking divots where the numbers are. Do you want some?' In the backyard they wrote their names in the air with sparklers and made fun of their resolutions.

Hours later, when people were beginning to leave, Audrey leaned against the kitchen bench to eat a plum. The linoleum was warm beneath her feet. Julian came in and kissed her very hard, very slowly, and he was so assured that Audrey didn't even have time to be surprised. He held her face. He touched her lips with his thumbs. When Pip walked into the kitchen they separated as though underwater.

'I just wanted—' Pip said. She looked at the two of them. 'I just came to get another beer, doyouwantone?'

'No thanks,' said Audrey. Pip left. Julian pressed his cheek against Audrey's and they kissed again. She was up against the fridge, his hand under her shirt, his knee between her thighs.

'I'm getting to know you,' he said in her ear.

Audrey stiffened. Julian pulled away.

'Sorry,' she said.

'Okay,' said Julian, holding up his hands. He left her there.

In her room she closed the door and took two paracetamol, swallowed them dry. She thought of Julian's hand on her ribs, breath on her neck. She'd almost forgotten what it felt like.

She watched the orange light fill the room, heard the dogs begin to bark, a few cars start up. She crept to the bathroom and stood under the shower. She lay in bed again with her wet hair wrapped in a towel, touched her thighs. She got up and rode her bicycle through the sleepy streets, coasting down hills with her arms outstretched. She called Adam lying on the grass by the foreshore. He said *Are you still drunk?* and she said *Yes, I feel fantastic*, and he laughed. He was antsy about a job interview he'd had before Christmas. He had a string of what-ifs for her to counter. Riding home, flashes of bougainvillea over the tops of fences, brown Christmas trees on nature strips, bottles and soggy streamers in the gutters.

She leaned the bike against the side of the house. Pip was flicking through a catalogue in the kitchen.

'Morning,' Audrey said. She set the kettle to boil. 'Is Julian gone?'

'Getting breakfast with Frank and Tess.' Pip licked her fingertip to turn the page. 'If you want to fuck him, just do it. Don't creep around, and pretend to be worried about changing the momentum, or whatever. I don't care. Just do it.'

Audrey poured herself a coffee. She handed a mug to Pip.

'Nobody's mentioned fucking. We were both wasted,' Audrey said. 'Happy new year.'

Pip dropped a sugar cube into her cup. She looked straight at Audrey. 'Just you wait,' she said.

Audrey felt a pulse of irritation. The light coming through the window was hitting something shiny. It was white and blinding.

In the evening she took herself down to the baths. Pip scoffed when Audrey unpegged her towel from the line, wound her goggles around her wrist like a bracelet. All day everyone had winced and said how bad they felt. *I am CROOK and El has a lot of things to say*, came a message from Claire. Audrey only felt tired. A small stone had settled in her chest. *Just you wait.*

Audrey spread her towel under the cover of the deck. The sting had gone out of the sun. She swam laps and laps. She thought about Adam, about her mother. Her muscles were burning. The water was turning thick, her blood was glue. She'd stopped counting laps. She reached the north wall and paused, panting, to look at the ocean. She wanted Sylvie to see it, to lie on her back and float here. She felt strong and alive.

'Oi, Dawn French!' Julian came down the steps. A few of the other swimmers turned to look.

'Dawn Fraser's the swimmer, idiot.' Audrey pulled herself out of the pool, water dripping from her hair and nose. She was ashamed of her flat breasts and sharp shoulders. Her flesh was translucent and goosepimply in the cool evening; the fine hair on her thighs stood up.

'I can't believe you,' he said. She found her towel, and wrapped it around her shoulders. 'I could barely get out of bed. Soon as Frank and I came home from breakfast, I passed out again.'

'I can't sleep in the day,' Audrey said. 'It was nice, being in the water.'

She picked up her bag and they walked back up the stairs. The railing was still sun-warm under her hand.

They sat down at the top, on the deck, on the plastic lawn chairs.

'Pip said I might find you down here,' Julian said.

'Did she.'

'Yep. She was really pissy.'

Audrey pulled her T-shirt over her head. 'Do you two ever sleep together?' she asked.

'No. How come?'

'Just wondered.'

'She didn't have a go at you about last night, did she?'

'No.' Audrey stood up. Julian stayed there, legs stretched out in front of him. The sun was slipping away. 'I just felt weird about it. Because of Claire, mostly.'

'Don't worry about Pippy,' Julian said.

'I'm not.'

'You're being really short.'

'I'm cold,' Audrey said. 'Are you coming home?'

She slung her towel around her shoulders like a cape and struck a silly, heroic pose. Julian did not quite laugh.

They walked back slowly, not speaking much. They were strangers at the front gate and strangers at the kitchen table.

Bushfire sky. The house was claustrophobic. Audrey lifted the heavy sash window in her room. The air was hot in her lungs. The

213

crickets hummed. Kids yelped and shouted in the street. She set the pedestal fan spinning. She lay in her underwear and tried to read. The bedsheets twisted around her legs. When she woke up the blinds were heaving and knocking at the windows so she knew the air had moved around the room and things had shifted.

In a bookstore, the one Claire had suggested, Audrey found a card: a black-and-white sketch of a bearded man wearing a kaftan, holding a stack of books. Underneath the picture it read *The Perennial Arts Student*. She bought it for Adam and wrote a quick note inside:

> Dear Adam,
>   Good luck with the potential job. You're going to slay it. This time in a few weeks, you'll have a roomful of teenagers calling you 'Mister Wilkinson'. You'll probably have to go on a school camp. My fingers are crossed. Let me know the minute you find out. XXX

She was on her way home, watching lightning snake across the sky, when Adam called.

'I got it!' he said. 'Year 7 and 8 English and History, Year 11 English.'

'I knew you would! Congratulations.' Audrey said. 'We must be psychically linked. I just put a card in the post for you.'

'I love you.'

'I love you too, you clever thing. Go and call your mum,' Audrey said. 'Maybe call Katy's mum, too. She'd love to hear.'

Going back to work in the new year she finally felt as if she'd got the hang of it. She was learning how she fit with everyone else: the parents and nurses and oncologists and nutritionists and psychologists and interpreters in orbit around the child, the patient. She learned about different types of paediatric cancer, mostly from the kids and

their parents. There were tumours with names that sounded invented. There were endless statistics on survival rates. The social work
department was on the lower level, with the dining area and the
gardens; the oncology ward was a level above it. She could have
navigated the stairs between them in her sleep. She saw the same
faces everywhere around the hospital: parents waiting in the queue
at the American coffee chain, on the phone in the narrow courtyard
of the Chinese Garden, standing by the ATM, watching their other,
healthy children on the playground. On Thursdays or Fridays the
Camperdown ward staff usually went to the pub opposite the train
station after work. A few times they took ciders to the park instead.

It was hard to have social energy at the end of the day. Audrey
checked her phone as she waited at the station, and then switched it
off until she got home. The train across the city sent her into a
torpor.

A friend of Julian's had an exhibition at the National Art School
Gallery for the Sydney Festival. Audrey had agreed to go, but now
she wished she hadn't, walking from Central to Darlinghurst: she
wanted to be alone longer.

She couldn't see Julian when she arrived. She moved from one
piece to the next clutching a glass of champagne, not feeling cool
enough for a gallery. The photographs were suburban scenes, but
tense, theatrically lit, like dozens of establishing shots from films.
Audrey did not know much about art, but she was transfixed. Each
picture was a new miniature drama.

A hand on her back, Julian's voice in her ear. She jumped.

He kissed her cheek. 'You smell like hospital,' he said.

'That's where I've been all day.' He was standing close. Italian
beer in his hand, tie loosened, a day's grime on the neck of his white
shirt. He nodded at the wall in front of them. 'What do you think?'

'I really like them,' she said. 'They suck you in. I feel like I'm
waking up from a dream talking to you now.'

'Reminds me of Gregory Crewdson's stuff.'

'I don't know who that is.'

He grinned instead of explaining. He went to talk to some friends and left her to look by herself, and she was happy, inventing her own stories to superimpose on the photos. *One day I might stand like this in front of something Bernie's made*, she thought. She wanted to call him and ask about Gregory Crewdson.

At last Julian reappeared, holding another two beers. 'Want to get out of here?' he asked.

It was warm out. The streets smelled tropical. They walked and drank, bought a couple more beers, sat beneath the fig trees in the big park near the busway. Julian tried to explain his job. He used a strange vocabulary, words whose meanings became nebulous in his mouth. He talked about *solutions*.

'We have to be the expert on whatever the client needs,' he said.

'But you can't be the expert on everything.'

'I guess it's more that we're doing the research so they don't have to.'

'But it's essentially about profit maximisation?' she said.

Julian drowned the rest of his beer, suppressed a belch. 'I guess. If you want. Is that unpalatable to you?'

'Unpalatable,' Audrey said. 'No. I don't care. It's just funny.' *I feel very public-sector*, she wanted to say, but she thought it'd offend him.

On the bus they sat side by side, knees touching.

The house was silent. Julian hollered *Hello*, and when no one answered he raised his eyebrows at Audrey.

'I'm going to have mushrooms on toast,' she said. 'Do you want some?'

'Can you be bothered?'

'Yeah. I'm hungry.'

'I'll get us some wine.'

Pip's essays were spread all over the kitchen table, where she liked to work in the afternoons. They took their dinner into the lounge room and ate sitting on the floor in front of the television, watching a film on SBS. It was about an Afghani woman caring for her vegetative husband. Julian had no patience for it. He groaned, invented his own dialogue. He took their plates to the kitchen and washed them noisily. Audrey wished he'd shut up.

When the film ended she said *Thanks for hanging out*. He stood up, held out a hand, pulled her to her feet. He reached out to straighten the collar of her shirt. They began to kiss. His mouth was wine-dry.

'Come on,' Audrey said. 'This can only get weird.'

'Claire doesn't care.'

'Even if she doesn't. It's like being in a three-person play.'

He laughed into her mouth. Last year had left her with a body that didn't want to fuck, or couldn't. She wanted to say *We're doing it wrong, this will mean something*, but she missed skin, she missed mouths. It was hard to stop.

They went upstairs holding hands, saying *Sh, sh*, went to Julian's room with its window over the sea. He kicked the door to, lay on the bed. She started to unbutton her shirt.

'Don't be a wanker about this,' she said. She kept undressing, dropping her clothes where she stood. Her hips moved against his, the skin of their bellies pressed together. Julian pushed against her as if their bodies were at war.

She'd imagined she'd fuck Julian once and that would be it: the end of curiosity, a small thing, someone other than Nick or a murky face in a strange motel room. Maybe they'd even laugh about it. But little stalactites of longing had formed in her, unsolicited. Not for Julian, but for that warm body, for the surety of hands.

She swung through the door after work. Pip was desperately chatty. She'd been marking for hours.

'Do you want a cup of tea?' Audrey asked.

'Ooh, thanks.' Pip got up and poked around in the fridge. 'I'm starving.'

'How's it going?'

'I've only got a couple more to do. They're all deadshits.' She pulled a tomato and a block of cheese out of the fridge. They faced each other. 'Speaking of—I'm sorry if I sounded narky the other day. About you and Julian.'

'You didn't sound narky.'

'I think I did. Anyway. I don't care what you do. And I mean that in a nice way. Just don't get sucked into his bullshit.' She rinsed the tomato. Water gushed from the tap and splashed onto the lino. 'I love him like I love my brother. We've lived together since uni. But he does exactly what he wants. He'll never think of someone else first.'

Audrey reached for the coffee tin. 'It's nothing serious. I just feel bad about Claire.'

'Claire wouldn't care.'

'That's what Julian said.'

'Ask her. She'd be more worried about you.'

'It feels kind of keys-in-the-bowl,' said Audrey. 'Or teenaged.'

'He *is* a teenager. He never changes. He always goes for the same girls.'

Audrey poured the hot water and took her own mug over to the table. 'Trust me,' Pip said, 'you're just like Magda. She was an OT, I think. Really sweet.'

'I'm mean,' Audrey said.

'You're so passive it makes me sick. Go on, then, what's the meanest thing you've ever done?'

'I was a really awful girlfriend.'

'I'm sure you once said *fuck* in front of his parents, or shrank his favourite jeans.' Pip cut fat slices from a loaf of bread. 'Julian's behaviour has a pattern. He had Claire, he had Sachini, he had Magda. That's not counting all the one-time girls. And now he's going to have you.'

'No he's not. We'd never do anything other than this.'

'That's what you think, but one day he'll lose interest and you'll be all cut. It's how he works.' Pip turned from the bench. The smooth silver breadknife was left spinning. 'So how tough can you be?'

Too late for tough: they'd started.

Julian only came to her when he got home late, or when he was drunk and wanted to fuck. Audrey only wanted him when the loneliness was hard to bear. They didn't talk about it. They fucked urgently, cared for as long as it took to come. Afterwards they rolled away from each other. They never slept together: Audrey would always get up and go back to her own bedroom.

Julian allowed her to be mean. He picked away at her weakest spots. He was triumphant when she eventually snapped. She never felt confident around him. She was not interesting or clever enough. 'Let me *see* you,' he'd say. She hid under the sheets, too pale, too sharp. She could have cut him right back, but he wouldn't have cared. He left behind little alluvial deposits of anxiety.

Audrey wanted to think it wasn't about control, but there were hundreds of small struggles.

They kissed each other through the plastic shower curtain. It was like suffocating. Audrey could feel his teeth.

She took care to remember that it was convenient. She worked to be unsurprised when he came home late with a woman from the office, the same one as before. She told herself it cut both ways. She could do the same. Julian fucked in a hurry. He almost always came before she did. Sometimes when she knelt before him it was with a horrible feeling of supplication. Sometimes she did it without looking up at him once, testing how remote she could be. He didn't notice. She'd clutch at the meat around his hipbones and feel it was just that—meat—and by the time he was finished her knees were tattooed with the impressions of the rug.

A few times he got home from work early enough to walk down to the baths, where he knew she'd be. He never paid to get in. He walked straight past the unattended window where Audrey dropped her coins, or explained to the kid standing there—surf lifesaving uniform, open face—that his friend had forgotten something, and could he please just run down and give it to her. When she told him she liked to be alone when she swam, he snorted. *Do you wanna piss on the rocks? Mark your territory?* but he stopped coming.

There were easy times, too. Morning, she was in her bedroom, scrabbling in her handbag for her Opal card. Julian hanging in the doorway, toast crust in his mouth. 'Can you drive manual?' he asked.

She looked up. 'Yes.'

'Wanna help me do something tonight?'

'What, move a body?'

He was looking at a bike, an old Yamaha. 'Sounds like it's almost clapped-out, but the guy reckons he's got a roadworthy on it.' Julian was going to fix it up. Audrey imagined it decaying in the shed in the backyard. He was saying something about a piston kit and timing chains, and Audrey almost laughed—*Do you know anything about timing chains?*—but something bright and childlike in the way he was talking made her think of her brother.

She said she'd come. The bloke selling it was up in Budgewoi. Audrey couldn't have found it on a map.

'What time?' she asked.

'I dunno. We just started a new case. I'll try to get away as quick as I can.'

The traffic was heavy. Julian drove with the window down, elbow resting on the sill.

'Ev-er-y-one is fucking off out of the city for the weekend,' he hummed. The music was down low. His face was tired and cheerful. He was concentrating.

Audrey wondered if they were friends. She'd thought the highway would follow the coast, but they were travelling inland, and it was all green through the windows. Once in a while Julian would say *This is the Hawkesbury* or point out a turn-off. She couldn't work out how far away they were from the sea.

The bike was in the front yard of the guy's house. It was more slender than Audrey had expected. She'd imagined something ostentatious.

Julian stood with his arms crossed asking questions, looking it over. Audrey didn't know if he was bluffing or if he actually knew things about motorcycles and their mechanics. The seller was a guy in his fifties, Audrey guessed, full in the face, easy smile, broad chest. She toed the pebbles edging the dry grass, half-listening to their conversation. Julian went to test it. She stayed behind in the yard, made small talk with the owner, drank the glass of ginger beer he offered her, scratched his dog's belly.

Julian came back. It was decided. He paid cash for the bike. He gave Audrey his car keys. 'Come on. Let's get dinner before we drive back. I'm buying.'

She followed him, parked facing the creek, sat looking at the water while he ran into the shop. They drove in convoy to the beach. Audrey was turned around by the lakes, the inlets, the ocean, the creeks, surrounded by water on every side.

He'd bought crayfish, wrapped in newspaper. They sat on the beach and ate with their hands, cracked open the claws with his Swiss Army knife.

Audrey looked at him sideways and he said *What, what?*

'Crayfish, motorcycles. It feels extravagant. It's nice.'

'That bike is a piece of shit.'

'I'm not talking about the bike.' She wiped her hands on her thighs. 'The other day Pip said to me, "Julian does exactly what he wants to do."'

'Yeah?' He folded up the paper into a loose square. 'That's good. Philippa, the ideologically pure altruist. Julian, the young libertine.'

'Don't twist it. I'm not passing judgement. I said it's nice.'

They drove home separately. Julian was in front, riding in the centre of the road. Audrey turned up the radio in his car and sang to herself all the way home.

Flint

Audrey saw a poster for a gig, a band she knew from home. They were launching an EP. Claire grimaced.

'Sorry, comrade,' she said. 'I've got no one to look after El. I can't ask Julian this week. He's being an arsehole. And my parents are in Cairns at the moment.'

Audrey asked a woman from work, shyly; she asked Julian, but he was lethargic about it, and she would not cajole him.

She went to Marrickville by herself. It was a warm evening, still light when she got there. The smokers were clustered on the pavement outside. Audrey could only dimly remember what it felt like to be a part of a group like that: the walks to friendly pubs where she'd always run into someone she knew, struggling into stockings at the last minute to go and see Minh's band on some filthy stage, saying goodbyes on the cold street afterwards.

Being alone made her timid. The girl at the door did not smile. Audrey got drunk while she watched the support acts, standing by the bar, then wriggled her way between shoulders to the front. Being alone made it easier. The crowd was gentle; it was a Thursday. Everyone stood patiently under the red lights.

Audrey had seen the band play before, an earnest, jangly garage rock that made her sentimental. Songs for drives on sunny days, windows down; songs for nights at the Corner, where she'd drink to get loose in the limbs; songs playing from the radio in the afternoons when friends came round. Audrey kept watching, kept her body moving in mild agreement with the drums, but she was bereft.

The room emptied out quickly. Audrey had another glass of wine. In a mirror she saw herself, drunk and blurry, and was glad she was alone with her hazy grief.

The buses had stopped running. She stood on the footpath trying to hail a taxi, and finally called Julian. He came to get her at once.

He watched her as she fastened her seatbelt.

'You didn't have to go by yourself,' he said.

'I wouldn't have wanted you to come along because of that. I just wanted to see some rock and roll.'

'Have you been crying?'

'Yes.' She wiped her nose and laughed. Julian switched on the interior light. She said, 'Oh, don't,' and he turned it off again.

'Are you all right?' he asked.

A groan forced its way up out of her chest, an ugly sound. She looked out the window at the unlit buildings. 'Thanks for picking me up.'

He edged away from the kerb. The streets flickered by, slow and yellowed under the streetlamps. Audrey saw signs for the airport. When they got to Anzac Parade he turned left, instead of down Rainbow Street, and she asked where they were going.

'I want a thickshake,' Julian said.

'Can't you wait till we get home?'

'Nah. I want chips.'

The McDonald's opposite the university was lit up. Its Australian flag flicked limply in the fuggy night. Julian paid for his food and they sat out on the stair at the entrance. He fished fries from the paper bag, saying, 'God, this is so good,' and Audrey watched him. His legs sprawled out on the asphalt.

'Don't you want any? You must be hungry. You're pretty fucked.' He wiped his hands on the cheeseburger wrapper. A bit of lettuce hung from his top lip.

Audrey began to laugh. '*I'm* fucked,' she said.

He stood and held out his hand. 'Come on. Let's go home.'

Her supervisor asked if she'd be interested in a five-day intensive family-therapy workshop. Audrey said yes. She was still photocopying pages from psycho-oncology journals to read on the way home. They had titles like 'Transitioning to Survivorship' and 'Psychosocial Inventories for Siblings of Children and Young People with Progressive Malignant Diseases'. It all made sense, but sometimes she still felt clumsy. In a family session earlier in the week, the child's mother and father had ended up just talking to each other, with Audrey barely facilitating. At the end they'd both shaken her hand and thanked her graciously, but she felt as if she'd done nothing at all. *That's okay*, one of the other workers had said. *Sometimes you just need to be there, providing the context for discussions they wouldn't have at home.* But Audrey wasn't sure.

'There's also a clinical skills course,' Henry said. 'It's not a professional development requirement, and I know you're on contract, but if you're looking at doing this longer term it might be worth a thought.'

Audrey hadn't thought past the end of her contract. He smiled. 'You're doing a really good job,' he said. 'You came into it with no warm-up. It's different from child protection.'

'I guess it's still child-focused,' she said.

'Yeah, but the goalposts are pretty different.' They were standing in the social work department, Henry with a hand on the door. He had a neatly trimmed beard, thick brows, eyes that made him look perpetually consoling. It was the right face for his job, Audrey thought. He reminded her of a German shepherd.

'Anyway,' he said, 'let me know.'

On the train she thought about her old job. She was careful not to remember it as easier than it had been. She'd felt out of her depth for a year, maybe more, at the Preston office. But eventually everything was easier. Whatever meagre reputation she'd had was of a nonjudgemental, dogged worker. She'd felt capable until she hadn't, at the end.

She got off the train early, hoping to catch Claire and Elliott at home. They were blundering through the front door. 'I'm glad it's you!' Claire said. 'I'm about to drop El at tennis near Mum and Dad's, but I've got to go to the wholesaler after that. Do you want to come for a drive? I can shout you some baby's breath.'

They drove through suburbs Audrey didn't recognise. She tried to map it all out in her head, but the city was still a stranger. The van's air conditioning cut in and out. Audrey felt sweat collecting behind her knees.

Claire knew everyone at the market. Audrey moved idly up and down the aisles, scanning the flowers, saying their names to herself. She could hear Claire's laugh. Once her face appeared above a bunch of gladioli. *Come here a sec*, she said, and tugged at Audrey's arm. She led her into a refrigerated storeroom. Audrey felt the chill of the concrete floor through the soles of her sandals.

'Isn't it better in here?' Claire said. She put a hand to Audrey's head like she was checking for fever. She crouched down by a bucket of carnations, white spattered with red. 'Once, when I was in TAFE,' she said, 'I pulled out a bunch of hyacinths, I think. They had fat stems. And I felt something against my hand, and it was a rat. It had gone stiff in the bottom of the bucket.'

• • •

226

Audrey came home to an empty house. She ate a nectarine right down to the stone, juice spilling between her fingers. She waited for Julian. She lined up her nectarine pits on the table. She made dinner. She lay on her bed and talked to Emy: her heart contracted when she saw the pixelated face on her laptop screen. She waited for hours.

When he finally arrived he was wasted. He collapsed on the couch and asked for a drink of water. Audrey filled a glass from the tap, but by the time she returned he'd already gone upstairs to his room.

She pushed open his door. His limbs were flung out at odd angles, the sheets puckered around his groin. Face crumpled into the pillow, lips parted, eyes half-open.

'Move over,' Audrey said, shutting the door behind her. 'I'm getting in.'

'Not tonight,' Julian grunted.

'Nice try.'

'Not tonight,' he said again. 'I'm really fucked.'

Audrey stopped short, arms poised to strip off her singlet.

'Oh—all right.' And he was asleep.

Her hands flew apart in frustration. She felt ugly and base, standing there in her underwear.

She was in the change rooms at the baths, peeling off her bathers, when her phone rang. She let it go, thinking she'd call back when she got home, but the ringing started again.

'Hello?' She held the thing away from her dripping hair, her face.

'Oh, thank Christ, Audrey, listen, do you know where Julian is?' Claire was crying.

'No, he's probably still at work, or—what's happened? Are you all right?'

'We're at the Children's. We've been in an accident. Elliott and me. Someone ran a red light and slammed straight into the side of the car. They've taken El into surgery, and I can't get on to Julian.'

'Oh, shit.' The blood had drained to her feet. She tried to think of what to do. 'He said he was finishing up on a case this week, but I can't remember when. He could be working late. What if—I'll come and meet you. We can keep trying him.'

Frank was in the kitchen cutting up vegetables. He lifted his face to smile at Audrey as she lurched through the door, but he saw her face. He'd turned off the stove, grabbed his car keys before she'd even finished the sentence. She dialled Julian's number again and again as they drove up Dudley Street.

'Where's his office?' Frank asked.

'I don't even know. Up near the state library, I think.'

'Right in the guts. I'll never get there in the traffic.' He pulled up to the kerb. 'Better if I just keep trying to call.'

He leaned over the console and gave her a quick, awkward hug.

Inside Claire was pacing. A cut above her left eye had been sutured. When she saw Audrey she stopped walking and held out her arms.

'Oh, Clairy.'

Claire's weight fell against her. They sat down on a bench.

'He's okay. He's okay,' Claire said. 'He's in recovery. It just took so long, and I didn't know what was happening, and I can't reach Julian. He was on the side that was hit.' She dragged her sleeve across her face. 'We were in the little Honda, not the shop van.'

'What did they say? Is he conscious?'

'Not yet. He ruptured his spleen. They had to remove a kidney. When the ambos took off his T-shirt his tummy was all purple.'

She put her head between her knees. She said *Fuck, I'm going to be sick*, but she didn't move. Audrey handed her a polystyrene cup of water. In the carpark she tried to call Julian again, reached his voicemail.

'Listen, Julian—' The anger evaporated the minute she started.

She began again. 'Everything's okay. Elliott's come through it all really well. If you get this, don't worry. Everything's okay.'

When she went back inside, Claire was talking to a young woman in surgical scrubs whose voice was too low for Audrey to hear. Claire had a hand over her mouth. Eventually she said, 'I'm really, really grateful, but I don't want to hear everything right now. I just want to see him.'

The doctor nodded, murmured something else. Claire glanced up at Audrey.

'Still can't get on to him,' Audrey said.

'It's okay. My parents are on their way. I can see him now.'

'Do you want me to go to yours and get you some clean clothes?'

'Oh,' Claire said, 'that's good of you.'

There was a mottled bruise across her chest where the seatbelt had done its job.

Audrey caught a cab to Redfern. The driver kept the meter on while she ran inside and collected things hastily. It was strange being in the house alone. It was empty without Elliott.

She tried Julian again on the way back to the hospital. There was an enormous, white-knuckled fist of a moon down low. She realised she was clenched, sitting in the front seat of the taxi. The plastic bags cut into her fingers.

After she paid she stood outside helplessly. She didn't even think she'd be allowed into the intensive care unit. Her phone vibrated in her hand: Julian.

'Where are you?' he asked roughly.

'In the carpark. I just got back. Where are you?'

'Here, with Claire and El. I'll meet you outside the ICU.'

Something heaved inside her chest when she saw him. He was ashen. His tie was choked into a knot, tugged to one side, like he'd yanked at it.

Audrey dropped the plastic bags at her feet. 'How's he doing?'

'Fine. He woke up for a bit, but he's asleep again. The doctor keeps saying how quickly kids bounce back from stuff like this. I reckon she's said it ten times. But she says the surgery went really well. Have you seen her? She looks about eight.'

'Where were you tonight?' Audrey asked suddenly.

'I was out.'

She looked at the flecked linoleum floor. 'Out.'

'Yes.' He toed one of the bags. 'I was in the office till eight. Then we went for drinks after. That all right with you?'

'And you didn't check your messages? You didn't hear your phone ring once? Claire's been trying to call since six-thirty.'

He rubbed his face. 'I had about a thousand missed calls from Claire and twice as many from you. I didn't think anything had happened for a second. I just thought Clairy was calling to chat. I thought *you* were being intense. I freaked out. It made me not want to call back.'

Audrey was so angry she could have hit him. The rage was in her bloodstream. In that second she was blind with it.

'Not everything's about you,' she said.

Julian looked at the wall. Audrey picked up the plastic bags. 'There's a thermos of coffee in that one. And Elliott's insect book is in there, when he feels like it.'

Julian said nothing. Audrey folded her arms. 'Say hi to Claire for me,' she said. She turned to go.

'I don't know what Claire plans on doing tonight, but whatever she does, I think I should stay with her,' Julian called after her.

'Yes.'

'Well, I might see if she wants to come to ours.'

'Do whatever you want.'

She pushed out of the hospital, took a second to work out which road led home. She walked halfway around the building and started down St Pauls Street, past the cinemas, past Bat Country. Somewhere near the park she burst into tears. By the time she got home she'd stopped crying, but her head was aching.

Pip and Frank and Tess were all sitting in the kitchen, three tender faces.

'Elliott's okay,' she said.

'We heard,' Frank said. He gave a small smile. 'Tough kid.'

She woke wanting to call Adam. The house was still. She washed her hair, combed it sitting on the couch in the lounge room. She and Nick had never celebrated their anniversaries, but she knew exactly when Katy had driven to the reservoir. She'd been counting down the days.

It was too early to go to work. She dressed in front of her mirror. Her wet hair left a cold patch on her back. She walked down to the park and sat on the burnt grass. Just before seven she called Adam.

'Did I wake you?' she asked.

'No, I've been up for a while. Couldn't sleep.'

'We're older than her now,' Audrey said. She was filled with a colicky sadness.

'Do you ever think about why she did it?'

'No. I understand that.'

It was a mild, airless Sydney morning, all pink light and rotting frangipani. Adam was silent, but she knew he was still there.

'You know when you're a kid how adults would go, "This year's just flying!"' he said at last, 'and you'd think, "What do you mean? A year's the longest fucking thing there is."'

'It's gone fast, hasn't it?'

'And it feels like all this stuff's happened,' said Adam. 'It's all changed. If somebody had said to me a year ago that you'd be up there, I'd have a real job—I wouldn't have believed it.' Audrey tried to picture where he was standing. Maybe in his kitchen; maybe on the tiny balcony with its view of the Grey Street beat, cigarette between knuckles. 'I'm going on an excursion today. To the Vic Market, with a bunch of thirteen-year-old girls. And Minh's started leaving his shit at my place. It's weird.'

'Yeah, but it's good-weird, isn't it?'

'Yeah,' he said. His voice was crackly with fatigue. 'It is.'

'I really miss her.'

'Me too.'

'And I know you're not supposed to say things like this, but for ages after she did it, I was so mad at her.'

'Me too,' Adam said again, and gave a watery laugh. 'The bitch.'

They said goodbye. Audrey took off her shoes and walked barefoot up the hill to the bus stop.

It was a long, strange day. She ran from family to family, room to room. In each one somebody was trying very hard not to die. A parent gave her a laminated card with a picture of the Virgin Mary. A child gave her a sheet of butcher's paper with 'A's scrawled all over it. *Your special letter*, he said, and Audrey tucked it into her satchel. At lunch she pushed out to the carpark and sat on the concrete stair with her coffee, sun-blind. She watched two ambos split a sandwich wrapped in wax paper. She thought of Nick, that courtyard at St Vincent's where he'd meet her, crunching a pear.

She took the slow route home. Bus down Belmore Road, head resting on the window. Audrey remembered the phone call from Katy's father, how she'd known something was wrong when she heard his voice. The air had gone right out of her, and Nick had said *What, what, what's happened*, crouched beside her. Later, when they were all adrift, Adam in his frenzied grief, Audrey had imagined she might have come across a signal or a clue. But Katy was a dark blur. She'd left no explanation, no notes, just an exhausting blackness that yielded no reason. She was an insect caught in amber, a leaf in resin.

She'd never be anywhere but in the front seat of that car with its windows sealed.

Up Oberon Street, almost home, when her phone rang.

Her sister's voice. 'Can you talk?'

'Of course.'

Audrey stepped out into the warm evening.

'I'm worried about Maman,' Irène said. 'I know you think I'm a panic merchant, but I wouldn't call unless I had to.'

'What's happened?'

'I think she's sick again. She keeps talking about money, but she still hasn't found a job. She's worried about you. She keeps telling me she's seen signs in number plates. Last week I took the kids to hers for the day. When I came to pick them up Lucas was screaming in his playpen, and she was in her bedroom with the door closed. With some bloke.'

'What?'

'They were in the bedroom, with Zoe watching TV in the next room, and Lucas beside himself.'

Audrey stopped walking. 'That's awful, Irène, I'm so sorry.'

'She's planning a trip to Europe by herself. I don't know where she's getting the money. I'm worried it might be a sort of last hurrah. You know, a big exit.'

'Shit.'

'I need to know what you did with her after Dad's funeral. I haven't been able to reach her since Friday. Does Dr Lawrence have a number? I don't know what to do. What did you do last time?'

Audrey reached the gate. Julian and Pip were sitting on the front porch drinking beers, and she waited until she was inside before she answered. 'I tricked her. I told her I was having a mental-health assessment, and asked her to come with me.'

The sisters were silent. At last Audrey sighed. 'I'll call Dr Lawrence.'

Sylvie's number rang out. Audrey sat with her back against her

233

bedroom door and called Bern.

'Have you heard from Maman?'

'Yeah, actually, she was round here this morning.'

'What, at yours?'

Bernie laughed. 'You could *not* sound any more surprised.'

'Is she all right?'

'She's fine. I'm helping her update her CV.'

'How about more generally? Irène said she'd been pretty intense recently. Something about Europe.'

'Oh, it was just one of those things—you know, like how she thought about moving to Bright a while ago? You know what Maman's like.'

'If she needs help, it's not up to you.'

Another pause before he answered. 'I think she's doing okay. She's rapid-cycling. She's probably not as bad as Irène said.'

Audrey could only get little words out. 'Thanks, Bernie.'

'For what?' he asked. 'I'm not doing anything.'

Audrey wished he'd have the grace to accept her gratitude. They mumbled goodbyes and disconnected. The phone was warm in her hand. It was still early, the evening sun streaming in. She wanted to sleep next to someone, but it'd be hours before Julian was home from work, and she didn't have the energy for another brush-off. She shut the blinds and crawled between the sheets.

She woke after nightfall, thinking it was very early in the morning, but downstairs the television was blaring and the others were eating and talking. The day would not end.

Still thick with sleep, Audrey made a cup of tea and took it back to her bedroom.

Julian loped down the hallway and stood at the foot of her bed, announced he was going down to the pub. She nodded and said *Have fun*, and he turned to go—but at the doorway he paused.

'D'you want to come?'

'Where are you going?'

'Just the big one up the street. You coming, or not?'

They sat overlooking the water. Audrey still felt disoriented. She was hungry. They ordered burgers, and Julian laughed at her appetite. They didn't have much to say to each other. They were both tired.

'All day I was looking forward to leaving work,' Julian said, 'and now I'm just thinking about all the shit I have to do tomorrow. Sometimes you can switch off, but sometimes your brain won't stop. I feel nuts.'

Audrey's fingertips had left greasy smudges on her wine glass. 'My dad used to have this saying—if you put a screaming man behind a curtain, you can still hear him,' she said. 'I think that's sort of what he meant.'

'I've never heard that.'

'I think he probably made it up.'

'I don't know if I get it.'

Audrey shrugged. She went back to pulling apart her bread.

'You okay?' Julian asked. 'You look a bit beaten.'

'I'm fine.'

Julian pulled out his phone, tapped at its lit screen as though he were alone.

They walked home along the beach, not speaking much. Audrey waded in the shallows. She stopped to look at a plane flying in and thought about how she didn't even notice them anymore. When she'd first moved here they'd seemed so loud and close she'd waited for one to crash through the ceiling. Julian was waiting up ahead, still wearing his shoes.

'That's a nice dress,' he said.

Audrey knew he was looking at the wet cotton plastered to her thighs, and she felt tired of him, but she kissed him anyway. He tilted his head to the air and said, 'I love how you just get it. It's like you've got no expectations at all.'

Audrey stared at him. His expression was oblivious, placid. They were still standing close.

'Don't be a dick,' she said. 'You can't just reel people in and out.'

'What do you mean?'

'I mean—there's a difference between having no strings, and treating somebody like shit.'

'I'm sorry,' said Julian. 'I didn't mean to be mean.'

'Are you an only child?'

'What?' He dropped back. 'I said I was sorry. Is this about the hospital the other night?'

'You seem to think I want to own you or something, and I don't.'

The two of them looked at the sand in speechless discomfort.

'We're not getting along any more, are we?' said Julian after a while. 'We'll just have to get a divorce.'

Adam came up to visit for the Labour Day weekend. He, Audrey and Claire went to dinner. They sat at a table on the pavement. They drank champagne. Adam and Claire had not caught up in years, and they beamed at each other, spoke in punchlines and bursts of laughter. It reminded Audrey of Katy, but in a happy way: she remembered what it was to share Adam with someone else.

Claire dropped them both at Neptune Street afterwards. She came inside to say hello to the others. They made a funny ensemble in the lounge room. Julian had been looking after Elliott. El was thinner after the accident; the anaesthetic had made him sick and he hadn't eaten for a week. But he'd returned to school. He'd bounced back quickly, as the paediatric surgeon said he would. He showed Audrey his scars. Still healing: they made her mouth taste metallic. *You don't even need your spleen*, he explained.

He and Julian had fallen asleep on the couch with eyeliner

236

moustaches pencilled over their lips.

'We tried to give El a Dalí one,' Pip said, 'but he looks more like Gomez from *The Addams Family*.'

Elliott lifted his head and gave a sleepy, wicked smile. 'Frank said, "You're shithouse at keeping still, mate,"' he drawled, and they laughed.

Adam did his wonderful trick of settling in, putting everyone at ease, making jokes as though he were the host of a party.

When he climbed into bed beside Audrey that night, he was quiet.

'You look really good, Spence,' he said. 'Since you moved up here, you look better. Come here. I'll spoon you.'

Audrey lay facing the window. The streetlight cut through the open blinds. She fit into the curve of Adam's body. They'd slept like that as teenagers. They'd top-and-tailed with Katy, the three of them squished into her bed.

'Adam?'

'Hm?'

'What do you want to do tomorrow?'

'Let's think about it tomorrow. Let's get up and eat breakfast and think about it then.'

'What do you think of the house?' Audrey asked.

'I like it a lot. I'm glad you've got friends to play with,' Adam said. 'But can I tell you something? I don't think I like Julian.'

'I don't think I do, either. We fuck. That's all.'

'Don't be so *hard* about it.' Adam was speaking into her neck, brushing her hair with his hand. 'I don't recognise you when you get like that.'

'It's just need.'

'I know. I know what it is.'

The powerline hummed out the window. Adam went on stroking her hair, as gentle and clumsy as a child.

Audrey had not been to the hairdresser in over a year. A sunny girl snipped at her head until the floor around the chair was covered in straggly dark locks.

At home Julian looked her over. 'I liked it better before.'

'I didn't do it for you,' Audrey said.

His chin was set in its impossible way. Audrey kept her face very still.

'Okay,' Julian said at last. He gave a short laugh.

But in the morning he lay beside her. The day had begun. Pip and Frank were already banging around in the kitchen. Little sprays of their conversation cut through the bedroom door. The window was open; the air smelled like cut grass, like a Sunday.

'Where'd you get that bruise?' Julian asked, stroking her thigh.

'I don't know.' Audrey bent her head to examine it, an ugly blue-yellow inkspill. 'Must have banged it on something.' She lay back. Julian traced its outline with his fingertips, pressed his lips to it. Audrey was looking at the sky through the window. She was thinking she had to get up and go to work.

'I'll be home early tonight. Do you want to do something?' Julian asked.

'Like what?'

'I don't know, go out somewhere. Or we could just hang out here. Watch a movie.'

Audrey was surprised, but she said *Okay*. He seemed pleased.

They ate breakfast together in a burst of shyness. Julian rinsed his cereal bowl and stood in the middle of the kitchen.

'I'll see you tonight, I s'pose,' he said.

A patient died at work, and Audrey got home late. Julian wasn't there. She washed her face and poked at her hair. She sat at the kitchen table. She called once, but he didn't answer.

She took her towel from the clothesline, draped it around her shoulders like a boxer before a match. She went down to the baths. There were fires in the hills again; the sky over the ocean was hazy, the air hot in her lungs. She made herself keep going. Nothing hurt until she hauled herself out of the pool.

She dried off and pulled on an old T-shirt of Nick's, pausing to smell the fabric. Of course it didn't smell like him any more. She'd been wearing it for years.

She heard someone moving around in the kitchen, but it was only Frank.

'*Bonjour*,' he said.

'Hello.' She dropped her bag on the table beside his. 'Where are you off to?'

'Townsville, actually,' he said, 'for my sister's graduation. She's a PhD now.'

'Oh, wow. What's she doing?'

'Something about immunology in tropical health? I actually have no clue. I kind of forgot I was going, things have been so busy.'

A horn blasted outside. Frank collected his bag and wallet.

'Have fun,' Audrey said.

'Thanks, mate. See you Saturday.' He started down the hall, and then turned around. 'Hey, Julian was looking for you. I don't know where he's gone now, though. Maybe call him.'

She called Sylvie instead. She helped her rehearse for a job interview, receptionist for a motel in Frankston.

'I don't think they're going to ask you these kinds of questions,' she said. 'It won't be like the bank.' But Sylvie made her ask again and again until she'd memorised responses, like a schoolgirl sitting an exam.

'I don't even have my *diplôme* at high school,' she said.

Audrey could imagine her skittish hand taking notes.

'They'll just want to know that you're trustworthy, that you can read and write and take bookings and stuff,' she said.

239

'Don't be patronising to me. I need this job.'

'I know you do. Okay. What are your weaknesses?'

She took a plate of toast to her room. There was a note tucked under the enamel mug of water by her bed.

> Audrey,
>
> I've gone out with Claire, hope you don't mind—she just wanted to catch up before the weekend. We're headed to the Crix if you want to join us.
>
> Julian

Fuck you, she thought dimly.

Pip came home around seven-thirty. They watched a report on the bushfires together, perched at either end of the couch.

'March is late in the year, isn't it?' Audrey said.

'It's been so hot, though. It's all so dry up there. All it takes is a lightning strike.' Pip shivered. 'Be an awful way to go.'

Audrey went out to water the garden. The heat was sticky. Pip leaned against the bricks, keeping her company, twirling a hibiscus between her fingers. Before Audrey turned off the tap, she said *Can you spray me with it, just quick?* and Audrey did it obediently, without thinking. Pip scrunched up her eyes, opened them again. Water was dripping from her lashes. She laughed.

'Now do me,' Audrey said.

Julian came home alone after midnight. Audrey had fallen asleep hours before. He walked straight in, collapsed on the end of her bed.

'Did you have a good night?' she asked.

'It was fun,' he said. 'You could have come, you know. It wasn't some exclusive thing.'

'Claire probably wanted to spend time with you.'

'We were just hanging out.'

She watched him pull his shirt over his head, kick off his jeans.

She turned back the quilt. He climbed in beside her and she turned to him.

'When I got your note I was disappointed. You said you'd be here tonight, and you weren't.'

There was a pause, and Julian laughed. He scratched his head.

'Fuck, Audrey. I didn't mean to *disappoint* you.'

'It's all right. I shouldn't have waited.'

'You don't sound mad,' Julian said.

'I'm not.'

'Do you want to sleep with me tonight?'

'No,' Audrey said, 'and it's not because you went out with Claire. I just don't feel like it.'

'All right.'

Somehow they fell asleep. It was the simplest thing to do.

Train home from work past the mason's, MON-U-MEN-TAL-ME-MOR-I-ALS, the stadium, the RSLs, the open drains, the water tower. Claire called.

'El's got tennis and then we're going to the Warren View for ten-dollar parmas. Are you still on your way home? Do you want to come?'

Claire picked her up at the station. Audrey said *Hi, Mum!* as she climbed into the van. Elliott held up his racquet as though he were about to hit her. Audrey flinched.

'Don't do that,' Claire said sharply. She swatted his arm.

Elliott looked wounded. 'I was only joking.'

They parked on Sydenham Road, and Elliott ran across the grass to join the other children. Audrey bought two cans of Coke from the servo next door. She and Claire sat on one of the vacant courts.

'I know this is awful, especially after the accident,' Claire said, 'but he's such hard work at the minute. We've just been at each other's throats.'

'It's not awful. What you're doing, with him and the shop—that's tough on your own.'

'We've both been out of sorts for the last month or so. I've been wondering if the anaesthetic did something to him.' She looked at Audrey hesitantly. 'It's silly. I'm not some anti-medication hippy. I just keep thinking, maybe it messed with his little brain.'

'There's the trauma of it, too,' Audrey said. The synthetic grass itched her thighs. 'It must have been terrifying. And he was very sick. He'd have a memory of it all somewhere. I believe in that stuff.'

'Julian doesn't. I tried to talk to him about it the other night. He was so dismissive, and I got to that irrational point of frustration, where you open your mouth to argue back and burst into tears.'

'Then you've lost all emotional credibility.'

'Yes!'

They smiled grimly at each other.

'He mentioned you the other day,' Claire said. 'He said you two had a bit of a thing.'

'We're only fucking.'

'I just wish you'd told me! I don't care.'

'That's what Julian said you'd say,' Audrey laughed, 'and Pip.'

'I don't! He's always going to be El's dad, but we do our own thing. He's the sort of person where you *can't* care what he does, or you'll have hurt feelings every day of the week.'

'I don't know why we're keeping on,' Audrey said. 'He makes me feel like I'm needy. I can't be bothered engaging with his shit, but if I turn him down it's like I'm playing into it.'

'I used to hit him. Really belt him. He can be such a deadshit. He'd go out for days and I'd be left with El, and I'd get so mad. I used to pummel him, and he'd just let me, as though he was accepting some kind of punishment.'

'I guess he was.'

Claire shook her head. 'Nothing punishes him. He's like flint.'

On the news they'd said it would be a cool night because there was no cloud cover. Audrey walked home, hugging herself for warmth. Soon it would be April and the baths would close earlier, and she'd only be able to swim on weekends.

The others were in the lounge room. The television was on, but Audrey sensed they'd been talking to each other, not watching it. Frank was sitting on the floor, a plate on his thighs. He offered his beer to her. She took a mouthful, handed it back.

'They're gonna sell the house,' said Pip.

Audrey dropped her bag. 'Wow.'

'We've got plenty of time,' Frank said. 'It'll take them months.'

Audrey glanced at Julian, expecting his face to be tight, but he grinned. 'It was too good to last, this place.'

'We had it cheap and easy for a long time,' Pip said.

'Reckon they'll knock it down and build apartments?' Julian said.

'Oh, don't,' Pip said, 'that's too sad.' She put a hand to the wall like it was a dog about to be put down.

Later Audrey sat on Julian's bed and watched him peel an orange. He could do it in one go, puncture it with his thumb and leave a curly corkscrew behind.

'My ex could do that,' she said. 'He used to peel them in the morning, then put them back in the skin to take to work.'

'Your ex.'

'Mm.'

'It's funny. I never thought about what you did before you came here. I mean, I know about your mum and your sister and your old job, but—I don't know. It was like you just appeared.'

'Sprang fully formed from someone's forehead like Athena.'

He stared at her.

'That's something else about Nick,' Audrey said. 'He knows all of this stuff about Greek mythology because his mum made him study classics in high school.'

'Did he become a teacher?'

'No. He's a paramedic.'

'Is his mum a teacher?'

'She works in a pharmacy,' Audrey said. They were both cross-legged, in their underwear. Julian held out half the orange to her and she took it.

'Where do you reckon you'll go after here?' Julian asked.

'I don't know. I guess it depends on what happens with work. Maybe somewhere around Marrickville or Newtown, if I stay at the hospital. What about you?'

'I've got no idea,' he said.

'You've got money. You could live anywhere. Double Bay.'

He looked at her, saw she was joking. She didn't want to fuck him any more. She went to the window, scissored open the blinds with her fingers. The black-and-white waves rolled in.

She turned back to Julian. 'Maybe you'll get a place by yourself.'

'I couldn't do that,' he said. He looked helpless, in pain.

'You are twelve years old.' She lay beside him, picked up the spiral of orange skin where he'd left it on top of the sheets. He watched her stretch it between her fingers.

'Go and get one from the kitchen,' he said, 'and I'll show you how to do it.'

Everyone was crawling. Audrey and Pip polished off a cask of wine in the backyard. After midnight Julian came and stood at the back door. The whites of his eyes shone.

'Me and Frank are going out.' He stuck his hands into his pockets. 'Come if you want.'

Pip sat up and looked from his face to Audrey's. 'That might be okay.'

'I'm drunk. I'm ready for bed,' Audrey said.

'Come on. It'll be good to get out.'

Julian stood there, looking at her from under his hair. Audrey shrugged.

Pip got ready quickly. Audrey caught a flash of her down the hallway: bare thighs, dark eyelids, loose hair. Audrey sat on the end of her bed and looked at her boots, at the cuffs of her jeans. She did not want to go. She felt nervous in a way she hadn't for a long time. Pip stuck her head around the doorway.

'Come on, you can't go out like *that*,' she said, but gently. 'See if I've got something.'

Pip was about Katy's size, but Audrey followed her into her room anyway.

'What are you two doing? It'll be morning before we get going,' bellowed Julian from the kitchen. Pip laughed and hissed. Audrey stood in her underwear as Pip fussed around her, pulling the clothes this way and that. She looked at herself in the mirror, ridiculous dress made to fit with tucks and safety-pins. Her shins stuck out like saplings. She was still wearing her flat R.M. Williams boots and woolly socks.

They took a cab. Audrey didn't know where she was; she wouldn't have known even if she'd been sober. The streets were unfamiliar to her in the dark. It began to rain. Water dribbled down the window. She watched the lit-up clinics and bars and theatres and peepshows running past in a stream of neon, backlit shopfronts, a church. Young girls ran out on stalky legs. They huddled together under awnings, cigarettes dangling from fingers, wearing identical dresses and matching grimaces. Beautiful boys with long eyelashes, moving like phantoms.

The taxi stopped on Oxford Street. On the footpath, Frank and Pip linked arms and sauntered off. Julian reached for Audrey's hand.

'You're freezing!' he said, and blew on her fingers.

They went into a warm cave. The throbbing of the bass matched

Audrey's heartbeat. Julian was in a generous mood. He handed her a shot of something honey-coloured. 'Here, this'll warm you up.'

She followed Pip to the bathroom, where girls leaned against the white-tiled walls. Pip squeezed between the bare shoulders in front of the mirror and dusted gold powder across her nose. Audrey leaned against the closed door of a cubicle and watched a pair of girls crouched on the floor as they extracted four white pills from a crumpled sheet of foil. One of them turned up her smooth face to the fluorescent light.

'Hot dress, babe,' she said to Audrey.

'Thanks,' Audrey said, laughing, 'babe.' She couldn't remember the last time she'd been in a place like this. She would have been seventeen, eighteen, still in school. She'd never liked the closeness of bodies, the boring, panicky thud of the music they played, the speed Adam had snorted cheerfully by the door. When he'd come up to visit he'd said *Let's get some drugs*, half-joking, but Claire found some pills. The three of them had sat on her living room floor, talking while they waited. It took a long time before Audrey felt anything.

'Are you in love with everyone?' Adam had asked.

'I'm not where you are,' Audrey said.

Claire stretched out on the floorboards. 'I am,' she'd said. 'I'm in love with both of you.'

Audrey sat back when it came, coldness in the arms, light and colour in her eyes. Adam started one of his stories: 'This one time a bunch of us went down to Blairgowrie for the long weekend and we had a party, and everyone got pretty fucked up. Audrey finished up spewing into the bathtub, and Katy and I were doing that sort of powerless laughing, where there's nothing you can do anyway, and after a while Audrey straightens up, wipes her face and goes, "I'm going to go and think about what I've done," like she was giving herself a time-out.'

'*The Naughtiest Girl Does a Vomit in the Bath,*' Claire said.

Audrey had felt better the next day, sailing on a wave of euphoria as she drove her friend back out to the airport. The stuff was still humming in her head.

The vibrations of the music echoed dully in the bathroom. The two girls with the pills were gone. Audrey couldn't watch Pip look at her mouth in the mirror any longer.

Out in the darkness the floor was sticky. Audrey had another drink by herself. She found Julian, and grabbed him by the wrists. 'Let's dance.'

'I don't dance. You don't, either.'

She dragged him into the thickness of bodies. He stood there and watched her spin. He leaned in to her ear.

'I feel like I'm watching a seizure.'

He was standing still while she danced, all staccato shoulders and jerky limbs.

'You're so grumpy,' Audrey said. She didn't know if he could hear her. 'You're so nasty about everything.'

'You don't care about anything,' Julian shouted over the music.

She reached up and kissed him to make him stop talking, hand behind his neck.

A shower of cheers from a nearby group. He took her hand and led her to a sofa in the corner, away from the bodies. She leaned her head on his shoulder. He petted her hair. She didn't care enough to move.

Pip reappeared and collapsed next to Audrey.

'I lost you,' she said, breathless. 'Let's go. I want some chips.'

Out on the wet pavement, they separated. Pip went home, and Audrey and Julian began to walk slowly through Hyde Park. Audrey felt dazed.

'I feel like I'll never get used to this city. I had no idea we were in Darlinghurst till the cab stopped.'

They walked all the way to the harbour, to the grassy flat by

Circular Quay, and sat by the water.

'This is where you bring a tourist,' Julian said.

'Your breath smells like whiskey,' Audrey said. Her ears were ringing.

'Your hair smells like a gross bar.'

They were too tired to speak. Audrey lay back on the wet grass and sang the Paul Kelly song about the bus between Melbourne and Sydney.

Julian groaned. 'Stop it. I feel like I'm in some bad suburban microdrama.'

'I sort of hate this view,' she said.

'Don't look at it, then.'

He took off his jacket and put it around her shoulders, and she was surprised.

They got home just after six o'clock, clattering through the door and down the hall, removing shoes and hissing *Sh* at each other. Audrey made some tea and two-minute noodles. They ate greedily. She sat at the table. Julian stood and slurped over the kitchen sink. Pip strolled out of the shower wearing a towel. She poured a cup of coffee.

'You fucking pig,' she snorted, watching him eat. Steam rose from her bare shoulders.

Julian shrugged. 'Morning,' he said, and went on shovelling noodles into his mouth.

Audrey couldn't stand him.

She'd been planning to fall into bed, but it was almost light. She put on her shoes again, and walked down to the beach. The air was still and cold. She saw the streetlamps glow off, a flock of gulls; people out with their dogs, wrapped up in sensible hats, waterproof jackets and walking shoes. Audrey was in Pip's black dress, safety-pinned under the armpits, and a big coat. The middle-aged walkers nodded greetings to one another, and offered tentative *Good mornings* to Audrey.

The sun went up and over the sea. Audrey sat on the sand. She turned up the collar of her coat to protect her ears from the wind.

The sky was grey and yellow. She was done.

She walked home with her hands deep in her coat pockets. At the corner of Beach and Carr she ran into Frank, out on his morning jog.

'I don't know why I thought this'd be a good idea. I'm going to spew,' he said. He stopped running on the spot. 'Are you all right?'

Audrey looked up at him. 'I think I need to go home.'

'Are you all right?' he said again.

'I mean home to Melbourne.'

'Well,' Frank said, and grinned. 'What an epiphany!'

They stood there in the grey morning. At last he nodded. He gave her a quick, tight hug. 'I just plunged a coffee. Go home and get it before Pip does.'

Tombs For Better Times

There was an afternoon tea for her at work, thank-you and good-luck cards, drinks at the Tavern afterwards. Audrey crossed the road to the station and thought it was probably the last time she'd ever walk out of that hospital. The last time she'd take the train out past Parramatta, maybe. The wine was warm in her arms.

It rained. Audrey and Julian went to a pub in Surry Hills, the Clock, sat on the balcony looking down at the wet street. In the cab going home they kissed once. Audrey leaned her head on his shoulder without expecting any tenderness, but he smoothed her cheek, her hair.

It was just turning dark when they got home. Pip was good-humoured. The three of them pranced around the kitchen and told stories. Audrey mostly listened. Julian and Pip were speaking about memories that did not include her, but not unkindly. When they fell silent Pip said *What about when we went to the snow this year and Audrey hooked up with that weird guy at LJ's?* Julian's face slid sideways, checking on Audrey. She smiled to show him it was okay.

'Remember,' Pip said to Julian, 'you followed them back to his room? Like the older brother.'

Julian was still looking at Audrey. 'You weren't well, mate,' he said.

'I don't think I'd had that much to drink.'

'That was just after you moved in,' Pip said. 'I hardly knew you. You were so quiet. I just remember looking up, and in the time it'd taken me to finish my drink, you'd pulled the moves on that guy, and I went *She's more of a loose cannon than I thought*.'

Audrey laughed with them because it didn't matter any more, and maybe it was funny, now.

Just before nine Claire turned up with Elliott in her arms.

'I've got five hundred corsages to do for this debutante,' she said. 'Please.'

Julian hoisted El over one shoulder and carried him upstairs. He looked back at Audrey. He mouthed *Sorry*. She said *Don't be*, and she meant it. She helped Julian tuck him into bed.

In the kitchen Pip was making hot toddies. Claire's face was wet.

'I'm sorry. I don't know what's wrong with me. I'm just finding him really tough at the minute. It's never been like this, and I know the timing's really bad, and I'm sorry—'

'Hey,' Julian said. 'It's okay. This is the deal, it's always been the deal. You call whenever you want.'

'He's got money for the tuckshop tomorrow, he just needs you to help him add up the order.'

'We'll do it in the morning.'

Claire stood up. She pressed her hands to her cheeks. 'I should go. I've got that much to do. Thanks. Sorry for being so nuts.'

'You okay to drive?'

'I'm fine, Julian.'

They stood at the front door to wave her off.

'It is actually a pain in the arse to take him tomorrow morning,'

Julian said to the dark street. 'Unless I drop him at seven-thirty. Is that legal?'

'I can take him,' Audrey said. 'Leave your car keys out.'

When she left Sydney Julian's beat-up motorcycle was still in the shed, untouched. She said goodbye to him in the morning. He was going to work and in a rush. Afterwards she went down to the baths. It was a cool morning. There were still tan lines on her skin, but they were already fading. They belonged to a different season.

Claire drove her out to the airport in the evening. Pip came too, sat in the back seat next to Elliott. They left the house hours early, went down to La Perouse for fish and chips. Elliott sang along with the radio in his high, breathy voice. The three women talked rapidly. They sat in the back of Claire's van to watch the sun go down. There were no flowers, just corrugated flooring that dug into Audrey's bum through the drop sheet.

'What'll you do when you get back to Melbourne?' Pip asked.

'I don't know yet. I feel as though I just left.' Audrey crumpled her paper napkin. She watched Elliott poking holes in his potato cake.

'You'll be fine,' Claire said.

Audrey nodded. 'I know.'

They cheered for the sunset, huddled together, the four of them shouting *Good job!* and *Thank you!* and *You're getting even better!*, clapping and whistling. The toilet block was already locked for the night. Audrey and Pip squatted in the long shadows beside it to piss.

They shared a few glasses of overpriced wine at the airport. Claire and Pip hugged her one by one. Audrey was surprised at how tender they were, how orphaned she felt. Elliott flung his arms around her neck. Claire stood there with her lovely yellow hair falling across her face, and then took Audrey in her arms again.

'See ya, sweet pea,' she said in her ear. 'El and I were thinking of taking a trip to Melbourne in winter, so we'll see you then.'

And then they left, waving and hooting out the doors. Audrey walked to the gate and sat by the window. Already it was strange to be alone. The airport noise hummed and hissed just loud enough to keep her from falling asleep.

The flight was delayed by one hour, two. Melbourne fog. She phoned Adam. *Don't leave yet.* By the time she shuffled onto the plane, it was due to have landed at Tullamarine.

Flying in over Melbourne she saw the glowing grid of streets below. The bay was just a black space. Adam was waiting in the terminal. She'd half-expected Minh to be there, too, but Adam was alone. She was relieved to have him to herself. He took streets she didn't recognise, past the shipping yards and factories under the bridge. He said *So how was it all left with Julian in the end.* She didn't know what to say to make it simple.

'He can do that thing Nick does,' she said, 'when he peels an orange.'

'That's not what I meant,' Adam said, and they were laughing and the streetlight was falling yellow across his face, and she wanted it to be the two of them in that car forever.

She waited for Vanessa in a café near the office. She was glad for the neutral territory. Something in her was scared of seeing all those people, her friends. She was afraid that she could walk back into the building and nothing would have changed.

Vanessa hugged her, made a fuss of her hair. When she said *Tell me about Sydney*, heaved her chair closer to the table, it was hard to know what to say.

'I had really good supervision,' Audrey said. 'I learned heaps. They seemed to have a huge budget for professional development. I read lots of trauma theory.' She watched Vanessa drop an artificial sweetener pill into her coffee. 'We had a meeting and they offered to extend my contract. I think if I'd started in a clinical setting like that, straight out of uni, I would have stuck with it.'

'Why didn't you?'

'The house I was living in—I was renting a room—they're going to sell it. I knew my unpaid leave here was almost up.' It sounded foolish. Vanessa waited. 'In paediatric oncology, all you can really do is make everyone more comfortable,' Audrey said at last.

'That's all we do,' Vanessa said.

'No, it's different.'

In the hospital there was no fight. Everyone was already on the kid's side. The parents trusted her. And still there was no stopping metastasis. It didn't matter how hard she worked: sometimes the worst still happened.

'We miss you,' Vanessa said, 'and I hope you come back, but I never expected you to. And that's not a statement on you, it's a statement on the job.'

'I want to,' Audrey said.

'I want you to, as well, but that's selfish. Have a think about it.'

Audrey said she would.

By the end of April it was already winter in Melbourne. She went to look at a flat in Yarraville. When she came out the sky was dusky. Walking back to the station she cut through a park where the leaves shivered in the night. On one side, a train clattered towards the western suburbs; on the other, the houses crouched meekly.

At home Adam was sprawled on the couch. He had a glass of wine waiting for her.

'How'd you go?'

'Okay.' She sat down next to him. He reached for the remote control, muted the television. 'I don't know if I want to move into another houseful of strangers,' she said.

'Wanna live by yourself again?'

'Yeah. I think I do.' She fiddled with a loose thread at her sleeve. 'It'll be all new. I haven't lived by myself since I was nineteen.'

'Have you called Nick?' Adam asked.

'I don't think he and I are very compatible as flatmates anymore.'

'To let him know you're *back*, you dag.'

'I was joking.' Audrey was itching in her bones. 'Do you want to come for a walk?'

It was the season for wet leaves on car windscreens. All the lights were doubled on the wet bitumen. The council bins outside the block of flats had been knocked over in the wind.

'This is the sort of air that gets in your lungs,' Adam said grimly, 'and makes you cold from the inside out.' But he looped his arm through hers. They crossed the playground, walking towards the beach. They went as far as the Esplanade, stood out the front of the Novotel huddled together while Adam lit a cigarette.

'You should come and live southside,' he said. 'You, me, Minh, Bernie—it'll be a party.'

'I don't want to party with Bernie. I'm looking at a place in Clifton Hill tomorrow. Until I get a car, it has to be somewhere close to work.'

'So you decided? You're going back to your old work?'

Audrey pulled her scarf up over her mouth. She wished her coat had a hood. 'I don't know. I think so.'

'Are you happy to be back?'

'Yes. God, yes.' She told him about the gig she'd been to in Marrickville, that crippling homesickness, calling Julian to pick her up.

'You're a funny thing, going by yourself,' Adam said.

'It probably didn't help. It just felt like something I should be able to do. I didn't have anyone to go with.'

'Come to the gig on Friday at the Retreat. That'll make up for it. You'll have so many friends you'll be smothered.'

They'd started back up Robe Street, walking in the centre of the road.

'It feels weird, being back,' she said. 'I'm scared that if I go back to my job, it'll be like I never left, and things will get bad again.'

She was embarrassed at how childish she sounded. They came to the roundabout and separated instinctively: Audrey went left, Adam went right. He grinned at her.

She thought of bushwalks down at Wilsons Prom, her father singing *You take the high road and I'll take the low road, and I'll be in Scotland afore ye.*

On the other side they fell into step once more.

'It wasn't only your job that made you sad,' Adam said. 'There were other things.'

'I'm just frightened of patterns.'

'I know you are.'

The gig was like Adam had said: an offer of asylum. So much love in the room, so many good faces. Yusra took her hands, made to pull her close, stopped short. She said *Oh, but you're so cold!* Johnny hugged her so hard he lifted her off the ground. By the bar Ben put an arm around her, said *It's like you never left.* She crouched at the front of the stage with a pint in her hand and watched Adam watching Minh on stage. The lights flashed amber and blue. Adam was standing alone, sucking on a wedge of lime, eyes fixed.

She ran into Tilly by the bathrooms.

'Here,' Tilly said, pressing a packet of tissues into her hand, 'there's no paper left.'

In these toilets Audrey had squished into a cubicle with Katy so they could go on talking without interruption, holding each other's handbags, knees pressed together in the stalls. In the courtyard at the Great Northern they'd spat cherry pits into the ashtray. In the courtyard of the Catholic school on Otter Street they'd posed beneath the icon, made up names for new saints, canonised each other.

Audrey hitched up her dress. The pub noise was dull through the walls. *Is this how it'll be here from now on?* she thought. *You and me everywhere.*

Yusra was outside waiting for a cubicle, fixing her lipstick. Audrey handed her the tissues. 'Here. You'll need these.'

Katy's mother still lived in the house in Northcote with its view of the city, but she and Steve had separated. Audrey had read about it happening to couples who'd lost a child. Your youngest daughter turns into dust, and you turn into strangers. Not even your grief is common ground. Audrey thought she could understand.

She asked careful questions, but Helen wanted to know everything Audrey had been doing.

'What made you decide on Sydney?' she asked.

'It was just where I got a job. I wanted to go somewhere new. There was so much context here.' She hesitated. 'It's silly. Last year I re-read this old book of Dad's, a Zola novel, *L'Assommoir.* Do you know it?'

'I read it when I was a student. A million years ago. It's all death and woe, isn't it?'

Audrey's heart beat light and fast. 'At the start, Gervaise explains what she wants. Simple things: a bed to sleep in, to make good citizens of her little boys, and not to be beaten. And in the end, she can't achieve any of it. When you get to the end of the book, you realise she was never going to. She didn't have a chance.'

'How hopeless,' Helen remarked.

'I got so scared that it was true, though.'

'Oh, Audie.'

'I know.'

'Nothing's ever immutable,' Helen said. 'It wasn't for Katy, either.

Things could have got better for her. We just ran out of time.'

Audrey reached across the table.

'It's all right, darling,' Helen said.

They sat for a long time. Helen stroked her hand absently. Audrey could not pull away. She wished she had more of Katy, something left to give her mother.

Adam and Minh went away for the weekend, to the country where someone had a house. Adam took his time over breakfast. Minh packed the car by himself. 'We'll leave when we fucken leave,' Adam said blithely. He was helping Audrey look over ads for houses.

'Remember that awful place in Flemington?' Adam said. 'What was that, first year of uni?'

'Yeah. That was bleak.'

'Feels like forever ago.'

Minh was pulling on his jacket. The groceries were stacked by the front door.

'Come on,' he said. 'We're never going to get there. I told them lunch.'

Adam stood up, bowl in hand, kissed Minh. 'I was waiting for *you.*'

In the evening she took the tram to the other side of the city. Factories and flats, leaves in the gutters, gold pas de deux of car headlights at the Hoddle Street intersection. Small clot of anxiety as she started up Charles Street.

The house was just as she remembered, as though it had been holding its breath. Audrey had enshrined it in her head: the flailing clementine tree, the car parked out front, the awning over the front door. The front verandah with its couch, picked up from hard rubbish, where they'd sat to watch the sky change colour. Down the side, over the cracked concrete pavers, the camellia would still be there, and the fire pit, and the plastic lawn furniture.

Audrey had always loved that house. It was a tomb for better times.

Nick came to the door with a cautious face. They smiled at each other. 'Hullo.' Audrey stood on her toes to kiss his cheek. Nick took her close. They let go quickly.

'Your hair's short,' he said. 'How are you?'

'Good, really good. What about you?'

'I'm all right. Just let me grab my coat.'

Audrey stood on the step and exhaled. She didn't know what she'd expected. If they couldn't speak to each other now, they never would, and maybe one day they'd see each other on the same tram, or at the Empress, and they'd still be bruised and teenaged. Pinned down to the back step where they'd sat, catatonic, in the morning; pinned down to the nature strip where they'd said a meagre goodbye.

She looked down the hall. She could hear Nick's boots on the floorboards. He was singing in an easy voice, something about lighthouses. She didn't know if he was relaxed or just making a show for her.

The music in the pub was so loud it drowned out the noise of other people's conversations, and Nick and Audrey leaned over the table to hear each other. It was nervous talk on newborn legs.

'Why did you keep living by yourself?' Audrey asked.

'I don't know. I thought about finding somewhere else. Paddy asked if I wanted to move in with them, but those guys—I just couldn't deal with it. Anyway,' he said, 'I like that house. It's close to work. I like riding around the river.'

'I missed that in Sydney.'

'What about you? How come you moved in with all those people? I thought you wanted to be by yourself.'

'I sort of was. I didn't know any of them.' The beer was making her hands cold. She pressed her palms together between her thighs. 'I spent the first week or so in my room. I thought they'd hate me.'

'You're a goose.'

'I know.'

He was wearing a shirt he'd had since she'd known him, a checked lumberjack flannel, sleeves rolled to his elbows. A hole in one arm that neither of them could mend. ('I never learned how to sew anything,' she'd said, bewildered, when he'd asked once.) His hair was clipped as though it had been shorn not long ago.

'Adam said you were seeing someone,' Audrey said.

'I was for a while. A girl called Jo. She was nice. She works at that gallery up past Ivanhoe. What's it called?'

'Heide.'

'Yeah.' Audrey waited for him to say more, but he said again, 'What about you?'

'Sort of. My housemate. He was…' Audrey pulled a face. 'He was okay. Sometimes he could be such a prick. I don't know if I just wanted to make myself feel bad, like punishment, some subconscious thing—'

Nick looked puzzled. She'd lost him.

They were learning to speak in ordinary sentences again. Audrey's mouth was dry.

'I'll be back,' she said. 'I'm just going to—'

She went up the carpeted stairs that led to the function room. It was quiet and dark. The bathrooms were empty.

Nick had followed her. Audrey backed into a toilet cubicle, watching his face. She could still hear the music, the dull thudding of bass and drums. Nick reached behind, fumbling with the lock. He kissed her neck, below her ear, her mouth. She opened her eyes. A pale square of light streamed in from the window high up on the wall.

How easy it was to come home again. Audrey tried not to think of anyone else he might have touched. She pushed herself at him harder at the thought. Nick was kissing her and mumbling something. There was salt in her mouth. They were as strong as each other. He fit himself into her and they fucked slowly: she worked to feel the rolling of his hips. Their bodies moved together, and as Audrey came she put her hands to the cold concrete walls of the cubicle and felt the vibrations of the music from outside.

Nick kissed her hair. She started to laugh.

'What? What's funny?'

'It feels like we're in a bunker hiding from someone.'

They were still clutching each other, but after a time Nick tucked his cock back into his jeans and said *Are you all right*, and she said *Yes*, and he said *I'll meet you downstairs*. After he'd gone Audrey sat on the toilet lid and sobbed. She stepped outside and washed her hands. She was leaning against the vanity unit with her back to the mirror when a middle-aged woman came in.

'Queue downstairs is atrocious,' she said. She glanced at Audrey. 'You okay, love?'

For a moment she imagined Nick would be gone when she returned to their table, but he was still there. They shrugged back into their coatsleeves without speaking. Outside the sky was pricked with stars. Audrey looked at the window and saw Nick's face reflected in the green glow.

'Do you want to come home?' he asked.

The rain set in while they were on the tram. They sat opposite each other, knees just touching. The lights made everyone look sickly. Audrey could only see bits of Nick's skin: his thin wrists sticking out from his sleeves, the parts of his face not covered by hat or hair or scarf.

'When did the beard happen?' she asked. She almost reached out a hand, but stopped herself.

'When it got cold. I feel like a bear.'

At Charles Street they went to the bedroom, and she undressed him, and they fucked again. The striped blue sheets were the same. The room was warm with their bodies. Afterwards Nick lay on the bed the wrong way, feet under the pillows, propped on one arm, and Audrey sat cross-legged beside him. They could not stop talking.

'What was it like, in Sydney?'

'There were sea baths at the end of the street. I got better at swimming,' she said. 'Not good like you, but I could do laps without stopping.'

Something rippled across his face, sadness or surprise, and Audrey was sorry for them both. She started again. She told him about living with Claire, the long commute to and from Westmead, all the time she'd spent with a six-year-old boy, how tropical and lonely it was in October when she'd first moved. Nick listened. Whenever she asked what he'd been doing, he dismissed it. 'Nothing exciting. You know, work, friends, the usual. I went and saw the Dirty Three with Pat last week. That's about it. Keep talking.'

She told him about the old house groaning on its stumps on New Year's Eve, Elliott and Claire's accident, the weekend at Jindabyne. When she got to the cold motel room—can of rum and cola, Julian at the door—Nick reached for her. Their knuckles brushed together. He said nothing.

Audrey got up and made a sandwich. When she came back Nick was sitting up in bed like a good patient.

'Did you think we were going to do this?' he asked.

'No. I just wanted to see you.'

The rain had stopped.

'Tell me what's been happening here with you,' Audrey said.

Nick was quiet for a long time. He set his plate on the floor. He said, 'My dad's got cancer. It's in his bowel.'

'Shit. I'm sorry.'

'Don't be sorry.'

'Why didn't you tell me?'

'There's nothing you could've done.'

'How is he?'

'Not too bad, considering. He's about to have his last round of chemo. Then they remove the diseased part of his colon.'

'When?'

'Depends how he takes this last dose. It knocks him about a bit.'

Nick held out an arm for her, and she lay down. She couldn't see his face any more.

'I wish you'd told me,' she said. 'Your poor mum. None of you deserve it.'

'We're through the worst of it.'

Audrey was silent. She pressed her mouth to his arm. He fell asleep after awhile, and she lay awake thinking she'd remember it for a long time: the smell of him on her hands, his legs heavy between hers, the sepulchral bed, the turned earth of the sheets.

By the morning they'd come apart again. Audrey took the train back to Adam's. He arrived home late in the day, full of questions and speculation. She began to think she couldn't stay with him much longer. His apartment had three rooms. Audrey slept on the fold-out couch when Minh stayed over. Every morning she folded the blankets like an amiable houseguest. They ate breakfast together and did the quiz in the paper. Audrey learned Minh's slow, deliberate sense of humour.

But it was three rooms. If she'd lain in the bath to read, pulled the curtain across for privacy, Adam would've been offended.

After a while she moved in with Bernie. Living with him was simpler. He was out a lot. Sometimes at night he'd eat the dinner Audrey made, and talk about art school.

'You'd fucking love it, Audie,' he said, eyes rolling. 'There's one girl who actually uses blood in her drawings. It's like a caricature. What else. A guy in my studio documents his acid trips, and tries to paint them later, only they're not very good. Last time he went tripping in the Botanic Gardens, and now he's working on this enormous canvas of squiggly green lines. It's horrendous.' He made her laugh. 'The words we use the most are *process* and *documentation*,' he announced. 'One of my lecturers likes to ask the international students whether they understand after every instruction. He goes, *Now, are we all following here?*'—slow, insulting tone—'and even they laugh because it's just too appalling.'

She slept in his painting room, where the light was best, and the wind chimes made a silvery noise in the mornings.

She went to a home visit in Fairfield. Vanessa said *Are you sure you don't want to ask a copper to come with?* and Audrey said *No, I know the family. I think I should go alone.*

The flat had been tidied: she could tell from plastic rubbish bags tied and waiting in the hallway, the filthy sneakers in a row by the door.

'Zak's at school,' the father said as soon as she set foot inside.

She smiled. 'Good. How's he doing?'

He shrugged, spread his hands. He had a likeable, ravaged face. 'Oh-h-h…they don't like it much at that age, do they?'

'He does Reading Recovery,' said a voice from the doorway. A much younger woman stood with a toddler in her arms. He looked at Audrey, buried his face in the woman's neck again.

'This is my niece Kim. She's living with us while her mum gets sorted out.'

'Hi,' Kim said. She shifted the baby in her arms. Audrey was sure she'd met her before. 'This is Cade,' she said.

They moved down the hall to the kitchen. Audrey was careful. At the office Vanessa had said *He's a Scary Dad*, as though the phrase had capital letters. Visits like this were like walking a tight-rope. Audrey knew she looked young, partly because she was small. Sometimes it worked in her favour, made her seem non-threatening.

There was a bad smell in the kitchen, but it was neat. The bench gleamed with dark streaks, the grotty sponge by the sink; Kim must have been cleaning it when Audrey arrived.

'Mr Horsburgh—'

'Mike,' he said. A phone rang in another room, and he jogged off. The movement was funny, almost farcical, in the cramped flat. Kim glanced at her apologetically. The baby had begun to grizzle, and she was swaying from side to side as she held him. He looked heavy. Her arms were like young shoots.

'Have you got a cot for Cade?' Audrey asked.

Kim nodded. 'It's just a portable, but it's okay with—um, it's SIDS-compliant.'

Audrey's heart squeezed at her earnest face, her rote-learned language. She was maybe eighteen.

They crowded down the hall together as Audrey made to leave. Mike turned to her. He looped a finger through her lanyard. She kept her face still.

'Listen, do you reckon you could take off that thing as you go? I don't want the neighbours thinking we're ratbags. Next door's already pissed about Kimmy being here. Cunt's threatened to call Housing.'

Audrey lifted the ID tag from her neck, tucked it in her coat pocket.

'I reckon they might work it out anyway, eh?' Kim said. She laughed nervously. Audrey smelled sweat.

Propped on a ledge above the doorway was a machete, impossible to see from outside the flat. Mike reached across to let her out. Audrey thanked him. The door closed behind her.

Halfway back to the office she pulled over by a football field. She called Adam. Her fingers were shaking. She couldn't stop giggling.

'That's fucked,' he kept saying. 'What are you laughing for?'

'It was just so simple. So clever,' she said. 'And here's me thinking I've done a good job with him.'

'You're nuts. That's not funny.'

'I know. I can't explain it.'

They hung up. She was calmer. Waiting to turn onto High Street, she realised she recognised Kim as a client from a couple of years back. She'd just started at DHS. That same small honest face, telling her she'd felt *relaxed* doing ice in the back seat of her friend's mum's car. *I've never heard of anyone being* relaxed *on ice,* she'd said seriously to Vanessa later. Vanessa had laughed.

She met Nick at the Grace Darling, but it was packed and there was nowhere to sit or stand or prop. They started walking and ended up at the Tote where some kids were playing noise rock. The gig was almost over and the man on the door waved them through. They stood at the back of the crowd and looked away from each other. Audrey couldn't see the band past the heads and shoulders.

She thought how strange it was to say *Yes* to his tentative text message when they'd taught themselves to be alone. She did not know what he wanted. She remembered the way he'd looked telling her *We can fix this.* Him saying *I love you and it's not enough.* She'd said *You like me when I'm weak, is that it?* and he'd snapped *Don't be fucken ridiculous.*

It was different now. She was trying to make sense of it.

The band finished and the smokers emptied into the courtyard. Audrey and Nick sat on the carpeted stair in the middle of the floor. They were not talking. The room was colder without all the bodies. Across the room a couple leaned against the bricks, kissing. Clinking glass and laughter came in gasps with the opening and closing of the door, and there was music playing over the speakers.

'Want another drink?' she asked.

Nick murmured a thanks. She looked back at him from the bar. He was rubbing his neck with one hand, watching the room's dim drama.

She crouched beside him. 'What are you thinking about?'

He took the glass. 'Do you remember when you put Katy's coat on?'

'No.'

'You wore it once, one night, you put it on—'

'What,' Audrey said, 'after she—'

'Yes.'

Audrey shook her head. She meant to say *I don't remember a thing*, but she said *I don't feel a thing* instead.

'I was really sort of appalled by it,' he said. 'I felt…disgusted? I think that was the first time.'

Audrey sat down properly. She wanted to touch him but she was afraid.

'What else?' she asked.

'Remember when we made the fort?'

'You made it,' she said. 'You did it for me.'

'I don't know if I can do that again. If that's what you want. And I'm sorry.'

'I'm not asking for anything.'

'I know you're not. You never do.' He was smiling like a sick child. 'It's hard being in love with the saddest person in the world.'

Audrey said nothing. Her hands were in the prayer position between her thighs.

'I know that's a dick thing to say. I'm not trying to make you feel bad. I'm the one who couldn't help you out of it. But it's hard. Or I'm not very good at it.'

'I want it to be different,' she said.

'So do I.'

The bandroom was almost empty. Everyone had disappeared into

267

the front bar or the courtyard.

'We're the last ones here,' Nick said.

Outside they started walking in the direction of Hoddle Street, towards the house.

Audrey turned to him at the traffic lights.

'Will it be like this forever?' she asked.

He kissed her gently. He said *I'm sorry*.

'We're both very sorry,' she said. 'I am going to get a cab.'

He's sad, she said to her sister. It was a Saturday afternoon. They met at a café, sat out in the courtyard because it seemed too sunny a day to waste, but they were both rugged up.

'Relationship break-up and dad cancer—they'd be high up there on the list of awful life events,' Irène said. 'I don't imagine either of us'd be cracking funnies, either.'

She had the baby on her lap. He was teething on a piece of celery, looking right at Audrey.

'He said *I don't know if I can do it again*, like I'd drained him,' Audrey said, 'and I understood it, because that's how I've felt with Maman. It's hard to be that person.'

'It's hard to be the sick person, too,' Irène said calmly.

They ordered a bagel to share. Audrey finished her half in the time it took her sister to manage a bite. She held out her arms for Lucas, bounced him on her lap. Irène reached across the table. She pulled the knitted hat down over his ears, smiled at them. She sat down and began to eat.

Nick phoned that evening. He apologised. His voice was threadbare. Audrey was alone at Bernie's, reading in bed to keep warm. She said *Do you want to come over*, and she heard him think about it, and he said *I'm pretty knackered, mate*. He said *Listen, Dad's last round of chemo's on Thursday. I know it's weird, but I just thought I'd*—and she was saying

Yes, yes, of course before he'd got the words out.

She hung up and wondered how long they'd keep running to each other, now that they'd started.

Audrey left the office at midday. It was raining lightly. She met Nick at the corner of Victoria Parade.

At the entrance to the Freemasons she paused. 'Maybe I shouldn't come. I haven't even been around, and your poor dad—I don't want to intrude.'

Nick looked at his feet. 'Honestly, he'd be happy to see you. But if you don't want to come, I get it.'

'It's not that,' she said.

It was warm inside. Nick knew the corridors. He paused outside one of the rooms and she dropped back. He put a finger to his lips.

'Sh. Wait here a second,' he whispered. He opened the door. 'Hey, old man.'

'Hullo! I didn't know you were coming in.'

'It's your last dose. We should celebrate.'

'Yeah, I told the doc to pump some champagne through the cannula, but she didn't listen.' Audrey leaned against the wall. There was a gentle mechanical humming, a sour hospital smell that reminded her of Sydney. She ran her fingers over the plaster and listened to their muffled voices.

'Listen, I've got a surprise for you.'

'Don't tire him out, darling.' Paula.

'It's okay, Mum. It's a visitor.' Nick stuck his head out the door, and ushered Audrey into the room. Nick's mother stood to embrace her. The room smelled of chemicals and Paula's perfume.

'How are you doing?' Audrey said, turning to Doug. His hair was white and downy. He was an old man in a chair with a hospital blanket over his legs.

'After today, it's all over, red rover. It'll be good to finish,' he said.

He motioned for her to sit. 'You back for good?'

'Yeah,' Audrey said, 'I've come home.'

They all looked at one another. Nobody said anything.

'Well, thanks for coming in, love,' Doug said. 'You've been the brightest face I've seen in a while.' It was raining harder now. A nurse came in. She turned on the brash fluorescent light. She checked Doug's intravenous line, asked how he was feeling. There were pearly beads of sweat on his upper lip. His mouth was waxy. Audrey could see his feet trembling beneath the thin comforter. *I'm okay*, said Doug. *I'm doing okay. This is Audrey*, he said. The nurse stayed to talk a while. When she left, the Lukovics all said how lovely the staff were.

There was a program on travel in Victoria on the television.

'That's what I'm going to do once this is all done,' Doug said, 'I'm going to buy a caravan. We'll go round Australia. What do you think, Paula?'

Paula was hemming a skirt. She looked up over her glasses, pins between lips, and smiled.

'If it's a nice caravan, with its own shower and toilet. And if you help to clean it.'

'You don't *clean* a bloody *caravan*, you whacker.'

'You do if you bloody *live* in it.'

Audrey looked at Nick, who looked away with a twisted face.

He got up and left after a while, and Audrey sat with his parents. They asked about Sydney, about her job and her friends. It was kind-hearted interest. It made her sad. She asked after Will. He'd finished his degree. He'd been travelling. They'd told him not to come home when Doug started treatment, but of course he did.

After half an hour, Doug closed his eyes and asked Paula to pass him the green plastic kidney dish. Audrey left them alone.

She found Nick on the steps out the front of the hospital, head bowed. She sat beside him.

'I'm sorry,' he said to his knees. 'He's going to be okay. He looks really good. The specialist said he's doing better than they could have imagined.' Audrey cradled him. He put a hand over his face. She felt him shaking. 'He's going to be okay. I don't know why I'm crying.'

He shook and she held him. They sat there until he was done.

They started walking in the wrong direction, through the Fitzroy Gardens. It had stopped raining. They moved slowly and without touching.

'Thanks for coming today,' Nick said. 'It means a lot.'

'I wish I'd known sooner.' She wrapped her coat tighter around herself. Her neck was cold, bare where her hair had been cut. 'We don't have to keep hanging out. I just wanted to see you.'

'I know. I missed you, too.'

'We could be better,' Audrey said. He smiled, but not at her. 'What?' she asked. 'What's that face for?'

'That's the Audrey Spencer defensive pose. Head bent forwards, arms crossed. Making yourself as small as you can.' Nick stopped walking to mimic her.

'The other night, when you said you didn't know if you could do it again.'

'That was a shitty thing to say.'

'It's okay,' she said. 'I get it. I'm glad you said it.'

'No. The way it came out made it sound like the onus should be on you all the time, and that's not fair.'

'What do you want to do?'

'I think,' Nick said, 'when it ended up so bad, it's hard to imagine things being good again.'

They blinked at the wind. Audrey folded her arms across her chest before she could stop herself, and Nick laughed aloud. 'What do *you* want, Audrey?'

'It could happen again,' she said.

'I know.'

She looked away. He bent his head and kissed her where her hair was parted. They were cocooned there for a second. 'Come on,' he said. 'It's going to rain again.'

In the kitchen at Charles Street she tried to put together the ingredients for a soup. Nick trailed after her.

'Hey Spence.'

'What.'

'Stop moving away from me.'

Lead-ring eyes, slow smile. It was almost normal.

They sat in front of the television. Nick fell asleep halfway through the show. When Audrey got up to switch it off, tell him to go to bed, he opened his eyes.

'I thought I might have some friends over for my birthday next week,' he said, 'our friends. Do a potluck dinner here. Would that be weird?'

'I don't know. Only as weird as you make it.'

'Tell me the rules,' he said, feigning panic, grabbing at her arms.

All she could think was *Give it back, give it back, give it back.*

They drove out to Tyabb together. Audrey watched the road. When she picked at her cuticles, he reached for her hand.

They pulled into the drive and sat for a moment, looking at the old house. The weatherboards were flaking, the hinges rusting in the salt air. The verandah had rotted away in places.

'It looks old, doesn't it.'

Nick said nothing.

Sylvie produced tea and biscuits. She sat twisting her hands, asking questions, telling stories. Her cigarettes waited in their pack on the coffee table. When Nick offered to go out and chop some wood for her, she accepted graciously. *C'est un vrai gentilhomme,* she muttered.

The wind roared in the rafters.

'How's the new job going?' Audrey asked.

Now Sylvie reached for a cigarette. 'I want it to be temporary,' she said. 'The pay is very bad. Fifteen dollars an hour.'

'That's absurd. Do you need money?'

'No,' Sylvie said. 'It's okay. I have enough.'

'Fifteen bucks—that's what I used to get working at the servo when I was at uni. You're worth more than that.'

An odd expression came over Sylvie's face. She sat forwards with her legs spread, set her elbows on her knees. She narrowed her eyes.

'Work has no intrinsic value,' she said, stabbing at the air with her cigarette. 'Only the value you fight to give it.'

She was imitating Neil. The two women were still giggling when Nick came back. He looked from one face to the other, gave a small, confused smile. He didn't ask.

Bitter, starry night, everyone in the backyard at Charles Street. Audrey was wearing a thermal shirt, striped in lairy colours, beneath her coat. Adam had already taken pictures of her in it, posing mock-sexy in her thick socks and tights in the kitchen.

She'd gone inside to get another bottle of wine, and now she stood by the back door watching her friends. They were crowded around the fire pit in their chairs. Their skin and eyes shone in the dark; their teeth gleamed when they laughed. Yusra and Mark playing mercy, Yusra's arm trembling with the effort; Bernie with a blanket wrapped around him like a mystic. Ben and Patrick poking at the flames, feigning indignation when Giulia said *What is it with blokes and being the boss of the fire?* Emy holding out her empty glass to Johnny, tilting her face, smiling like a queen. The light fell clammy and dramatic from the floodlamp. *Some kid comes past the tent and goes 'Have you guys got any nangs?', and Johnny yells 'Don't put that shit in your body. Go to bed, son. Take care of yourself.'* Meredith with her American sweetness. *We don't think you're psychic.* Plastic buckets for the mussel shells, dew collecting on the streamers they'd hung along the fence.

It was almost too good to bear, this home, these friends. Audrey was in love with them all.

'They're such good value. The other day I took a sub for Father Wallace—' Adam was saying.

'Father Wallace.'

'Yes, Nicholas, turns out you get those at a private Anglican school. It's very reverend, tra la la, anyway, I had to take the big guy's Year 9 ethics class. So the first thing I said was *Who can explain briefly to the class what euthanasia is?* And this girl's hand shoots up, and she goes, "Once I had a cold for, like, three weeks, so Mum took me to the naturopath and she said I had a really bad immune system? And she gave me these euthanasia tablets?"'

'Fuck *off*,' said Ben.

Their laughter rang out in the night. Audrey watched them. She realised she'd stopped expecting the worst, or waiting for it. The thought was a magnesium flare in her.

Nick glanced up at her standing in the shadow. He held out his hand. She came flying across the grass to join him.

Acknowledgments

Much of my time editing this book was spent as a fellow at Glenfern. I'm indebted to Writers Victoria, the Readings Foundation and Glenfern's Iola Matthews for the time and space.

Thank you to Toni Jordan, Sam Cooney and Clare Renner, judges of the 2014 Victorian Premier's Literary Award for an Unpublished Manuscript, for shortlisting this novel, and to the Victorian State Government for their continued support of the prize. To Sam Twyford-Moore, Jen Mills, the Emerging Writers' Festival, the Wheeler Centre and the many others who encouraged my writing.

Heartfelt thanks, too, to Melissa Manning, Tom Minogue, Yasmine Sullivan and Kieran Stevenson for their tireless insight and encouragement, for all the late-night conversations around kitchen tables and through laptop screens. How lucky I am to workshop with people whose work I admire so. To Laura Stortenbeker, my brain-twin, for being a beautiful friend first and a sharp reader second. To Carrie Tiffany for reading first in Tuesday-night TAFE classes, and ever since; for finding the possibility in my work.

I'm deeply grateful to everyone at Text, particularly my wonderful editor Alaina Gougoulis and Michael Heyward.

To the gang, for so many years of love: Tasha, Kathleen, Bianca, Bridget, Clairy, Jasna and Steph.

And to my family, especially my parents, for their good hearts.